FAITHFUL ARE THE WOUNDS

BOOKS BY MAY SARTON

POETRY

Encounter in April
Inner Landscape
The Lion and the Rose
The Land of Silence
In Time like Air
Cloud, Stone, Sun, Vine
A Private Mythology
As Does New Hampshire
A Grain of Mustard Seed
A Durable Fire
Collected Poems, 1930–1973
Selected Poems of May Sarton
    (*edited by Serena Sue
    Hilsinger and Lois Byrnes*)
Halfway to Silence
Letters from Maine
The Silence Now
Collected Poems 1930–1993
Coming into Eighty

NOVELS

The Single Hound
The Bridge of Years
Shadow of a Man
A Shower of Summer Days
Faithful Are the Wounds
The Birth of a Grandfather
The Fur Person
The Small Room
Joanna and Ulysses
Mrs. Stevens Hears the
    Mermaids Singing
Miss Pickthorn and Mr. Hare
The Poet and the Donkey
Kinds of Love
As We Are Now
Crucial Conversations

A Reckoning
Anger
The Magnificent Spinster
The Education of Harriet
    Hatfield

NONFICTION

I Knew a Phoenix
Plant Dreaming Deep
Journal of a Solitude
A World of Light
The House by the Sea
Recovering: A Journal
At Seventy: A Journal
Honey in the Hive
Among the Usual Days: A
    Portrait (*edited by
    Susan Sherman*)
After the Stroke: A Journal
Writings on Writing
May Sarton—a Self-Portrait
Endgame: A Journal of the
    Seventy-ninth Year
Encore: A Journal of the
    Eightieth Year
At Eighty-Two: A Journal

FOR CHILDREN

Punch's Secret
A Walk through the Woods

ANTHOLOGY

Sarton Selected: An
    Anthology of the Journals,
    Novels, and Poetry (*edited
    by Bradford Dudley
    Daziel*)

"*Faithful are the wounds of a friend*"

FAITHFUL
ARE THE WOUNDS

May Sarton

W · W · NORTON & COMPANY · INC · *New York*

MACLEAN LIBRARY
SIERRA NEVADA COLLEGE

First published as a Norton paperback 1985; reissued 1997
COPYRIGHT © 1955 BY MAY SARTON
COPYRIGHT RENEWED 1983 BY MAY SARTON

Library of Congress Cataloging in Publication Data

Sarton, May, 1912–
  Faithful are the wounds.

  I. Title.
[PZ3.S249Fai 5]   [PS3537.A832]   813'.5'2   72–1812

ISBN 0-393-31715-3

W. W. Norton & Company, Inc., 500 Fifth Avenue, NY, NY 10110
W. W. Norton & Company Ltd., 10 Coptic Street, London WC1A 1PU

1 2 3 4 5 6 7 8 9 0

For Eleanor and Kenneth Murdock

The Author wishes to express her gratitude to Bryn Mawr College which awarded the Lucy Martin Donnelly Fellowship to her in 1953, thus making possible the writing of this novel.

PROLOGUE

Isabel lay on her bed in a fog of fatigue, too tired even to undress. She could hear Henry splashing about in the shower, giving a shout of pleasure as he turned the taps from hot to cold, and in her mind's eye she visualized him, brown, compact, his very skin prickling with resilience, and she smiled. It was astonishing to realize that John and Lillian were almost grown-up, that she had been married nearly twenty years, safe, she thought, for nearly twenty years, and still it could seem like a miracle, so that she never wrote her name "Mrs. Henry Thomas Ferrier" without pride. She was rehearsing this pleasure in her husband and in her life, because all evening as they sat playing backgammon, and for weeks before, she had been fighting off the sensation that she was walking on very thin ice, that just below was darkness, black despair—the more frightening because there seemed to be no reason for it. It was impossible to fight an anxiety which had no name, which one couldn't face with reason because it wasn't there, because as she told herself again, "it's all imagination," forcing herself through an organized pattern each day, taking more trouble than usual with the cooking, dressing with more than usual care, keeping the house immaculate. She pulled a blanket up because her teeth had begun to chatter. Yet all around her the room spoke of peace, order. She had chosen this exact shade of salmon for the curtains with care, chosen the texture, nubbly against the pale gray surface of the walls. . . . She opened her eyes and forced herself to pay attention, to be in this room, in her life and not somewhere else, where the unknown chaos waited to invade her like the cold fogs which swept over the harbor these October evenings and shut out the lights of San Francisco across the bay.

When the phone buzzed, she thought, Let Henry go. There was silence in the bathroom—couldn't he hear it? But now he was brushing his teeth noisily; she would have to answer—some drunken friend no doubt—noting that the clock at her side said midnight.

"Boston calling. A person-to-person call for Mrs. Henry Ferrier."

"This is Mrs. Ferrier."

"Go ahead, Boston."

But she did not have to hear what the hesitating old voice was telling her. She hardly listened. She knew, had known, it now seemed, forever, had waited for this call all her life, and now it was here she felt absolutely calm. She heard herself saying that she would find out about planes and wire within the hour, that she would be there by late that night, "for it is morning there, isn't it?" she heard herself say. And then the voice stopped talking.

2

It was all over. She put the receiver back and heard it click. She sat there, waiting to feel.

"What is it, darling? Pretty late to call up, it seems to me." Henry stood there in his pajama pants, rubbing himself red with a rough towel, drops of water standing in his rather heavy gray eyebrows, and she looked at him without a word, seeing all this, knowing that he was over there and that she loved him, registering the sudden focusing of his glance, the surgeon's clear look that could meet emergency with reason. He was at her side, his arm around her. He was holding her tight against his naked side. She could feel his heart beating against her. "What is it?"

"Safety," she said, "you're my safety."

"What's happened, Bel?" He said it sharply this time. It was a command, and she had to obey it, break the film somehow, get through again.

"Edward," she said.

"What in hell makes him call up at this time of night?" She could feel him resisting, feel the tension in the ribs, for Edward, her brother, had been this, the disturber of the peace always.

"No," she explained speaking quite slowly and distinctly, "it was not Edward. He threw himself under an elevated train. He's dead now."

Henry held her tightly against him as if to keep her from falling, as if she were falling down, down, and he were holding her back by sheer force of will. And she talked against this because she knew she had to fall, had to feel, there was no way of staying suspended any longer. "A professor called. He sounded very old. He had an Italian name. He said he had to tell me now because"—here she hesitated—"because it will be in the papers."

"Yes, of course," Henry said. "You had to know."

"I've always known," she whispered and knew she was crying because she felt hot splotches on her hands. She pushed Henry away almost roughly, pushed her hands up to her face as if they were someone else's hands and rubbed the tears away. "I shall have to find out about planes. Can you come with me?" No, of course not. She knew the answer before he said it. He had two operations, one serious one. They could not be put off. "Of course not," she said. "It's just that"—she got up and walked up and down in her stocking feet, wringing her hands—"I'm scared, Henry."

"Take it easy, darling," he said, picking up the phone. "The first thing is to get a reservation."

Very far away she could hear him talking, noting the time and time of arrival. She gave him the address she had written down and heard him send a wire to Cambridge, Massachusetts, where Harvard University was, where she had never been, where she must go in a few hours alone.

"There's a seven o'clock plane. That means I can put you on it and just make it at the hospital. I'm going to make you some hot chocolate now," he said, moving toward the door.

"Don't go. Don't leave me. Please." For now panic seized her. "I can't stay here alone."

"Come along then," he said in his kind, careful voice, his doctor's voice. "You can sit on the kitchen stool while I make it." He took her by the hand and she followed as if she were blind.

She walked into a stranger's kitchen; she was, she felt, in a stranger's house. It had never seemed quite real and now she was set way outside it, looking in, looking at the carefully planned shelves, the automatic dishwasher, the little herb cupboard, the red tiled floor, looking at herself Isabel Cavan—no, Isabel Ferrier—and her husband, the distinguished surgeon, pouring milk into a saucepan with all the care with which he might have used a scalpel, as if nothing else for the moment existed.

For so long she had fought off the sensation that all this was make-believe, that reality was somewhere else; now she did not fight it. She sat, passive, on the high stool and knew that only Edward was real. Edward lying on a stone slab, she imagined, with his chest crushed to a pulp. He had not suffered, the old professor had said. Suddenly she laughed, a loud rude laugh.

"What?" Henry said.

"No, don't worry," she said quickly. "I'm not hysterical. But that professor said Edward didn't suffer. It was too quick, he said. Just a lifetime—just under fifty years," she said with heavy irony.

"There," Henry said as if he had not heard. He put two cups and saucers on a tray. He even remembered a little white cloth and spoons, sugar, cream in the silver pitcher. "We've got lots of time. Let's sit down and drink this."

So she followed him into the living room, the room she had dreamed of and planned and agonized over, spending weeks looking for the curtain material to match soft blue and white handwoven rugs, the one sea-green chair, this room that had come to mean that she had emerged into her real life, trusting her own judgment at last. As she sat down she put her hand out and touched the arm of the chair as if to prove that she was not dreaming. Yet even this house, this room had, after all, been invaded by Edward. Just there at the fireplace he had stood three years ago, scorning them (oh, how she felt his scorn), first being icily polite, then suddenly raging at Henry, for no reason, because Henry had said something perfectly sensible about the refugee doctors, that there were enough Jewish doctors already for their own good and it was absolutely necessary that the exams be kept stiff. Hot shame shot through her again. Why did Edward have to be so difficult, so raw? And why did it hurt so? Even Henry had understood that she must make it up somehow, forced her to write Edward afterwards, for it was true—and Henry sensed it—that always somewhere in a deep layer of her consciousness Edward existed, an unsolved problem, something with which she could not cope, deeply disturbing.

"People will talk, of course; we've got to face that," he said, then, "Maybe it's just as well you'll be away for a few days, honey."

For the last few moments, she had been alone with Edward. She had faced Edward and his anger and suffering here in her own house alone. Now it was as if hundreds of faces were peering in through the great glass windows, pointing at her and at Henry, innocent dear distinguished Henry; sneering and accusing faces, or just curious faces. She would never be alone with Edward again, then. He had deliberately pushed himself and her and all their lives onto the front pages. She put her face in her hands, trembling with the force of the image.

"How could he do it?" she said, and she meant "do it to us."

"He was a sick man, Bel. You can't blame him." This was the tone Henry had always used about Edward, the tone of understanding, as if he were dealing with a patient.

Always before, this tone had helped her because it made Edward seem unreal, not to be taken seriously, not to be allowed to invade their marriage, someone outside in a kind of self-made hospital in which his agony could be medically examined, but did not need to enter into anyone else. And when she said to Henry, "You're my safety," she always meant, you're my safety against Edward, against pain.

"Why is he so important?" she asked almost angrily. "Why the papers?"

"He was a distinguished professor, I understand," Henry answered gently. "And after all, he wrote all those books."

"Nobody we know ever heard of him," she answered bitterly.

"Well, it's a different world, Bel. In his world he was pretty famous, you know that as well as I do."

"Why didn't he stick to what he knew about? Why did he have to come out here to campaign with Wallace? That's all people here know about him." She hated the harsh vulgar tone in her own voice, it was as if someone else were taking her over, an angry person she didn't know, who frightened her.

"Well, we feel the same way about that, Bel, and there's no point in going over it all again. He's at peace now."

"Yes, *he's* at peace," she said in her new bitter voice.

"Drink your cocoa, honey. You know you don't really want to talk this way. It's just the shock. Give it time."

"Don't say 'take it easy' again or I'll scream." She was caught in a spiral of anger which she couldn't break. Henry was frowning into his cup, his lower lip thrust out a little.

If you battered your head against this man, she felt, it would be like battering it against rock. And she felt that she was sitting opposite a stranger; it was as if Henry was so sure of himself that one element had been left out of him, and that he was so human just because he was really so inhuman—he had never heard the voice of anguish breaking through his flesh like sweat, the little creeping whispery scream of anguish. But I mustn't go on like this, she thought. I must get out of this. It's dangerous. "I'm sorry, Henry," she said in a flat voice, "you must get some sleep—those operations."

She was so used to putting planned activities, lists, between her and that feeling of despair just under life, that now she was able to pack quite efficiently, even to plan a menu for the next day's meals, write out the address of the cleaning woman who might be persuaded to come and take over for Henry, and when John came in she insisted on telling him herself. He stood there in the hall outside their bedroom at half-past one, a smear of lipstick on his chin, a little bewildered, a little ashamed, it seemed (had he had too much to drink?), saying, "I'm sorry, Mother," and not looking at her, casting furtive glances at his father until Henry said,

"Go on to bed, John. And wipe that lipstick off your face."

Isabel watched John walk slowly down the hall, his shoulders stooped a little, go into his room and close the door very quietly. How awful that such innocence had to be involved, that no one she loved would be untouched by the talk, the curiosity, the stain that was creeping across the continent towards them, that couldn't be stopped. Already she herself was infected with it, so much so that she resisted the temptation to go in and kiss the sleeping Lily good-bye. Lily would take this hard. She was so vulnerable under her funny freckled little face, thirteen, and worried about everything, just as Isabel had been.

"Here," Henry was saying firmly. "Drink this. It'll give us about four hours' sleep, and you're going to need it. I've set the alarm."

Where is grief, she thought, with her cheek against Henry's back, breathing with his breath as it came from deeper and deeper down, until she herself went down with it into that numb sleep you can buy in a bottle. Where is grief, she asked. But the answer was: Sleep. This is our last night of safety alone. Tomorrow the world will have crashed in. It was the first time in years that she had gone to sleep without saying Edward's name, without his coming alive into her mind, without the wave of anxiety beating down on her.

They drove to the airport through fog, fog drifting down in billows across the road, then half lifting. It was a relief to come out at last on the three-lane highway which would take them right through, to be able to follow taillights ahead, though it was still a slow process. "Don't worry," Henry said, "we have plenty of time."

"I'm not worrying." She rather liked this limbo. There was nothing she could do, nothing except talk, and she could talk out into the fog, knowing that Henry, concentrating on the car ahead, was only half listening. She felt lightheaded, almost as if she were a little drunk. She could say whatever came into her head, it would not matter. And she had woken up, not knowing where she was, thinking for a moment that she was in bed at home in Medfield.

"It's so queer that you never saw that house," she said.

"What house, honey?" he said, swerving out past a bus.

"The house in Iowa, of course. What I remember, funnily enough, is the way the stained-glass window on the stairs made a colored pattern on the floor, and then the velvet window seat, brown velvet. Everything in the house was golden oak or brown," she went on dreamily.

"Gloomy?"

"Well, maybe." She felt doubtful. No, it had not been gloomy exactly, sitting in the window seat looking through the diamond panes, waiting for Edward to come home from school, sewing a doll's dress, those long winter afternoons which seemed timeless, wonderfully safe and timeless now. "It was one of those solid houses built about nineteen hundred, shingled, with turrets, and seemed awfully grand at the time. All the other houses were white frame with green shutters and lawns going right down to the sidewalk. We had a hedge."

"You were big shots," Henry smiled.

"I suppose so," she said, but it had not really felt like that.

"Anyone who's president of the bank in a town that size is a big shot. I can't see Edward, though, in all that. What was he like?"

"A stranger," she said, without thinking how peculiar it must sound. "From the time he was about nine or ten years old, he was always off somewhere, playing with the Donovan boys for instance, people my father spoke of as 'Irish riffraff.' He was always doing the opposite of what Father would like—on purpose, perhaps."

"Like what?"

"Like playing with the Donovans instead of the Chesters who lived right next door and were 'nice boys.' Then

10

he wouldn't hunt, and Father was a great hunter. The only thing Edward really loved as sport was baseball, but he never did make the team. He always wore glasses, you know, but that didn't keep him from getting into fights. I hated the fights— I used to run away, crying. I couldn't bear to see Edward get beaten, to see Mother's face when he got home with blood all over his mouth and that funny little look he had, as if he felt somehow—somehow—as if he'd crashed through. I don't know how to say it, as if coming in to the house which was always so quiet, all bloody and dirty, he had won even when he had really lost. Of course Father approved. That was about the only thing Edward did that Father approved of, as a matter of fact." Yet the strange thing was that Edward got into those fights when he was so bottled up with rage that it was the only way out, when he hated his father so much that she sometimes had been afraid he would kill him, sitting there at the table at mealtime glaring out of his deep-set blue eyes.

"What did your father really want of Edward?" Henry was asking. It was an effort to pull herself back to the rational plane, to be reasonable when the old anguish was rising in her like a wave, the anguish of being a witness in a family torn to pieces, of dreading every mealtime for fear the storm might break. And perhaps the worst was that the storm so rarely did break, that so much emotion was all the time held in suspense, never precipitated and played out.

"What did Father want?" she repeated the question aloud. Surely not just that Edward should wear white flannels or play golf. What then? "You know what I really think"—she turned to Henry—"I think he was afraid of Edward."

"That's queer. Why? I should have thought——"

"Father was terribly afraid of feeling, you see. And that fear made him cruel, especially cruel to Edward. They were like two highly charged batteries that short-circuited each other. If only once the current could have flowed through . . ." she said, knowing as she said it that it was like crying for the moon. For their father had been incapable of a spontaneous gesture. For a moment Isabel was silent, seeing her father coming toward her as if from a long distance away, so stiff-looking in his pince-nez and high collar, in his severely cut suit and black boots, a brief case in one hand. Every evening when she was a little girl she had waited for him at the corner, run to meet him, to be swung up into the air, to walk sedately the rest of the way holding his hand, and this was possible just because it was a routine she saw now, because in fact it asked nothing of her father, nothing that he could not give. Whereas Edward wanted only to break the routine, to get through, to be recognized as himself, not as the idea of a son, wouldn't compromise, wouldn't take a crumb of love when he wanted the whole loaf.

"Did Edward have many friends?"

"Where are we anyway?" Bel peered out into the fog.

"Nowhere," and Henry chuckled. "We've got another half hour of this, don't worry. But you might light me a cigarette."

She lit the cigarette, thinking about Henry's question. "He had friends, but they were always queer people, bums like the Donovans, not kids he could bring to the house. It seemed as if in the house there was only Mother. He and Mother had a real thing together——"

12

"I thought so."

Bel remembered how when their mother looked at Edward her whole face seemed to light up from way down inside. . . . "He'd come running up the path with a report card to show her, or a poem he liked, always something wonderful."

"Mothers and sons," Henry said a bit ironically.

"I expect it's an old story," Bel answered, flushing, "but when I was growing up, it didn't seem that way to me. I minded terribly. You see she always treated Edward as if he were her equal, grown-up—even when she scolded him, it was different. She was hard on him, and with me she was indulgent, but I would have given a good deal to see that severe look in her eyes."

"And she didn't mind about the Donovan boys?"

"She always took Edward's side against Father. I can see her now at Sunday dinner—a huge dinner, you know, chicken and ice cream and all the fixings, and mother sitting there, flushed from the cooking in a white frilly blouse, her eyes very bright blue, saying that Edward thought there ought to be a ballfield down on the other side of the tracks, as if God had spoken."

"And what did your father say to that?"

"Asked for more chicken," and Bel smiled. It was all so clear and bright in her mind as if she were seeing it on a screen. "Or else Father gave a lecture on the kind of people who chose to live in slums and wouldn't work themselves into decent surroundings. Often it seemed as if he wanted to bait Edward, did it on purpose. There was never any peace," she said, and now she was not looking at a bright screen, she was inside the old pain and wishing Henry would drive faster, drive her out of it.

"I shouldn't have started to remember all this," she said, lighting a cigarette. Her hands were shaking.

"I don't know," Henry kept his eyes on the road, but he reached over and laid his right hand on her knee. "Maybe it helps." But what helped was this touch, was this contact, as it always did, and she squeezed his hand hard. The terrible thing with families, she thought, was the aching tearing love that never could express itself simply like this. All through her childhood she had looked and looked at Edward, as if through a pane of glass, but she could never hug him. It was never simple.

"I suppose you and Edward were quite close," Henry said, giving her hand a gentle squeeze before he let it go.

"I don't know. I used to follow him around, down by the river where he and the Donovans had a secret place. It seems to me I was always calling, 'Edward, where are you?' and often he didn't answer. After all, little sisters are a nuisance. Everybody knows that."

"But you minded."

"Oh, Henry." She said what she had never said to him before. "I felt I was always outside everything." And then she stopped, amazed at what she saw. "But that's what Edward felt too. Only he could break through in his own way, and I didn't have any way." She realized that she had without even being aware of it, let down the walls she had maintained all these years, that the walls were sliding away. She could talk to Henry about Edward, at last. "I keep forgetting," she said, wrenched back to the reason, "what this is all about, why we're doing this." She peered out through the fog, in a panic suddenly. "What's the time?"

"There's ten minutes—take it easy, honey."

"If only you could have known Edward then. You see, he seemed so much more alive than other boys. He cared so much." She faltered, for how could she describe him to Henry who had only seen an exasperated difficult middle-aged man, Henry who couldn't imagine that redheaded boy, swinging a baseball bat, always off somewhere in a hurry?

"What did he care about?"

Isabel thought about this for a moment. "You know, I used to steal up to his room when he wasn't there and try to find out. Once it was photography. He said he wanted to make a record of the town, the real town was what he said, and that seemed to be things like empty lots and the shacks where the colored people lived, things like that. Then he had a big black notebook where he copied out things he liked, Walt Whitman at one time, then Shelley, then all kinds of things I couldn't understand about socialism, government. Even then I hated all that. I was jealous, I suppose."

"Maybe you were just right," Henry said, smiling at her.

"No," she frowned, "I didn't care about such things." She wanted now terribly to try to say it to Henry, just once, to bring these two parts of her life together just once, to explain how Edward felt responsible, also ashamed of their father, how he always wanted to make up somehow for their being rich. But just then the car swung into the airport, and Henry clamped on the brakes.

Bel took out a mirror and powdered her nose nervously, meeting herself and surprised at how neat and pulled together she looked, a middle-aged woman with cool gray eyes, in a soft blue hat. No one would know, she thought. No one would guess all the images that crowded behind her eyes and that now she would never be able to tell Henry.

"You're going to be all right," he was saying.

"But I wanted to tell you— I wanted to explain."

"There's no time now, honey."

At the very last minute she clung to him, just as they were wheeling out the bags. The huge silver plane made everything look dwarfed and out of proportion. The people who were rushing around in little trucks looked like insects; the people who were waiting to get on looked like insects too. She had become an object, she felt, a thing to be transported, cut off from everything human and safe.

"I can't, Henry," she breathed. "I'm too scared."

"They won't eat you." He turned her around and kissed her hard on the mouth. "I wouldn't be scared of a lot of old professors."

"It's Edward," she said, but there was no time to explain. She was being gently pushed on her way. She was walking up the shiny steep steps alone. She had to do it alone.

Now she was inside, the plane looked small and crowded. She went far up to the front, and sank into the chair, so deep that she felt she would never be able to move, get out again. There seemed to be no air, nothing but a steady vibration though they were still not moving. She looked out of the window, but Henry had gone— yes, he would have to hurry to get to his operation while she sat in this shaking cocoon and waited, waited for what seemed like hours, so tense her hands were clenched tight round the safety belt. Then there was a jolt and they were bumping out onto the field. But just as she began to relax,

16

they stopped again, while the whole cabin vibrated and she felt wildly claustrophobic. Was it too late to plead illness, get out somehow, get back to Henry and safety? But now they were jolting along again, faster and faster until quite suddenly the jolting stopped. "Airborne," she said to herself, looking down as some trees whizzed past below them, as they circled back over the airport and then everything tilted away, the whole world tilted away sideways, fields shot out from under them, houses disappeared, the cars on the roads looked like beetles. It was a still humming emptiness, rather like ether just before you go under, and she was going under now, down the long tunnel of air alone. There had been so many words, so many images floating behind her eyes, and now there was nothingness. She had become a vacuum. "Edward, where are you?" she said silently to the sky. She tried very hard to cry so that no one would see, wiping the tears away surreptitiously with her handkerchief, leaning her head back against the chair, her eyes closed.

She would never be able to tell Henry, this is why she was crying, she reminded herself. All her life she had wanted safety, peace, to be accepted. But even Henry could not accept that part of her which was, in spite of everything, Edward's. These last years when she and Edward hardly wrote to each other, when she imagined she was through with him, when she imagined she had made a choice once and for all, and his unreasonable anguish, his continual war, had been firmly labeled in her mind childish and neurotic, she had really borne him inside her like a child, had never been able to bury the anguish, had lived with it always just under the surface of life. You can't break off from family, she thought, the tears squeezing their way down through her lids, even if you try. And now it was too late. She couldn't hide; she was caught here—was that how Edward had felt when he—when he—Edward, where are you? The tears flowed down behind her fingers.

"It can't be as bad as that, honey. Take a drink of this." She saw first the hairy hand, offering her some whiskey in a paper cup. Where was she? The throbbing of the plane, steady now, had become the throbbing inside her. Then she realized that there was a man sitting beside her, a middle-aged man in a rather flashy pin-striped suit, offering her whiskey in a paper cup.

"Th—thank you," she said. "I'm sorry." She drank the whiskey carefully in little sips, felt its warmth creep down inside her. Then she blew her nose. There was no point in pretending anything here. He had seen her crying. And he had rather a kind face, she thought, lined, with wrinkles round the eyes, a balding head. If she didn't say something, she would begin to cry again.

"Families," she heard herself saying to this perfect stranger, "are cruel. They murder each other."

The man had rather tired blue eyes. "You've taken a beating," he said. "You're all upset." He poured out a little more whiskey into her cup. "Tell me about it," he said. "After all, we'll never see each other again."

She put her hand over her eyes to hide them. "My brother committed suicide last night—in Boston," she added. "He was a professor at Harvard." She felt frozen with shame. These were not things that would ever happen to the man in the pin-striped suit beside her. The tears flowed down her cheeks behind her hand.

"That's bad," she heard his voice say, but not as if it

18

were shameful. "Your brother, you say"—he shifted a little in his seat. He reached over and gave her a big white handkerchief—"It's all right, honey. You just cry. It'll do you good."

"We hadn't ever had a quiet talk for years. We just f—f—fought," she blew her nose in the handkerchief, gratefully. "That's what's so awful."

The man was saying, "Sometimes talking doesn't help, but sometimes it does. We've got a long time before St. Louis where I get off, and I have nothing in the world to do. I'd like to know more about all this." She felt him waiting there in the seat beside her and she knew she wanted to tell him everything, to say it all out to this perfect stranger, just because he was a stranger. "When you said 'murder'—that's a strong word, but in my experience I would say it's not too strong a word, at that."

"I've tried so hard to get away, to be—to be—myself," she said, "but Edward was always there, doing crazy things like campaigning for Wallace, being a Socialist, always digging under everything I believed. No"—she sat up straight and turned toward him, as if she were pleading a case—"none of that is the point. I'm not telling the truth. We disagreed about nearly everything, you see, but that isn't the point."

"No, I expect not," the man said, rubbing his chin vaguely. "Could you tell me a little more about your family?" He smiled as if he were smiling a bit ironically at himself. "I'm a lawyer, you see. I like to get everything straight from the ground up."

"Oh yes"—Isabel sighed a long sigh—"I know." But she did not know where or how to begin. It all seemed a tangle, and she had lost her way now, as she always did when she tried to express anything important to her in words. "It all happened in one year," she said, "the family broke up. When Edward graduated from Cornell, Iowa, he got a Rhodes scholarship to Oxford. Father was awfully proud, you know, but all he said was that Edward had better get some decent suits over there." She laughed that same bitter laugh that had surprised her long ago with Henry. "It's silly what little things seem like the last straw. But I knew what those words did—they were like the final closing of a door. Edward never talked about Oxford after that, just to Mother. Then he went away to England and I couldn't tell him—I had promised Mother not to—that she wouldn't be there when he got back. She had cancer of the lung. So I read his letters aloud to her while she fought to keep alive, just so he could finish his year and not be brought home. The last weeks, she couldn't even hear the letters, just held them in her hands, just looked at the handwriting, and when I kissed her good night used to slip the last one under her pillow. And when he was on the boat—"

Isabel was crying again. She put the big handkerchief up to her mouth. When she laid it down again, she felt a strong firm warm hand, clasping hers. It didn't seem strange. She was grateful for the pressure, grateful that he held her hand hard and didn't let it go. "Only those last days Mother said she wanted to die. She couldn't quite make it."

"When Edward came home she wasn't there. I can see that was pretty tough," the man said gravely.

"He never forgave us," she said. "You can't imagine what it was like in the house. You see, we never had talked very much at meals, but Mother was there to make it seem somehow all right. Then, afterwards"—she hesitated a second—"we hardly said a word to each other. I used to pray for a caller, just someone to come and force us back to normal. Finally Edward went East—he had his first job as an instructor at Columbia. We closed the house and never went back, my father and I. We went to California. Father married again."

"You married too," the man said, unclasping his hand from hers and offering her a cigarette.

She nodded, turning the wedding ring on her finger. "My husband's a surgeon," she said, feeling as if she were coming out into sunlight from a long tunnel, and this must have been reflected on her face, for the man smiled at her suddenly, as if he too were happy that she was married, as if almost they were coming out together into the sunlight.

"It's queer about my father," she said in quite a different voice, as if some ease were there now, "he and Mother were never really happy together—at least it didn't seem that way—and he did marry again, most unsuitably we thought, but something went out of him just the same when Mother died. He gave up the bank, he lost his grip on life. I expect marrying again was just a way to try to get it back. Poor Father," she said. "It's idiotic to keep crying like this," and she blew her nose hard. "I'm going to stop."

"Your brother never married, I take it?"

"Oh no."

"Not the marrying kind?"

She considered this. "I don't know. He wanted to help people—he was always taking up with lame ducks, a waitress in Medfield—that's where we lived in Iowa—for instance. He stood there looking out of the window, I remember and told me, 'People shouldn't be so starved, Bel. It's all *wrong.*' I just sat there very still, because it was too strange. I couldn't really imagine it—the girl's mother was a cleaning woman at the high school. I didn't dare ask him if he was in love with her or what. It must sound crazy to you," she said, appalled, as if she had given away a secret, exposed Edward.

"Why crazy?"

"Well, she wasn't anything I knew about. She was too far outside. . . ." There it was again, that word "outside" which kept coming back again and again like a key. "Maybe that was why, maybe Edward needed to get outside."

"That would be my guess." The stranger smiled. "And what happened?"

"Edward went away to college, and for a while it seemed as if"—she hesitated—"as if he were going to be all right. He was brilliant, you know—and then Oxford seemed just the right thing." But Isabel knew she was walking round and round, spilling out a ribbon of facts and that she was still not telling the truth, still far from the truth.

"And then your mother died. Yes, that was bad," the man said quietly. "I can see how bad that was."

"I can't tell you after all." She felt the tears rising up again and turned her face away. "I can't say anything." For a few moments she was fighting off the sobs that came back again and again, breaking through her like blows from the inside. There was no coherent way to follow through now and what came out was a stammered, "He w-wouldn't listen," she cried. "Did c-crazy things like joining the Socialist Party." It was as if these words woke her up, made her angry just to say them. "Edward was not human," she said quite coldly. "He wanted to be more than anything, but he wasn't."

"Well that Socialist stuff is hard to take— I can see

that. But I don't quite follow about his not being human."

"He hurt people."

"Yes, people with strong convictions often do."

"He had to be right, you see." She turned to him now, a little irritated by his tone. "Is that the way men are? I mean, must they always be right and everyone else wrong? I don't think women have to be. I think they can take people more as they are."

"And yet, you couldn't take Edward, could you?" He said it quite gently but it fell like a blow, and she defended herself.

"He disturbed me too much," she said. "You see, he could make everything I have look cheap. That was a rather cruel question, wasn't it?" She could not look at him.

The plane had become very noisy in the last few minutes and they had had to raise their voices. They were swooping up and down into waves of air, buffeted, and Isabel felt a little sick.

"I'm sorry. As I said, I'm a lawyer. I've got interested in this as a problem." He sat back, his hands clasped loosely between his knees. She felt that he had something on his mind and would have liked to know what it was.

"Tell me," she said, "I want to know."

"You used the word 'murder' awhile back. I don't quite get it," the man said quietly, as if he were very gently probing a wound. "From all you say——"

"But I can't say it," she said, shouting at him over the noise. "I don't know."

Then for a while because of the noise, they were silent. Isabel did not look at the man, she was busy trying not to be sick. She closed her eyes, but all the time she had the curious sensation that she could feel the man's thoughts beside her, she could feel him wondering about the word "murder." It's because the love could never get through, she said to him silently. And it seemed extraordinary, like a miracle, that here in the plane she had talked to a perfect stranger, that a perfect stranger had held her hand, that she had trusted him, that in some way he had spoken for Edward, forced her to accept him—but could she? Perfect strangers can let the love through, she thought, and she was crying again.

Was it hours later that she felt her head being gently lifted from a shoulder. "You'd better fasten your belt. We're landing."

She opened her eyes. "Where are we?"

"St. Louis. I'm getting off here."

"Oh dear." She smiled up at him, a little shyly, wondering how long she had lain like that against his shoulder like a child. "I shall miss you."

"I have an idea you'll sleep the rest of the way."

Such a kind man, she thought, holding his handkerchief crumpled up in her hand. I tried to tell him the truth—what is the truth? The plane gave a big jolt and landed. She knew well that she had not told it, that Edward was more than anything she had said, more disturbing, more . . . Who was he murdering when he threw himself under the train? But the kind man had not asked her that and, if he had, she could not have answered. She could only have said, "I did not know my brother very well." Had that old man who called her from Boston known him? What face of a stranger would she have to meet in a few hours, what accusing face? What face which had looked deeply into Edward's eyes and could tell her the truth?

part I

I

A week earlier in that October of 1949 George Hastings in his rooms in Kirkland House at Harvard flung down his pencil and stood up to stretch. He went over to the window and looked up at the bright blue sky, then across the court-yard at the white cornices and sills of the windows and the red brick glowing in the late afternoon sunlight. There was no one around except a gardener raking the leaves. Some-where far off a bell tolled the hour. I've got it in my hands, he thought, and excitement flashed through him like a wave of physical desire. He went to the desk and read over once more the headings of the ten chapters of his doctor's thesis; there it was, then, at last. All the minute detail he had been buried in for months, the endless cards which had so long been a barrier between him and what he really wanted to say had focused in the last twenty-four hours. He had been able to encompass and synthesize all the little parts like the parts of a complicated machine, and now the machine was purring and alive. Just a single sheet of paper, but it was magic, he thought. It was a book. Looking at it again, his heart thumped inside him like a big animal. This was the thing no one could talk about, but that he supposed they all felt once in a while, like an athlete when he secretly breaks his own record, when he knows what he's got. And what people may say afterwards, and whether he can ever do it again, doesn't really matter.

For just a few moments the excitement, the pride, flashed through him, and then he looked around the room, at the disgusting ash tray filled with cigarette butts, at the wastebasket overflowing, the unmade bed, for he had told the cleaning woman to leave him alone when she came in late that morning. There was still a little cold coffee in the percolator, and he poured this out and drank it down. It was time to get out into the air, to walk this excitement out until he could go somewhere and have an enormous meal. He put on a clean shirt, then looked at himself absentmindedly in the mirror and burst into laughter. The face he looked at was so very unlike the way he felt, for what he saw was a frowning boy with black crew-cut hair, rather sharp gray eyes, and a funny wide mouth which made him look like a freshman. The contrast between this grotesque mask and his sensations a moment before of being a giant, full of magical powers, was ludicrous. No wonder Pen couldn't take him seriously. Pen would find it hard to believe that he had finally got through, that he was on the brink of writing what he had been talking about for so long. She would raise her eyebrows in that ironic way she had— Oh Pen, he thought, with an unspoken sigh. There was no point in calling her at this hour. She wouldn't be in.

If only there were someone like God to whom he could breathe praise and thanks, as for a dangerous journey safely completed. But tomorrow he would write to his father and say, "I think I'm about ready to begin the writing on the thesis. I'm pleased about that." He always had the feeling that his father didn't read his letters through, or if he did, then only with the surface of his mind; he couldn't be blamed for he was overworked like all G.P.s, now that so many of the younger men were drafted. But George's mother would read every word, sitting in the kitchen, perhaps with flour on her hands. Would she understand? She had understood his loneliness at the beginning, his sense of being an outsider, because that still had its roots in home. When he first came to Graduate School, he had poured out all his doubts and frustrations to her, but gradually the thread, so taut in the beginning, the root-thread, had loosened. Lately—and especially since he had got into Cavan's seminar—he had found it harder and harder to communicate with his family. It was a little like being in love with Pen. He couldn't explain about Pen either. They already thought of her as "his girl," in terms of a formal engagement, no doubt. How could he explain that Pen didn't want to feel "engaged"? Just because she was such a serious person, not because she wanted to be free to experiment elsewhere. He could see her face, turned away from him, looking out of the window, a little remote, thinking her own thoughts, wanting to think her own thoughts. For this he loved her, though it hurt him, his own desire so remote from hers, reaching its greatest intensity—or so it seemed—at the instant she withdrew.

He closed the door on this image and ran down the stairs. He was not going to allow indecision, doubt, the revulsion which followed a long bout of work to reach him yet. He was going to hold on to his exultation still awhile longer, take it to the river perhaps and lie down in the grass there, find his real self again, that self which the mirror had temporarily taken from him.

Outside, the day greeted him like a clash of cymbals, one of those New England days that make up for all the rain and gloom, the air clean and salty, and light so brilliant that it makes the red brick pavement glow and a single leaf falling seem on fire. He ran towards the river, as if he had an appointment there, as if this light might go before he reached it. The river—that was another thing about which he couldn't write home—Cambridge itself, the river, what it had come to mean. He stood now on the grassy bank and took a deep breath. All around him couples were lying on their stomachs, with books open between them, or just lying there looking up into the sky; four boys were throwing a football around in a desultory way. In his state of exhaustion, hunger and excitement, he saw all this as if for the first time, with the sheen on it. The freshman crew went flashing past, the steady stroke setting up its inexorable rhythm against the nonchalance of everything else. The sky was now a deep orange, making the grass emerald green, turning the blue river to flame. And beyond it on the other bank even the Business School, so new in fact, looked ancient and rosy. He turned back and looked the other way to his own land, the pink, white, and gold of the Harvard Houses, the little shapely towers and the hundreds of windows suddenly taking fire as the sun reached their level and made them blaze. All this seemed given to him like a present, the vision of the university as it might look in a dream. He was so full of it, that he hardly needed to look at it; he lay down with his arms under his head and closed his eyes. Far away he could hear the "one-two" of the crews, then an oar slapping the water—some-one had fumbled. There was a sweet smell of warm grass, of smoke from burning leaves.

Yet beautiful, romantic as all this appeared, George, remote in his private excitement and power, lying with his eyes closed, pushed it aside as irrelevant. For the meaning of it all was something else. The University, he saw, was no building, no great collection of books, no classrooms, and certainly not the students—they were the college. The University was intangible, it existed in the persons of a few great men, in a few faces—at this moment Edward Cavan's especially, Cavan not as a teacher, but in a way George would never see him, bent over his own work, fighting out a book alone, the long arduous lonely work of a scholar. This was the University, and the clock towers, the libraries, the Houses by the river might all be blasted away—yes, even the river—but this image of a man's thinking face would remain.

George rolled over on his stomach and chewed a piece of grass. It occurred to him that at last, with his book on the way, he might actually do what he had never dared to do, invite Cavan out for dinner at the Oyster House, even tell him in that informal atmosphere about Pen, for he imagined that in Edward Cavan he had found the man who might be to him all that his father could not be, to whom he could pour out his whole heart and mind.

Except for conferences in the dingy atmosphere of the office at Warren House, George had only seen Edward Cavan once in a personal way, on Christmas Eve. He would never forget that party, for it marked the turning point. At that moment he knew that he belonged at last, that he was accepted. For not everyone by any means was invited, and the invitation made it clear that this was a personal and not an official matter. "I invite a few of my friends to drop in on Christmas Eve and I hope you will want to join us." George had preserved this brief note, written in Cavan's small precise hand, as if it were the entrance to a secret society.

He remembered everything about those rooms, the second floor of a house on Chestnut Street. They were all that such rooms should be, just elegant enough with their good old pieces of furniture, their walls of books, the few carefully chosen paintings by artists of whom George had never heard—just elegant enough, but comfortable and unself-conscious too. Cavan himself looked relaxed and happy, standing against the mantelpiece. They drank punch and talked about Wallace Stevens, and about Faulkner, he remembered. And they laughed a great deal. All the time George had wished that Pen were there, so they could talk about it afterwards, savor each detail together. He did not know most of the people there, except by name, but they all took him for granted. He did not feel like a stranger, bound to explain that he had gone to Rutgers instead of Harvard. He was one of a company of scholars and teachers, and his heart was full.

Remembering this in his present state of more than usual self-confidence, George got to his feet hurriedly and looked as his watch. Why not go over to Warren House and ask Cavan out to dinner now? Ridley was having his orals this afternoon and they would still be at it. It was the day for a daring adventure, his day. Why not? After all, he had something real to tell Cavan, a reason for such a celebration. George left the river without a backward glance, walking fast, hardly looking where he was going. There by the river it had been possible to contemplate the University in essence. Now as he drew closer to the Square, to the Yard itself, as he made his way through the college men and glanced in at the windows of smart clothing stores and tobacconists, as he walked past the Clubs and the fancy bookstores, he could feel the compulsion, the ambition in the balls of his feet. The people he met were his enemies, his competitors. And the University which had appeared to him as serene and pure as the City of God, a company of devoted scholars, showed him its other face. For it was also, he thought, a machine for turning out Ph.D.s, for getting people like him jobs, for measuring and discarding the almost adequate, for reserving its honors often for those men who could play for position. George took out a cigarette and lit it as he skirted the Yard.

"I'll see that you get a real chance, I'll do all I can," Cavan had said months ago, hinting at a possible instructorship for the following year. Then he had stopped, sat down, played with a pencil and added in a curiously abrupt, embarrassed way, "Of course it's not entirely in my hands, you know. These things are department matters. I sometimes think I have become an outsider." He had looked up at George with a hesitant smile, seemed to want to say more, instead changed the subject. It was George's first glimpse of the fact that even the great felt insecure, that even they were caught up in the matrix of ambitions, even they were vulnerable. Since then he had heard enough gossip and rumor to be quite aware that Cavan was considered a maverick in some quarters, not entirely sound for political reasons. It had done him no good to stand up and fight on every liberal issue for the last ten years. "But after all," George had answered hotly when this came up in a bull session, "his work is absolutely first-rate. You can't deny that."

"All I know is they get letters of complaint from old grads; people talk, you know, and it doesn't do the college any good."

"It doesn't do the college any good to be full of second-rate pussyfooters either." George had been furiously angry, the more so because he was not interested in politics and felt slightly bewildered himself by this side of Cavan.

"Hi, George." Jack Warner almost bumped into him, on purpose it seemed. "What's eating you?"

"Why?"

"You look like a bat out of hell—what's the rush?"

"I have an appointment," George said stiffly and walked on. It was a stupid thing to say, and out of sheer exasperation George broke into a run. He rounded the corner past the Union and jumped the three steps of the Warren House porch as if he were bringing the message to Garcia. Then, inside, he was greeted by silence and the dead bulletin board, every item of which he must have read a hundred times. Was it all over? The whole place had a dank academic smell as if the students sweating out their fears had infected it; how many of them had waited here, as he was waiting, smoking because there was nothing else to do, reading over and over the announcements of fellowships and lectures, trying to think up a new excuse for a late paper?

A door upstairs opened and closed. Ridley appeared, visibly shaken, took out a handkerchief and wiped his face, then disappeared again. He had the air of a condemned man. It was silly to let this atmosphere get you, but George himself felt wildly nervous now. If Ridley failed, Cavan would be upset—especially if Goldberg had had his say. Rumor had it that he and Cavan were archenemies, but one never knew; the affairs of the faculty reached the students rather as the peccadilloes and fallings out of Greek gods, enlarged by gossip and wishful thinking, turning quickly into myth. At any rate, Goldberg with his icy passion for perfection would be a formidable examiner. They must be arguing about poor Ridley now, no easy decision evidently. George looked at his watch. Five minutes. You could damn a man to hell in five minutes, or you might just manage to tip the balance of judgment in his favor.

"Mr. Ridley, will you come in here, please?" It was Edward Cavan's voice, dry, without emotion. No way of reading what it meant.

Why in heck am I putting myself through this? George asked himself. Ridley came down the stairs, his hands shaking as he took out a crumpled cigarette pack, dug around and found it empty.

"Here," George offered his. "How was it?" he asked in a toneless voice. The poor guy was obviously in a state of shock. But you never knew. He himself had been near to tears when it was safely over.

"Lousy," Ridley's face grimaced into an attempt at a smile. "I lost my head."

"Bad luck." George's instinct was to turn away, not to have to witness the shame or the bravado of a man facing failure, and, seeing Cavan at the top of the stairs, he slipped into the big empty office off the hall. It was no time to make a social engagement.

"What happened to you, Ridley?" he could hear Cavan asking with clinical concern. "You were doing all right, and then suddenly you went right off the track, spectacularly off the track."

"I—I don't know, sir," Ridley's voice cracked.

"This sort of thing happens all the time," Cavan sounded thoughtful as if he were settling down to a philosophical question, treating the miserable Ridley as a peer. "The trouble is that we haven't found a better way to find out how a man moves around in a lot of material. Maybe we ask the wrong questions. You got thrown off. I'm sorry." There was a slight pause, in which perhaps Cavan was shaking Ridley's hand. "But don't go into a tailspin—you'll do better on a second try."

"Thank you, sir."

As Goldberg and Beatley came down the stairs, Cavan turned into the room where George Hastings stood twiddling his thumbs. The front door slammed on Ridley's exit.

"Hello, Hastings, what are you doing here?"

Cavan stood under the garish electric lights, peering out like some animal caught unaware, and blinked a smile. But it was not a real smile.

"Just hanging around." Warren House was not so cozy that anyone would choose it to hang around in for no purpose. "I dropped in," he explained, ridiculously embarrassed now, "and then sort of got suspended on Ridley's oral."

"You know him?"

"Slightly."

"Well," Cavan said curtly, "come out and have a cup of coffee." Dazed by the simplicity of this moment which he had planned and rehearsed so many times, and which had just happened when all seemed lost, George followed Edward Cavan out without a word. They walked down Massachusetts Avenue past the men's clothing stores, tobacconists and banks, none of which Cavan noticed. He seemed compressed, hardly aware of the boy who walked beside him. "Hideous mess," he muttered to himself once, nodding to a passing student. They were held up at the Square by a red light, and again George had the image of a small compact animal always on guard, or a prize fighter at ease but ready for a blow. Why was this?

"Where shall we go?" Cavan said, as if he were coming to, aware for the first time that he was not alone.

"St. Clair's?" George offered tentatively. This and Schrafft's were the posh places.

"I refuse to pay fifteen cents for a cup of coffee," Cavan said irritably, as they finally got the light and crossed over. "Albiani's—it's more human."

"Well, it's empty at this time anyway." It was, to George's view, dismal, a huge room full of empty tables now, at rush hour filled with high school kids and bums. It was inhabited at the moment by two old ladies, a Negro workman in overalls, and a stout elderly man eating a complete dinner in a booth.

"Sit down, I'll get the coffee." He wondered if they would be able to talk after all. He felt frightened.

"A clean well-lighted place," he quoted nervously, for effect, as he brought back the tray with two cups of coffee and two jars of cream on it.

"You see some real people here," Cavan said quite seriously.

This George recognized as completely in character, this nostalgia of the intellectual for the workingman. He recognized it, but it seemed to him rather childish. The coffee was poor, and all he himself felt here was loneliness.

"That silly fool let himself get baited by Goldberg," Cavan was saying, "lost his head. It was quite unnecessary —Ridley knows the sort of thing Goldberg is after perfectly well."

"Goldberg has everyone scared to death," George confided.

"I know." Cavan lit a cigarette, then drank down half his cup of coffee at one gulp. "He sets a high standard. I have nothing against that." He set his cup down firmly and frowned. "At least you've got a passion for what you're doing, Hastings. The trouble with Ridley is that he's so dull about it all. I don't get any sense that he's gripped by the subject. Oh well"—Cavan shrugged as if to shrug away something unnecessarily disturbing—"he'll get through next time with a little luck. What have you been doing with all those cards and files lately? Got anywhere?"

George choked on a swallow of coffee. Tears started from his eyes. He felt ludicrous. He had been running toward this moment all through the day. For months he had dreamed of this moment, and now he was coughing and trying to catch his breath and Edward Cavan was giving him a heavy slap on the back and laughing at him. Finally he was able to say in a squeaky voice, "I outlined the book today. I think I'm ready to begin." He wiped his face with a handkerchief and blew his nose. He felt utterly humiliated. Some of the coffee had spilled on his shirt; he tried to wipe it off with a paper napkin.

"Good, I'm glad to hear it." Cavan looked at him hard, without smiling. "Better be prepared for a letdown," he said unexpectedly. "You'll never see the book as clearly again till it's finished—and even then all you'll see is the enormous gap between that flash of real mastery and what finally gets down on paper." Cavan was leaning forward now, not looking at George, and George watched him, the way his mouth clamped shut tight when he was thinking, the way his eyes seemed to get more intense and smaller. For Cavan the act of thinking was a physical act, a physical conflict, and this was rather disturbing.

"You didn't feel that about the American giants book surely, did you?" George said, trying to fit together what looked like anguish and the classic masterpiece.

"Of course," Cavan said impatiently. "I rewrote some chapters five times. When I finished it, I was in despair." He laughed a short laugh with no humor in it. Then he looked across at George with one of his rare warm smiles, blinking a little behind his glasses. "It's all in the game," he said almost cheerfully.

"Is your own book finished, sir? You said the other day you were near the end." He hoped this was the right question, the question that might open their sealed relationship like an envelope and all the things he wanted so much to talk about—Pen, his father—fall out.

Cavan looked startled as if he had forgotten all about it, rubbed his forehead with one hand abruptly. "I've been busy with other things," he said. He looked over at George, as if he were measuring him. "I've been troubled, too troubled to do any work lately. It's a bad time, George."

The first name made the difference. "Yes, sir." George fumbled for the right answer, but couldn't find it. As he raised his eyes he met in Cavan's a look of naked appeal, but for what? He did not know what he was being asked now, what the question in the air between them really was.

"It's like a creeping paralysis of the nerves—you don't know where to begin, how to fight it." George felt as if an enormous cloud were settling down over Cavan now. He sat hunched over, looking down into his cup, everything in his face withdrawn.

"I don't think I know— I don't understand—" he stammered.

The look Cavan shot him was like a blow; it was hostile. "You never knew what a liberal world was like," he said harshly. "How could you? You were four or five at the time of the Spanish War; you can hardly remember the New Deal."

It's not my fault, George wanted to say, but he just waited.

"But it should mean something to you that professors in our colleges and universities are being fired for nonconformist ideas, that it's becoming a crime to subscribe to the *Nation*, that everywhere in this country fear is taking the place of reason." The words fell hard and fast as if they were meant to shock.

"It's bad, I know," George said, "but isn't there always a period of reaction after a war?"

"The historical point of view is nothing to hide behind. My God"—Cavan brought his fist down on the table—"I heard people say about Hitler that all tyrants fail eventually. Let's be detached and wait while millions of human beings are slaughtered; it'll all come right in the end, won't it?" He was furiously angry, it seemed.

"I didn't mean——"

"You have to fight at the very beginning—otherwise it's too late."

"Yes, sir," George said helplessly.

The deep-set blue eyes focused on him—bleakly—and then looked away. Cavan put out his cigarette with a gesture of impatience. "I'm sorry," he said. He smiled, but it was the smile of effort and the effort told. He looked ten years older suddenly. "We'll talk about all this some other time," he said, getting up to go.

I've failed him, George thought miserably. I had the chance and I couldn't say the right thing. Cavan paid for the coffee and then left him on the curb with a curt, "Good luck on the book." George watched him run between the cars and disappear into the subway station.

What was it all about anyway? At first it seemed as if at last he was going to have a chance to talk to Cavan easily, like another human being. But somewhere along the way, something had happened. He as a person had ceased to exist. He had been given a riddle to guess, that was it, and because he didn't know the answer, couldn't participate, he had ceased to exist. "I am troubled," Cavan had said, and "You have to fight." But what did you have to fight and how? George stood there on the curb in the middle of Harvard Square, filled with silent longing, the longing to know all those things he didn't know, the Spanish War and whatever that meant to people like Edward Cavan, the longing to be as rich and complex, as eaten up by life as the man with whom he had just failed to communicate at all. Was the thinking man of his vision, the man who represented the University really in danger? Was Cavan in danger himself? What did all the books mean if you couldn't answer these questions, couldn't meet another human being on his own terms—failed out of hopeless ignorance and indifference? Could politics matter that much?

II

Every month on the day of the Civil Liberties Union meeting Grace Kimlock stopped to pick up Edward Cavan on her way in from Cambridge to The Hill. She got off at Charles Street and enjoyed the walk across to Chestnut where Edward lived. She allowed plenty of time to stop and peer in at the antique shops and especially at a spectacular florist's where new great pots of deep ochre, orange, and dark red chrysanthemums were set out on the sidewalk between orange trees. All this was a rite, filled with anticipation, for she looked forward even more to seeing Edward, to the further steep climb up the hill with him, as if this monthly custom had become a sign, precious to her, of their intimacy.

On this particular October afternoon, Grace Kimlock rang his bell several times, but there was no answering buzz. She began to wonder if Edward had started off without her; no, that was unthinkable. But he did seem absentminded these days. Could he have forgotten all about it? Decided not to come? She felt suddenly agitated, standing there on the steps, exposed to the curious glances of the passers-by. The erratic pumping of her heart bothered her and she rapped sharply with the man's umbrella she carried, as if to make it stop.

Grace Kimlock, daughter of a beloved Harvard dean, considered herself a kind of emeritus dean herself, now that she was in her seventies. It was certainly true that she had a gift for bringing members of the faculty together and getting them to talk, as she put it, "about the facts." What this really meant, of course, was "the feelings"; she dearly loved a row, the chance to watch two enemies fight it out in the open. The passive, the indifferent, or those with little life to spare were frightened off; she needed resilience to strike her flint against. Weakness of any sort upset her and she reacted, quite unconsciously, by being cruel. It was in the order of things that she and Edward Cavan recognize each other in the early years when he had come to Harvard from New York, "an unlicked cub," as she loved to remind him. She belonged to an older, less complicated generation, the generation of Darwinians and Socialists for whom Debs, Huxley and Shaw were heroes. Edward Cavan, of the Eliot era, called himself a Christian Socialist; she would spare the adjective as irrelevant. But they had seen eye to eye in the Spanish Civil War of course, had thrown themselves passionately into the Republican side, speaking as a team before factory groups and at women's clubs and colleges. This was in the early days of their friendship. Since then these strong intellectual and emotional ties had been firmly cemented. She regarded Edward as her dearest friend, almost as a son.

She tried the bell once more. Finally at the end of her patience, she went out into the street and shouted, "Edward! Hurry up!" in a piercing voice. The silence of the street echoed her cry. "I feel ill," she said to herself. "It's ridiculous to be so anxious, damn him!" She had tears in her eyes. She was trembling. For, in her seventies, Grace Kimlock was still a passionate person; the source of whatever ills she knew, neuralgia and that fast-beating heart, came from exasperated nerves which she had never bothered to control.

"It's the state of the world," she told herself. "We're all as nervous as cats." Really it was the worst year she could remember. As if it weren't bad enough that the Communists had taken over Czechoslovakia—how wrong Edward had been proved about that, poor Edward—the fear of communism was taking over the United States. Even the conservative old Civil Liberties Union seemed changed and was all at sixes and sevens. Edward felt these things too much, that was the trouble—and where in thunder was he? Actually she had been standing there little more than two minutes, her heart thumping out its questions, when Edward Cavan ran down the steps.

She gave him a single piercing glance and turned to walk briskly up the hill beside him, scolding him as they went. "You forget that I'm an old woman, Edward. I get agitated when I'm kept waiting."

"I'm sorry, Grace, but you're always early, you know."

"What if I am?" Relief after anxiety took the form of irritation. She stopped a moment to lean on her umbrella

44

and catch her breath. "You should wear a coat, Edward— you'll catch cold," she said crossly. But it was not the lack of a coat, it was something in the way he walked, his shoulders hunched over, that made him look vulnerable to her, as if he were holding himself down, holding down some acute tension by sheer force of will.

He did not answer, did not seem to have heard her remark, and they took the steepest part of the hill in silence, then turned down Walnut Street, a little apart, for Grace had drawn away in order to be able to see his face. He's troubled, she thought, and I can't ask him about it. Was it the book? Was he again in one of those periods when he wrote each morning and then threw the morning's work in the wastebasket? Was it something at Harvard? Whatever it was, it could not be deciphered in his face. As they emerged into the open spaces, high up at the top of the Common, she drew a deep breath and stood for a moment surveying the scene. Somehow the vista of trees, the colonies of pigeons, the bums feeding the pigeons from crumby bags, the frog pond just below, so familiar and safe, cheered her.

"I feel like a child dragging his feet to a horrid school. What has happened to us? I used to enjoy the meetings . . ." she said, as if aware for the first time what a change had come upon everything lately. "Pay attention, Edward!"

"I'm sorry." He shoved his hands down into his pockets, forcing a thought down there out of sight, or so it seemed. "What was it, Grace? What did you say?" He turned to her and smiled, a young smile, his deep-set blue eyes regarding her with humorous concern.

"I said that I hated these meetings and I wonder why. What's happened to us, Edward?" and this time there was a plaintive note in her voice.

"Nothing's happened to us, nothing at all. We're just what we always were, that's what's the trouble." Movement was clearly necessary to him now and he increased their pace.

"The sense of the meeting has changed, you mean? Don't walk so fast, Edward. I'm an old woman."

At this, he took her arm and slowed down. "It's a liberal organization, Grace, after all."

"It used to be a fighting organization."

"The trouble with the liberals is that they see *all* sides. It paralyzes them." He was half-smiling now, that ironic smile she knew well. "It was quite all right to be radical twenty years ago—at least in these parts. Now I frighten my students if I mention the New Deal. Actually they've never heard of the Spanish War. They're not interested in politics—even the best of them," he said bitterly, "like Hastings." They were close to the State House, standing back from the hill up its serene flights of steps, the red brick façade turned a warm rose in the late afternoon sun, the cupola, bright shining gold.

"Dear old thing." Grace gave it an affectionate glance. "Isn't it lovely to have the dome gold again? Lovely." She stopped a moment here in the final open space before Beacon Street grows dark with office buildings.

"Yes, the dome's gold again . . ." He left the sentence in the air. But she knew what he was thinking as the current of intimacy flowed between them again. She knew very well what he was thinking as he turned and looked about him, a slightly quizzical expression in his blue eyes.

Certain elements of Boston are gathered in this block in concentrated essence. Beside the office buildings, where the Civil Liberties Union is squeezed in among various Protestant Church organizations, stands the Athenaeum, that private library which is also a private heaven (Good Americans may go to Paris when they die; good Bostonians go to the Athenaeum). Just up the street on the same side is Goodspeed's, for rare books and prints, and across from it the Bellevue Hotel where, at lunchtime, boys from the State House and Protestant ministers elbow each other. All this debouches into the wide hilly expanse of the Common. This Boston may look sedate, ancient and settled to an outsider, but to Edward Cavan and Grace Kimlock, standing on the corner, its tradition was a living one, a tradition of reform, protest, fierce belief in general enlightenment and in the rights of minorities. Not for nothing was their final glance for the corner where Robert Gould Shaw stood in bas-relief leading his Negro regiment into battle.

Then, as the lights finally changed, they cut across to the narrowing street and quickened their pace. "Yes, the dome's gold again," Edward had said, and what he meant of course was that the hot war (when the dome was camouflaged dark gray) might be over, but the cold war was on, and was on in the Civil Liberties Union as well as everywhere else: The question as to whether some of the members of the executive committee might be too radical had certainly never occurred to anyone until lately. Grace really dreaded going in, so much so that she stopped at the door, gave Edward a shy look, and said, "You go on ahead. I'll just pop into the Athenaeum for a moment. I'll be right there," she called over her shoulder, already ashamed of herself as she saw Edward standing where she had left him, his head bowed, his hands shoved down into his pockets, lost in that thought of his she could not read.

She found the last issue of the *Economist* and stood leafing it through nervously, but it was no use. The vision of Edward, outside, haunted her. In some ways she knew him very well; someone who knew him less well would not have been anxious. But Grace recognized the signs of depression in his lapses of attention; she knew by the look in his eyes that he was not sleeping. She knew that much, yet standing here with the thick wall of the Athenaeum between them, she also recognized that she knew nothing. Our real lives are secret, she thought, frightfully secret. No one knows anyone else. Friendship, even love, fails. We are alone. She stood there with the *Economist* in her hands, while it seemed everything disintegrated round her; the walls flew apart; there was no safety.

"Come along," she commanded, as she found Edward again just where she had left him. "We might as well get it over with." Before the slow-moving elevator crept down to them, they were joined in the marble hall by Damon Phillips, his pockets bulging with newspapers as usual, two brief cases, one half-open, in his hands, and that air of perpetual harassment and gusto which made him endearing. Phillips was a Harvard professor in physics. In him everything that seemed bottled up and tense in Cavan spilled over; it was the thing to say that if only Phillips would stick to his last and not try to be Universal Man, he might end up with a Nobel prize. If Edward Cavan's students sometimes thought of him as a small compact animal, a woodchuck or hedgehog, Phillips might be caricatured as a long-legged heron, all angles and awkward sudden flight. The two men had always been friends, meeting often at Grace Kimlock's house. So it had been until the year of Wallace's Progressive Party. Phillips, after considerable soul-searching, had cast his vote for Truman, and since then there had been a rift between them which no amount of geniality on the surface could quite conceal.

But at least here, Grace thought, greeting him with a pat on the shoulder, we still see eye to eye. I do not have to feel nervous about Damon.

"What's up today?" he asked, and then, without waiting for an answer, crumpled up a paper from his brief case and threw it on the floor, "I'm sick and tired of these meetings. What makes us keep on exposing ourselves to such boredom and frustration, eh, Edward?"

"Well, at the moment some pretty dirty bills are brewing, little Dies Committee stuff," Edward said drily.

"Hey, wait for Beatrice," Damon called, as the elevator door was closing on them. "You're just in time. The Old Guard is now complete."

Beatrice Carr laughed. "Are we really the Old Guard? I prefer to consider us the Radical Wing." She was a middle-aged stout woman with short-cut gray hair, an old black suit, and held two bulging rubber bags since it was her habit to go to Faneuil Hall and load up on groceries before these monthly meetings. Beatrice had been on the committee in one capacity or another longer even than Grace; she was a professional, had even run for Governor on the Progressive Party ticket. Many people suspected her of being a Communist, a fact which she knew perfectly well, but she believed that if you begin to explain yourself you have already capitulated, and she went her way, quite fearless.

In the few seconds while the elevator rose slowly to the third floor, a kind of warmth crept about these four. The precious thing, Grace thought, the thing it was quite impossible to put into words was this feeling of solidarity. They had been through a lot together through the years. And they were bound so closely not only by hard work and conviction, but even, she told herself, by having shared the boredom of innumerable meetings like this one. She felt suddenly happy, ready for a fight should there be one just ahead down the dingy corridor in the dingy little room where a faded protrait of Lincoln looked down on three rows of folding chairs. Why is it, she asked herself, that in spite of myself I can never come here without being moved? Perhaps it was that here one felt the roots of democracy at work, in such small organizations as this, always in financial trouble, always near collapse but somehow persisting, lifted on the belief of a few devoted people willing to gather month after month and year after year, willing to expose themselves to ridicule and to each other's often difficult temperaments, to go out and dun friends for money, to spend hours addressing envelopes—and all this for the purpose of standing, a bulwark against hysteria, to see that fundamental human rights were upheld and not forgotten, in fact to defend the Republic. But it was a dreadfully slow process, and as Grace picked up the agenda and read over the familiar items, she gave a loud sigh.

"Surely, Grace, it's not as bad as all that," the chairman teased. One of the new young men guffawed nervously, and everyone chuckled.

"We'll see, Mr. Chairman. It's a moot point," Grace said, bending on him a fierce eagle eye.

"We have a quorum," the chairman announced in his official voice. There was some dull business to go through, and while the minutes of the last meeting were read and passed on, Grace was busy making drawings in her notebook, a large childish sunflower, an elephant trumpeting, a house with smoke coming out of its chimney. She never could keep still. Phillips had taken over two chairs, and was ferreting about in his brief cases, emerging now and then with some document on which he doodled, a cigarette hanging from his lips and impetuous volleys of talk bursting from him at intervals. Edward Cavan, on the other hand, sat as always, with his head bowed, his hands clasped between his knees in an attitude of tensely watchful waiting. Only Beatrice seemed quite calm. Such they were; such they had always been. They made up the quorum but, far more than that, they electrified the room by sheer force of character.

Item two on the agenda had been safely reached. It looked innocuous enough, some request for information from the National ACLU, and no one showed much interest at first. But the way the chairman coughed before he began to read, Grace sensed that something was up. She left the elephant without any tail, her pencil suspended in the air, and devoted her whole attention to what followed. The chairman read on smoothly without lifting his eyes from the letter. It seemed that the national organization would like written assurance that the executive committee of its Boston affiliate contained no Communists or fascists. This was the dynamite; it was followed by a word to explain that of course all they needed was an informal statement, that they had the utmost faith in the affiliate and so forth. It was signed by the executive secretary. Very quietly the chairman laid the paper down and leaned forward to listen. "I would like to have your views on this——"

"Preposterous!" Grace said loudly, without waiting to be recognized. She scribbled furiously on her pad. She wrote "damn" on the elephant's behind instead of making a tail.

Edward raised his head and at a nod from the chairman said rapidly and angrily. "I move that we spell out to them in no uncertain terms that for an organization set up to defend Civil Liberties to institute what amounts to a loyalty oath among its members is tantamount to betrayal of all that we stand for."

"Second the motion," Beatrice said clearly.

"Any discussion?" The chairman looked around with a twinkle in his eye.

Damon raised his hand and was recognized. He spoke directly to the chairman without looking at anyone else. "It has always been our policy and principle that our political views were our own business here, as long as we were whole-hearted believers in civil liberties for all citizens regardless of their political affiliations—" He is spelling it out for the new members of the committee, Grace thought, resuming her drawing. This was all old stuff after all. But she did not draw for long. Damon proceeded to say, "But in the case of members of the Communist Party today things are a little different. I think the national association has reason and is wise to want to be quite sure that no one on this board has a higher loyalty than that I have expressed. If we could be smeared with a political label, we might as well go out of business. We have to be realistic, for God's sake," he said, feeling, no doubt, that Grace's hackles were rising.

"That is the liberal view, isn't it, Damon? When it comes to the point, always back down." These brief words of Edward's, directed at Damon personally, fell with the impact of a blow.

"We shall be labeled anyway," Beatrice broke in, "Even if we spend money and time explaining how anti-Communist we are like the ADA. We shall be called Reds because it's absolutely inevitable that we shall have to defend Communists for some time to come. The question of the rights of Communists *is* the frontier of Civil Liberties today, after all. Ten years ago, as some of you perhaps do not know," she said turning round to face the younger members of the committee, "we defended the rights of fascist organizations, Gerald K. Smith's for one."

"But," one of the young men answered, "just because we shall be defending Communists, Miss Carr, mustn't we ourselves be impeccable?"

"Hasn't the national affiliate a right to know that we are?" another broke in.

Above their voices Damon's could be heard. "This is not a personal matter, Edward. I have a right to say what I think, and I object to your tone."

Everyone was now talking at once except Grace, surprisingly enough. She was trying to measure the damage already done. Here it was again, she thought. Instead of getting down to business, we are fighting among ourselves about things which should be absolutely taken for granted. She sat up as straight as a ramrod, her cheeks flushed, and finally shouted, "Mr. Chairman, Mr. Chairman, we have a motion before us."

By now some people had forgotten the motion and Edward repeated it for their benefit. It was put to a vote and voted down, with only Beatrice, Edward and herself in the affirmative. Grace could feel the tension in Edward as painfully as if he were twisting her arm and not sitting, as he was, with his head in his hands. She knew very well how he felt and that for him this was a crucial matter. She had heard him say often enough that if you begin to compromise on matters of principle, you are lost. To the others, it might seem a small matter—after all, there were no members of the Party on the committee and why not say as much? But to Edward—and she felt sure he was right in essence—the first compromise led inevitably to others; if you give in on small matters, you haven't a leg to stand on when the big things come along. That was the position. How Damon could fail to admit it, she could not understand.

While she was turning all this over anxiously in her mind, Damon was making a motion about the kind of letter they might write, giving the necessary assurance, on the chairman's word, with no further inquiries among themselves. Once while he talked he turned to Edward, as if to plead with him, but Edward did not raise his head. His hands were clasped tightly between his knees. Let's get it over with, Grace thought. Damon's motion was voted.

"Well," the chairman said with a beaming smile, "so that's all settled."

But before he could go on to the next item, Edward had risen to his feet, stood there, glaring as if he wanted to shout something, then instead turned on his heel and walked out, closing the door quietly instead of slamming it as the violence of his move had seemed to require; this gentle closing of the door was curiously disturbing. The chairman waited a second with the agenda lifted in one hand, then proceeded without comment. From then on the meeting passed in a blur through Grace's mind. They agreed to give legal aid to a mathematics teacher from the Boston public schools who had just been fired without trial, having been accused of being a Communist. They talked about who they might get to speak before a mass meeting which would include support from some of the Protestant Churches. But all the time Grace felt the awful desolation of Damon's surprising stand seeping in and wondered all the time what Edward was doing now, where his rage might take him.

How could it have all happened so quickly, almost before she was aware of it? Like a thunderstorm it had come and gone, leaving them changed. Was it only a half-hour ago that they had come up in the elevator so cheerfully together, that she had rested in the feeling of solidarity and trust? She did not dare even look at Damon and hoped she could get away alone as the meeting broke up. But she was waylaid by Beatrice first, and then Damon was there at her side saying, "I've got the car. I'll take you home, Grace."

Yes, we must talk, she thought, torn between the obvious necessity for that and the part of her which only wished to run down the hill to Edward.

But Damon was standing there beside her, looking at her a little ruefully, puffing at his cigarette. She could not abandon him now, just when perhaps he too felt forlorn.

One did not, she knew, take this kind of stand without suffering. Certainly Damon did not.

"All right, Damon," she said, "Edward's gone."

"That," he answered stiffly, "is an obvious statement of fact."

They did not speak at all until they were in the car, parked on Mt. Vernon Street.

"Why don't we go and see Edward now?" she said on an impulse. Couldn't it still be mended, this rift which seemed to be growing larger every second?

"I'd like to," Damon was now hunched down in the seat, playing with the car key nervously. He looked haggard. "But you know very well, Grace, that it wouldn't be any use."

"I can't see that it's all so important," she said crossly.

"You can't?" Damon gave a shocked short laugh. "I thought the whole point was that it *is* important."

"I mean compared to friendship, I suppose. I can't bear it, Damon. It shouldn't be like this between you and Edward."

"It shouldn't be, but it is." He started the car jerkily, throwing Grace forward like an old stiff doll. "Sorry, Julia tells me I'm the worst driver in the world. Did I hurt you?" he asked, more anxiously than the moment warranted.

"I'm quite all right, thank you."

Stopped at a red light at the foot of the hill, Damon lit another cigarette and turned to Grace. "The trouble with Edward, Grace, is that he's too passionate about these things. It isn't his real self—because when it comes to the things he really cares about—Wallace Stevens' poetry, say—he can be judicial and balanced. Why is it? It's like some illness he has, and it's much worse now than it

56

used to be. Am I wrong? I'm not trying to justify myself. I may be wrong about this political thing. Maybe I am just a liberal, as Edward would say with contempt. Only"—the car jerked forward again—"I'm proud of being one, that's the difference. Liberalism implies generosity and it seems as if, politically speaking, Edward were incapable any more of generosity."

"He would call your generosity compromise and cowardice, Damon."

"Do you?" he asked as at last they turned off down Beacon Street and had a clear run for a few blocks.

"I don't know what I think. I'm upset," she said. "What's going to happen now?" she asked in a frightened voice.

"As far as the Union goes this is a minor matter, Grace. There's no point in making a mountain out of a molehill. There are no Communists on our board, as we all know. It's easy enough to write an informal letter of assurance——"

"Edward's lonely," she said, off on her own train of thought. "I'm anxious about him."

"He's always been lonely," Damon said thoughtfully. "I wonder why." She didn't answer this. They had come to Massachusetts Avenue now and turned onto the bridge to cross the river. There it lay, deep lacquered blue with the lights reflected in it and Boston, the great city, suddenly small and intimate along its rim. This sudden view of the river, so calm, so beautiful and quiet, upset her. She was in fact, near to tears, and felt absurdly nervous in consequence. She was not a woman for whom tears are a relief. Anger was the only emotion she could handle and enjoy. Anything else terrified her.

"Partly perhaps he has laid too great a weight upon friendship, for lack of love—or because of love—which is it? I'm upset too," Damon said quietly now. "Just as upset as you are."

"You'll have to go to him, talk to him—you'll have to, Damon. He won't do it. You know that."

"I think Julia will have to do it."

"Why Julia?" Julia, Damon's wife, had always seemed to Grace one of these cowlike women whom one looked on simply as appendages to a man.

"Because Julia has a real relationship with Edward, just as real as mine—and because she's a woman."

"Why because she's a woman?" Grace Kimlock, ardent feminist though she was, really disliked women.

"Whatever gentleness there is in Edward comes out in relation to women, that's all. He's less thorny with Julia. He used to come and have tea with her two or three times a week. I often thought he was a little in love with her, but of course he would never admit it, even to himself——"

Grace gave a deprecatory sniff.

"The queer thing is that we none of us really *know* Edward, do we? And lately it's been hard to know him, he reacts so violently, like a wounded bear if you touch him——"

"With me he's not like that," she said firmly.

"No"—Damon gave her a quizzical glance, tender and amused—"I expect not. You agree with him, you see. You don't raise any troubling questions. Politically, Edward is on the brink of an abyss, he's just balancing himself somehow on the *will to believe*. I don't suppose any of us can measure what the Czechoslovakia business did to him, Grace."

"I don't see that you have to give up believing something just because in one instance it hasn't worked," she said, flushing. And there it was again, the rift, the ache, the sense that at some point now communication broke down.

"Never mind," Damon said, impatiently swerving round a truck and nearly colliding with an oncoming car. "That's not the point really . . ." He was himself, Grace thought grimly, near exasperation.

"What is the point, Damon?" she asked. "Slow down. I want to see the river," she commanded. For whatever else failed, the river was always there, a quiet glory, darkened over by the curving bridges, reflecting all the points of light of student rooms in the Harvard Houses, in the Business School on the far side. Whatever loyalties might fail, this loyalty to the University remained steadfast, and rose up in her like a balm.

The traffic slowed down, stopped at a red light, just under Eliot House. For a moment Damon said nothing, though he was much too impatient and nervous a driver to pay attention to the river, his hands gripping the wheel like a racer, as if he could leap forward when the light changed and would not be stopped by the slow crawling crescendo of cars ahead.

He did not answer her question until they were out of the worst traffic and swinging along under the avenue of plane trees. Then, as if emotion had suddenly drained out of him, as if the moment had exploded for him some time back and now there was no vital energy left, he said quietly, "As a scientist it shocks me to see someone as blindly, as emotionally committed to an idea as Edward is to the idea that Communists and Socialists can work together. Don't you see that he's on the defensive? He's too intelligent for that, Grace—don't you see?"

"But people who are not emotionally committed, as you put it, never get anything *done*, Damon. Look at the Civil Liberties Union."

Damon jerked the car to a stop in front of Grace's house on Fayerweather Street.

"What about Fosca?" she said suddenly.

"What about him?"

"He could talk to Edward," she said with immense relief as if she had caught hold of a life preserver. "People are what matter, Damon. At least we can agree on that."

"Don't give me up for lost, Grace," he said, turning to her now and searching her eyes, "will you?"

"I hate it all so," she said as he helped her out. "I'm so tired, Damon," she said leaning on his arm a moment, as if this were actually true and she was a very old lady.

"You, tired? Nonsense," he teased, but it was a perfunctory response after all. He was already gone.

She watched the taillights of the car vanish up the street and stood there a moment, leaning on her umbrella, the damp leafy smell rising up from the earth all around her like solitude itself. She stood outside her garden on the street dramatizing her own sense of being abandoned, old, lonely, and somehow unable to cope any longer. Every day now it seemed as if chaos and uncertainty came a step nearer—now, at the meeting, this flare-up between Edward and Damon. "The state of the world," as she called everything that troubled her, was breaking into the most secret places, the intimate circle, the final bastion. And for the first time in many years, she doubted herself. She felt frightened of what lay ahead.

Then she stooped down to caress an enormous black cat who was winding himself round her legs.

"Oh, Horace," she said, relief flooding her as if this animal warmth and trust had given her back her strength, "you funny old puss," and turned and went in, the black tail waving triumphantly up the path before her.

III

To his landlady, who liked to think that intellectuals were helpless and inferior beings, Orlando Fosca seemed the type of the absent-minded professor. Actually his life was as tightly organized as a fugue, in which a number of themes wove themselves in and out under expert control. Now, for instance, when Mrs. Cram had taken his supper tray down, he would smoke one pipe and read some poetry (a volume of Leopardi was open beside him) or listen to records, Vivaldi or Mozart. Then he would work for three hours before going to bed. "Work is my rest, you know," he was fond of saying, a slightly mischievous look coming into his blue eyes. "It's what keeps me alive."

He had laid down the volume of poems and sat smoking, looking around this room which had become like another self. Every wall was lined with books to the ceiling, and between and among the books were photographs, one of his wife taken many years ago before her death, one of Goethe, one of Mazzini, several of associates, among them Edward Cavan standing under a tree by the Charles. Fosca's eyes rested on it a moment, seeing it freshly, as one may at times see a familiar object as if for the first time. Damon had given it to him in memory of a long walk they had taken that day, a spring day long ago. Damon and Edward had been young men then, enthusiasts—yes, he smiled a slight smile—but he himself had already been old, old enough to be armed against all that had happened since. It was some time since Edward had dropped in to drink cup after cup of coffee, to wander about picking out books from the shelves, often sitting on the floor—perhaps a month or more. And now Fosca's eyes rested on the photograph because he was expecting Edward in a few minutes.

Tonight it would be Edward and not work, after all. Tonight it would be the troubled troubling Edward of recent times, and he found that he somewhat dreaded this interruption. Edward at his most intense made great demands. But this, after all, was what friendship implied. Americans did not on the whole, he considered, ask enough of personal relationships, or expect enough. Edward Cavan and he shared the conviction that a true friendship must dig down deep enough to be at times painful, or it had no truth. Over a period of twenty years the young man and the old man had shared a great deal, not everything, but a great deal. When Orlando Fosca's wife died after a long illness, Edward had come regularly over a period of months, had shown a comprehensive tenderness which did not find its way out in words but in acts. For instance it was he who remembered that Sylvia had always kept fresh flowers on her husband's desk, had seen to it that this small rite be continued when Fosca finally moved into this small apartment at the top of an old house on Lowell Street. So now there was a bunch of dark red Korean chrysanthemums in the Chinese jar on the desk. Edward had discreetly added to the record collection; he had come late in the afternoon, not once·but twice or three times a week at a time when he knew Fosca was apt to take a short walk, to accompany him, padding along, Fosca thought like some soothing quiet animal at his side.

It had seemed then to Fosca that he had found a son, a most unexpected gift to an old man whose life was closing in on itself, rather than reaching outward. But now for some time, Edward had not been available, not in any deep sense. For one thing Fosca had watched him spend alarming amounts of time and energy in the Wallace campaign; he had watched him allowing himself to be sucked down into the whirlpool of politics, too involved, too passionately, to see clearly. And this had been painful to watch. How long was it since Edward had come to read poems and talk about them? Or to say, "Come for a walk, Orlando, we must look at the leaves before they are all gone." That was the Edward who looked out from the photograph on the wall. On an impulse Fosca got up and took it down, to hold it in his hands a moment. It seemed almost incredible that Edward that day had laughed, for he was laughing at Damon who took the photograph. He stood with his hands in his pockets, the wind blowing his baggy tweed suit, his head bent a little, laughing. Eight, ten years ago? He had not been so angry, so difficult, so untouchable then. Then the various parts of his life had been harnessed together—the

64

big book on the American roots in literature, the Teachers' Union, just then being founded, the Radical Club of students where Edward felt so at home and at ease, the New Deal which seemed the very proof that at last the intellectual was to be assimilated into the political scene, used instead of isolated. In Edward, Fosca had thought he saw a new type emerging, an American type, which would perhaps come closer to the ideal of the whole man, totally responsible, than the world had yet seen. He smiled a slightly ironic, slightly weary smile as he put the little photograph back on its hook. And now? Now he must put water on to boil on the little electric range he had set up in the bathroom. Very carefully and precisely he set out two blue cups on a tray, brought the milk in from the window sill, sugar and spoons from a shelf under the range. Now it seemed to Fosca that this small act of kindness was all that he could do for Edward, that—and to listen.

The bell rang three times, short rings, Edward's ring. Fosca heard his feet coming up the first flight, quickly, then slowing down, finally pausing at the door which Fosca flung open.

"Come in, come in, *carissimo*." He shook Edward's hand warmly, holding it a moment in his own, for Fosca was Latin enough still to make such natural gestures of love without embarrassment. Then he took Edward by the shoulder and said, "Sit down, make yourself comfortable, I have just started the coffee."

When he came back into the room, Edward was sitting, quite still, his hands between his knees, his head bowed.

"I have been looking at these Korean chrysanthemums

all day like an old Chinese poet." Fosca looked at them again, standing away as if he were looking at a painting. "Aren't they fine?"

He watched Edward raise his head and look at them, unsmiling, as if he were looking through a screen, as if nothing outside himself had at this moment any reality. A large dark cloud had settled in the room—the room which a moment before seemed so rich and human, full of small bright objects, such as the paperweight of a penguin in a snowstorm, the little wooden donkey from Jerusalem, the brilliant enamel ash tray covered with flowers which his wife had given him years ago for a wedding anniversary. There had been flowers, music, the warm presences of all the familiar books, the soft gold curtains at the windows. There had been something airy and brilliant about it all. And now it was as if a great dark cloud had settled over it as Edward said, "I was wrong to come," his voice excited and strained.

"Well, I don't know. How do I know?" Fosca said gently. "You haven't come for a long time. I don't know what is happening to you." Then he disappeared into the bathroom again, to measure out the coffee and fill the cups with water. Perhaps if he gave Edward a few moments, he would manage to relax a fraction, and then perhaps he would be able to talk.

"There," Fosca said, as if the making of this coffee were a triumph, "you see."

Edward got up quickly to take his cup, to insist that Fosca sit down now while he himself poured the milk, performing the familiar rite very precisely, then stood with his own cup in his hands and drank it half down at a gulp.

"Well, what is it, Edward?" Fosca looked up at the

somber man before him, who had seemed like a son. But Edward was wandering about the room; he stopped to pick up the penguin paperweight, tossed it from one hand to another, then watched, absorbed, as the snow fall began.

"Wherever did you get this?" he asked.

"Grace gave it to me—isn't it rather like her?"—Fosca smiled mischievously—"such an unmoved object, so irrefutable, so absolute in the middle of his snowstorm——"

"Enviable state," Edward smiled and put it down. "Poor penguin."

"Poor Grace, you mean?"

"I suppose so." Edward flung himself down in the deep armchair. "I don't know why I said it. I suppose I rather envy that solidification into certainty. What she doesn't know won't hurt her."

"She's not invulnerable, Edward," Fosca said gently.

"Who is?" Edward said testily, and then more quietly, "I expect she's bothered about me right now, as a matter of fact. I walked out of a Civil Liberties Union meeting this afternoon, idiotic thing to do. I had a brainstorm."

"She probably was delighted." Fosca kept to a light tone. "She loves a fight, as you well know. What was it about, this tempest in a teapot?"

Edward raised his head and looked at Fosca with such intensity that the old men retreated, "It was not a teapot, Edward? Are you serious? What is all this about? You had better try to explain. In the first place I didn't know you took the Civil Liberties Union to the very center of your heart——"

"No, no," Edward said impatiently. "It's just that Damon has finally come out into the open. He can't be trusted any more."

"So?" Fosca brought his two hands together, the tips of the fingers meeting judicially. "And what exactly do you mean by that?"

"I mean that on a matter of absolute principle, Damon backed down, ratted. Oh, it doesn't matter about the specific thing. It's just a straw in the wind. But that Damon of all people should back down, now——"

"Drink your coffee, man, and sit down like a human being and talk to me." Fosca followed the pacing figure with his eyes and quietly relit his pipe. "Now begin at the beginning."

While Edward briefly outlined what had happened at the Union meeting, leaning forward in his chair, speaking in short clipped angry sentences, Fosca watched him, but what he listened to was not the words. For some time now he had had the feeling that Edward, the real Edward, was imprisoned somewhere trying to communicate, that somewhere there was a prisoner desperately rapping on a wall, and it was these intermittent attempts to communicate to which Fosca listened.

"You see?" Edward ended. "It's finished between Damon and me. I can't see him again." He took out a cigarette and lit it, sitting hunched up now, emptied of his anger and his story.

Fosca puffed at his pipe for some moments in silence.

"You do see?" Edward asked again, and this time he wanted an answer.

"I see that you feel personally betrayed," Fosca said quietly.

"I have a right to, surely."

It was a strange image which went through Fosca's mind—that if he could only bring Edward into the room, if he could open some door that would bring Edward really into the room, into the atmosphere of the room, instead of locked away in some blank arid room of his own, that would solve everything. But how to do it?

"I'm prepared to see that from your angle Damon has betrayed you, but I am not so sure that he has betrayed himself, Edward."

"Of course he has. He used to be uncompromising and militant—when that was the prevailing atmosphere. Now that the atmosphere is full of suspicion and doubt, he's changed under it."

"You suggest, my dear, that to change one's mind is to betray. I cannot agree with you."

"But one has to take a stand somewhere, Fosca—you must see that. There are some things about which one does not change one's mind."

"I wonder—faith has nothing perhaps to do with evidence, or with facts. Politics has everything to do with facts. Its essence is compromise, Edward. What frightens me a little is that you seem to have confused these categories. This is the mark of the true believer—and, alas, also the fanatic— No, don't interrupt me," Fosca said sternly, "you must let me say my say." Edward sank back into his chair, his head in his hands. "In your real work, Edward, when it comes to literature, you have always exercised great intellectual control; you have exposed passion to the most delicate and severe investigation. You have been able to judge without ferocity, with real understanding. Why is it that here, in these matters of political belief, you cannot be dispassionate?"

"I'm not ashamed of being still an uncompromising Socialist," Edward said quickly. "I'm not ashamed of having made a fool of myself in the Czechoslovakian affair, if that's what you're talking about."

Somewhere under the words, Fosca could hear the prisoner tapping, but how, how to communicate with him, through the stone wall? At the moment, his only means was silence. He did not answer, carefully refilling his pipe, tapping down the tobacco, carefully and slowly lighting it, prolonging the pause on will. When Edward spoke again, he lifted his head and for just a second Fosca looked through the screen to the haunted eyes.

"I care too much," he said angrily. "That's what you're saying. And it's true of course."

"Maybe. I don't know," Fosca said gently. "I don't know if that is just what I'm saying."

"I have the sensation of screaming in a high wind," Edward went on.

"I hear something else"—Fosca waited a second, then decided to say it aloud—"like a prisoner tapping against a wall——"

"I am in prison, Fosca. It's true." A moment before Fosca had thought that if he could bring Edward into this room, he could help him. Now he had the sensation that instead, it was he who had been locked into the prison with Edward. Edward walked again from the window to the desk, to the armchair where he had been sitting and back again. It was very like the walk of the great cats in zoos, back and forth, back and forth, his head down in his shoulders, his hands clenched in his pockets.

"You have felt like this before," Fosca probed very gently. "It has to do sometimes with finishing a book."

"I know. I've told myself that. Fosca"—he stopped and

looked down at the old man, as if he were standing very far away looking down—"have you ever despaired?"

Fosca puffed on his pipe. "Yes," he said, "when I was young."

"Not since then?"

"I think not—what is it? Responsibilities—one is held to life by so many little threads as one grows older. If one snaps, there is always another. One imagines that one is needed."

"I feel cut off from the students," Edward said, sitting down again.

"They don't feel cut off from you, Edward," Fosca said earnestly. "You know"—he was deliberately changing the tone to a more relaxed one—"it's a queer thing. But the very things that tear you to pieces, Edward, are what make them respect you. They know you're really involved, you see. You're not screaming in a high wind to them. You know you're not."

Edward visibly relaxed as if some almost unbearable strain had been eased. The shift from politics to teaching, Fosca thought. Now he's in his element again—and it seemed so fantastic that Edward could not understand this himself, strapped himself again and again to the wheel of torment. "Quite a wail I've been making," he was saying, smiling now across at the old man and putting his feet up on the footstool. "You are patient, Orlando, I must say, when crackpots come to call." He lit a cigarette and smoked it really in the way a man emerging from physical pain smokes, "Of course my strength as a teacher is in seminar and as a tutor. I'm merely adequate at these big lectures—it seems so inhuman—and I'm not a performer, by nature," he said ironically. "I have no desire to hypnotize six hundred students at a time, or to hypnotize anyone for that matter; it seems always slightly cheap."

Fosca watched him silently, glad that at last Edward was here in the room, a fact made tangible by the way now he looked around him, looked for the first time at the chrysanthemums, then along the wall of books, and back at Orlando, his eyes gentle and thoughtful again and that strange look, as of an animal trying to get out of a prison, quite gone.

"How's your book, by the way?" Edward asked then. "The last time I saw you, you had almost finished chapter four. You were happy about it . . ."

Orlando Fosca raised his eyebrows. "I had been feeding the donkey carrots," he said. "Lately I have had to beat it. And then all these committees, you know"—he made an impatient gesture. "The administration"—and he made a wry face.

Edward chuckled, "Come the revolution, we'll eliminate the deans, blow up the administrative offices, hand over the running of the college to a janitor as they do at the Sorbonne. Ah!"—and Edward laughed a short unamused laugh—"what a machine it's all become, Orlando."

Orlando sighed. "In a way," he granted, but unwilling to spoil the moment of pleasure, he would not argue, or defend. "Let us listen to some Mozart, Edward. Would you mind? Lately I have found it a good idea to end my day with Mozart. I feel the need of purification," he said, "to remove the clutter"—he was already slipping a record out of its case. "Order," he said, laying it on the machine, "harmony—"

"Yes." Edward leaned forward, prepared to listen. One

of the bonds between these two men was this one, the fact that they listened to music in the same way, not as a self-indulgence, but poised, even a little tense perhaps, in an attitude as far from daydreaming as possible.

Orlando had chosen the clarinet quintet, one of the records Edward had given him a Christmas some years ago. They had not listened to it together for some time, and now it seemed to Fosca that they were walking together through a formal garden. The world had dropped away, anxiety, torment, it all flowed away. Yet the range was still human, included all that was human, never became *exalté*—this was the miracle of Mozart, he thought, to feel all human griefs and joys and yet transcend them quite simply, quite unself-consciously. Edward caught his look and smiled.

And when it was all over, they said nothing for some minutes, as the music left them, and the silence bore it away like a long receding wave, still heard long after it had vanished.

"The saving grace," Edward said. Then he got up and put the record away. "I suppose I must be going," but he looked around the room, as if he hated to leave it, as if he dreaded the night waiting for him outside, waiting to pounce.

Orlando rose and faced him. This, this last hour, had contained whatever he had to give, but he knew that Edward would not sleep. If one could give sleep to another human being that would be the real saving grace. But Edward had always been cut off from this human sleep. His nights were brightly lit, nightmarishly alive. Now he would probably walk for hours, drop in at some late night bar, dreading to go back. All this Orlando knew. But tonight for some reason, it troubled him more than usual.

"You could sleep here, Edward; I have a cot, you know," he said tentatively.

"Thanks"—Edward rubbed his forehead—"but I'll be all right."

He turned toward the door.

"Edward——"

"Yes."

"Don't cast Damon into outer darkness. For your own sake. The price is too high."

"I don't know." Edward did not turn back. "I'll have to think about it."

Fosca laid a hand gently on his shoulder. "Think about it," he said, and then Edward was gone.

Fosca stood there a moment, facing the closed door. At the end Edward had made an effort, had actually perhaps for half an hour forgotten himself and the anguish he carried around these days. Yes, for a half-hour or more, Edward had come out of his prison.

The big door downstairs closed loudly and then he could hear, amazingly clearly in the silence, Edward's footsteps, quick, definite, first quite staccato and loud, then gradually fading out into the silence. Fosca went to the window and raised the shade to look out at the amber leaves lit up by a street lamp in a great flaming arc, then at the black tarred road below. In the house opposite, light burned in the attic windows where some student lived. Far off a streetcar ground to a stop, then grated forward to a harsh singing cry as it regained momentum. And then again, the silence poured in.

It was just after ten, he noted. That meant that he had two hours at his desk, and he went automatically to sit down there, to take out the neat pile of manuscript, wide lined pages across which his small definite script ran in an unbroken stream. It was a book in which Fosca was passionately interested, an assessment of Italian thought and letters since Mussolini, and he was now engaged in the very core of the first part, an evaluation of Croce. As he took out the cards on which his notes were inscribed, he felt as if his mind were a great sea bird, a seagull perhaps, circling and circling round in the dark and the silence, waiting to dive down to seize an idea like a fish. It was an intricate, but at the same time exhilarating, act, this act of pure thought. Very carefully he unscrewed his pen, moved some little pads to within easy reach and then reread the paragraph he had set down the night before.

The sharp imperative ring of the telephone seemed at that moment a violent attack. He picked it up automatically, cursing himself for a reaction he could not control.

"Orlando—" the old familiar voice asked his name like a question.

"Oh, hello, Grace dear, what is it?"

"You sound cross," she accused.

"Well, I was just getting to work, as a matter of fact. Edward has been here."

"Oh, I'm glad. That's what I called you about. You know then——"

"Well, I gathered there had been some sort of argument at your meeting. Edward takes it much too seriously, of course——"

"You're so balanced, Orlando. I hate balanced people."

"Oh, very well," he answered sharply, "it is serious, I suppose." Grace and he communicated always on a tone of irritability which concealed tenderness.

75

"The point is that I'm very worried about Edward. Damon can take care of himself, make a fool of himself if he chooses, but Edward is in a bad state, Orlando."

"Yes, I know," he said quietly.

"Isn't there something we can do?" He could see her as clearly as if he were in the room—sitting up in bed, surrounded by piles of *Nations, New Republics* and books, wide awake, looking like an old hawk—and seeing this image so clearly moved him.

"We can try to go to sleep," he said gently.

"Don't be preposterous, Orlando. Tell me what happened," she commanded.

"We talked. Edward told me the whole miserable affair. Then we played the Mozart clarinet quintet, and then he left—just a few minutes ago."

"I don't know what's the matter with me. I feel so anxious."

"It's hard to stand by, but Edward has got to come to terms with his life, Grace."

"Whatever do you mean by that?"

"I mean you can't allow yourself to be torn to pieces by what *has* happened and hence what cannot be changed, in this case the Czechoslovakian business. But that's only a symptom—we'll have to talk, Grace. I really must get to work." For what had happened was that Orlando felt suddenly exhausted. He might appear to be balanced, but everything that had happened and was happening in the world affected him deeply. To be summoned out of his quiet, when he had just reached it after the long day, to be confronted once more with these painful matters, to have to bolster Grace up as well as Edward—he felt wildly impatient with the telephone. His instinct was to slam down the receiver.

"You'll come to tea tomorrow?"

"Of course. And now try to calm yourself. Is Horace there?"

"No, he's out, the wretch, making fearful noises and infuriating Professor Stone, no doubt. I shall have to go and get him in."

"Yes, perhaps you had better."

"You're a great comfort to me, Orlando," she said meekly.

"You are one of the furies in disguise, but I love you just the same. Good night, dear." This time he did put the receiver down. Then he sat for a moment with his head in his hands, gave a sudden short laugh as he imagined Horace keeping the whole neighborhood awake, and then, still smiling, picked up his pen.

IV

It was really too dark to see, but Julia Phillips stayed on in the dilapidated old garden, cutting down the phlox, tying up the chrysanthemums (why had they grown so very tall and floppy?). She stopped every now and then to look up from the shadowy garden to the extraordinarily luminous lavender sky overhead, where already the moon was brightening, white gold over the deep red gold of the maple leaves. Has the light in October always been like this? she asked herself. She did not remember an autumn of such radiant skies, an autumn of such pure gold, and she lifted her head to drink in the amplitude of it. How dark the house looked, how dark now the garden. It really was time to go in and light the lamps, for Damon would soon be home.

Still she lingered on, feeling about for her tools in the dark, smelling the bitter sharp smell of the earth and the leaves, not wanting to break this quiet mood. There, working for long hours till her back and legs ached, she felt sane, she recaptured some deep rhythm which these hectic days destroyed. She was a large Junoesque woman who had been a beauty and still had the carriage and air of a beauty, a deceptive surface calm which concealed strong feelings and which had made her the kind of woman people lean on and expect comfort from. She had long ago grown used to giving to life what was expected; the revolt—and there was revolt—was buried very deep. No one guessed what her life with Damon had been, that the other side of his enormous gusto and love of life was an abyss of self-distrust. She had lifted him again and again, patiently, quietly, and with what she imagined was love, but it had seemed to her for some time now that she was acting a part, the part of the perfect wife. Lately she had felt a wild desire, to escape, to run away, to find out at long last what she herself was like, to live her own life, though she was very vague as to what this might be.

She felt that this autumn, so outwardly calm, was moving toward some crisis, a crisis which she would not have the power to avert. And now since that fatal afternoon at the Civil Liberties (was it only three days ago?) Damon was in his very worst state. She stayed in the garden because she dreaded going in to light the lamps, to put away her natural self, which at the moment longed for a deep sleep, longed like a hibernating animal to hide away somewhere and no longer have to respond. She stayed in the garden, in the dark, as in some kind limbo, gathering her courage.

In fact she stayed too long. She was startled suddenly by the headlights of the car as Damon swung in, erratically, barely not grazing the garage door, arriving as he always did with a loud bang, dropping his brief case, slamming the garage doors shut (it was so bad for them) and calling out to her, "What are you doing there in the dark?"

"Looking at the sky, Damon—have you noticed it?" she called back, already running ahead to open the door, light the lamps, jerked back into his staccato tempo in spite of herself. Quickly she set a match to the wood fire in the study, lit the lamps there and disappeared behind the swing door into the kitchen to take a look at her casserole. In the distance she could hear Damon, crashing up the stairs, running water, his every gesture, it seemed, snapping another thread of the peace she had carefully built up in the last hours. In these moods he was like an engine running too fast for itself, a dangerous engine which might at any moment explode.

They met, she felt, at the end of each day like strangers, extending to each other the formal politeness of strangers. Damon mixed an old-fashioned; she took off her apron and sat down for the ritual half-hour or so when the entanglements and irritations of the day would be consciously laid aside. He had put on his red slippers, his old sweater, and stood, lanky, a little stooped, his lined irregular face which could look so distinguished, or—as it did now—so curiously disturbingly unfocused, the nose too strong, the mouth sensual and at the same time prim, his hair, as always, disheveled.

"God, I'm tired," he announced, as if this were someone's fault and could have been avoided.

"A bad day?" she asked automatically, as a nurse might ask an invalid.

"No worse than any other; we had a long committee

meeting. Goldberg was in his element, laying down the law, arriving with masses of neat graphs and God knows what— Oh, it's not that," he said, running his hands through his hair.

"You haven't heard anything from Edward, I suppose?"

"I don't expect to." The tone implied that she would have done better not to ask. He kicked a log with one foot, turning away from her, to lean his forehead on the mantel, an awkward gesture which she found unexpectedly touching.

"It's rather childish of him, Damon, isn't it really? You've been friends for twenty years."

He flung himself down at last in the worn leather armchair, looked at his wife quietly for a moment and then said, "It's so hard to be sure you're right. Maybe I *was* wrong"—he looked at her imploringly. And she knew him well enough to see here his generosity, knew that if he could persuade himself that he had been wrong, he would make an apology, knew that he longed to do just this.

"Oh, darling," she said warmly, "you and Edward have been drifting apart for some time. This is only the final straw—it would have been something else eventually."

"It's a hopeless mess." Damon took a sip of his drink. "We'd better talk about something else."

"I must send that sweater to the cleaner's—it's covered with spots, Damon."

"The damnable thing is that I envy Edward his conviction"—Damon paid no attention to her remark. Of course they would not be able to keep away from the one painful subject which was eating Damon up. There was little use in trying.

"Am I just becoming a doddering old fuddy duddy, Julia? Am I crazy?"

"You know what I think? I think that we are having to grow, to change in fundamental beliefs and it's a painful process—at our age. We took an awful lot of things for granted, Damon, you know?"

"Like what?" he asked suspiciously.

"Well, like that the unions must be right about everything, that Socialism *is* the answer, that"—she smiled shyly —"oh well, you know what I mean. It's very disturbing to have to admit that people you hate and despise and know to be narrow in vision, have been, after all, right about a few things." But Damon had not been listening. He never listened to the words she said. "It's humiliating," she said.

"Edward thinks any compromise is a sin. My grandfather would have agreed about that. 'Stand up and be counted!' he would roar at the boys, terrified into admitting things they had never done just to give the old man what he wanted." And Damon laughed suddenly. It always cheered him up to remember his grandfather, whom he had so admired, so hated too, but who appeared to Julia always rather like God in the background, a presence which loomed up before Damon whenever he was troubled in mind.

"Your grandfather was a perfect child, Damon."

"A lot you know about it," he said irritably, glancing over at the portrait of John Phillips on the wall, as if he half expected the old boy to speak out. John Phillips had founded a preparatory school for boys which was now a household word. He was still headmaster when Damon and his brother went to the school and had always preferred Waldo, Damon's brother. But for some reason Damon adored him and, whenever he had something to drink, told stories about the old man, never would listen to a word against him, loved to quote the famous sayings: "A boy is born with personality; he is taught character." "To hell with the intellectuals: give me the whole man."

"Don't tell me he was a whole man," Julia said, remembering this saying. "For he wasn't."

"You know," Damon went on on his own track, "Edward has something of that quality. The old man would have liked Edward, oh, disagreed with him of course, but I can almost hear him saying, 'Edward Cavan has moral stature. He's all wrong of course, but he'll stand up and be counted,'" and Damon laughed again, then stopped laughing abruptly. "I feel absolutely gone, Julia." He was slumped down in his chair, and looked quite ill.

"You need your supper. I'll go and gather things together——"

"No, let's talk. It's not late." For just a second Julia felt like a prisoner. They would have to go over and over the same problems now, until Damon had talked himself out of his depression. Her job was to listen and to say appropriate things. She felt mean to think in this way and, because she felt mean, was determined to be kind. She settled back, tucking her feet up under her, her chin in her hand.

"It's not only Edward. I've come to a blank wall in my work, six months or more on a completely false trail—the joke's on me all right."

Damon's saving grace was this, this lightness about what mattered most to him, this humility and persistence which had to do with being a scientist, she supposed, but always it moved her. He's a great man, she thought, and most of the time I misjudge him because I have a mean little nature. What was Damon like in that mysterious paradise of his where he sat poring over equations which she could not even read, let alone solve? Was he quiet then? At peace with himself? Centered? She would never know. They had been married twenty-five years and still she would never know.

"Well, darling," she said warmly, "at least you know that now."

"Yes," he sighed, "but it's a bore having wasted all that time."

"I should think it would be restful in a way, because you can get an absolute answer at least——"

"Relatively absolute." He smiled across at her indulgently. "One man's blank wall turns out to be another's open door—sometimes. It's not as black and white as all that, Julia. It's more like walking in the dark, feeling your way"—he swallowed down the last of his drink and stood up, leaning on the mantel, rubbing his face with his hands as if to rub out the deep lines.

"Do you think I've wasted time?" he asked her suddenly.

"How?" For she did not follow his thought. He had leapt off somewhere else now.

"Oh, by all the things I can't resist having a finger in like the Civil Liberties Union, or the Institute of Contemporary Arts. My colleagues think I'm a crackpot, the seedy end of some sort of old-fashioned liberal tradition, you know—that's what Goldberg thinks."

"Unregenerate curiosity, that's all," she said answering his half-smile. "Oh, I don't know, Damon"—it was true that he had wanted everything, that he had always been avid as if there was some hunger in him that nothing could satisfy—"but surely Goldberg is the type of the scholar in blinders. I'd hate you to be like that."

"He's a thorn in Edward's side. They had quite an argument at the meeting today, went off together afterwards though, magnetized by their disagreement. There's no one I can talk to," Damon groaned.

"You talk to Hinton and Couperin, don't you?" These were colleagues in his own department, but Damon had never chosen his friends from among his colleagues.

"Oh, in a way, Hinton tells me dirty stories and Couperin teases me in one way or another. I've always been a maverick in the department. The mathematicians think I'm a philosopher and the philosophers think I'm a mathematician— I feel lonely," he said in a cross tone of voice, "damned lonely. It's Edward" he came back to the sore point, in spite of himself.

"It's time we had something to eat," Julia said firmly. She felt she must have some food before they got onto this again.

Putting on the coffee, mixing the salad dressing, Julia was free to think. She knew why Damon was haunted by Edward—or thought she knew. There was something violent in Edward, passion perhaps, which Damon always seized on in other people. For with all his curiosity, his multiple interests, his sense of being driven, it was not after all passion which drove Damon. It was hunger. Fame was what he starved for and all these things were substitutes, *ersatz*—the committees, the chairmanships, the little essays in *The Atlantic*—they filled the hole but did not nourish. Julia guessed that his disappointment over whatever it was that had not worked out these last six months was greater than he admitted. He had worked too hard, all summer—she put the casserole on the table, water in the glasses, feeling all her love flow out into these habitual gestures. Strange, how quickly it happened, the change— we are this warmth and this coldness, strangers, lovers, friends, enemies. People talk about "a happy marriage" and it meant, she supposed, all this, the complex creation hour by hour and minute by minute, the revolt and the acceptance. And now the meal ready, arrival at the end of the day.

"It will be all right, Damon. You'll see," she said out of all these thoughts.

"I wish you'd call Edward." He ate ravenously, too fast, as he always did, coming back for more when Julia herself had barely begun, pouring out the coffee in the middle of the meal out of sheer restlessness. Their two children had nervous indigestion as a result.

"We haven't heard from Bess for ages," she said irrelevantly. Bess, their younger one, was at Bryn Mawr. The boy, John, in the army at a camp in North Carolina.

"You never listen." Damon was cross. "I asked you a question."

"Oh yes—" She came back from her thoughts about baking a cake for Bess tomorrow. "But why should I, Damon? After all——"

"He's always liked you in a rather special way," Damon said carelessly.

She was staggered by the indifference of this. For Edward, it was true, had used to come nearly every day at teatime, sit and talk or be silent, always there, like a still pressure which she did not understand or know how to handle.

"That was two years ago. He doesn't come very often now."

"Still, you're a woman——"

"What has that got to do with it?"

"I don't know. He's a queer duck. He doesn't really love women, but he needs them, gets on with them some-how. Do you know what I mean?"

"All I remember is the fearful strain," she said. It had been like an undertow, the light going, and Edward sitting in the dark, smoking always, asking her about the children absent-mindedly, sometimes talking about his work, then suddenly getting up to go, not saying whatever it was he had come to say. "I'll try, Damon," she said, but in such a tired voice, that he reacted at once.

"Oh well, if you're going to be a martyr about it."

"No, no"—she got up, glad of the chance to go out into the kitchen, brought back grapefruit—"I'll do it after supper. I really will. Perhaps you're right," she said. "What about Grace Kimlock? I should have thought——"

"Oh, the old darling, she's awfully upset. I drove her home, as a matter of fact. Didn't I tell you?"

"No," Julia said. She didn't like Grace Kimlock. There was something tangential about her, fierce old maid, taking out her repressions in politics. Julia did not like intellectual women, they disturbed her.

"Poor old girl," Damon shook his head. "She's in a perpetual head-on collision with the world as it is."

"Bloody but unbowed?"

"She and Edward see eye to eye," he said morosely,

taking out a cigarette. "Well, I must get to work, lecture tomorrow. I haven't even looked at it."

After all, Julia thought, with relief, we have been spared. Damon was emerging from the worst of his mood of the last days. The least she could do was to call Edward.

His voice sounded excited and wary on the phone, but he agreed to come to dinner on the Friday, agreed right away, much to Julia's surprise. After the call, she sat for a moment on the little chair under the stairs where the phone was, wondering if all Damon had been through in these last days was madness. When he was in one of his down moods, everything got out of proportion. Perhaps, after all, Edward was going to be sensible. Perhaps they could all be friends.

V

Cambridge at eight thirty on a bright October morning was one of George Hastings' secret pleasures. He was smiling as he walked along Garden Street toward the Radcliffe dormitories, smiling because in a few moments he would see Pen, smiling at the gray-haired lady winding in and out of traffic on her bicycle, the basket filled with books and papers, at the stream of students moving in the opposite direction to his, so he caught them in full flood, a parade of girls in bright coats, enormous notebooks under their arms, or a green bag slung over one shoulder, and threaded through by their elders, the tweed jackets, the gray flannels, the distinguished worn faces as the professors also made their way to nine o'clock classes. Among these, solemn packs of small children moved toward the public school—late ones, subdued by their lateness. It seemed at this hour as if the whole city were a learning city, as if everyone's chief concern were school. If, by chance, a wife in slacks on her way to market, or a Babbitty banker carrying no books, appeared for a moment among them, it was only rather a joke, so incongruous did anyone with different concerns appear. George thought it all rather like a ballet, the beautiful girls, the books, the leaves golden in the gutters, for everything in the clear autumn sunlight seemed so airy, so graceful and alive. And in a few moments he would see Pen. Unless—he glanced hurriedly at his watch—she had already gone. But it felt like such a lucky day, she could not have gone. He had so much to tell her. Her presence and the excitement it raised in him, made it possible for him to see all kinds of things he didn't know he knew, to discover shades and nuances, a form of showing off no doubt—but such a pleasure as a beginning to a new day. Pulled forward as he turned into Shepard Street, he began to run and almost missed Pen altogether, as he skirted a group of girls talking on the steps of one of the houses, and she at the same moment was making a detour round the other side.

"George"—it was she who saw him first. "Where on earth are you going?"

They stood in the path, her face as always intent, unsmiling in the first second, as if she must always rediscover him, was always a little surprised to find him there, perhaps not even pleased till she could get used to the idea.

"I was looking for you of course. I want you to come to Cavan's seminar today—if you can"—for he caught the hesitation in her eyelid, as she dropped her eyes. "It's at two."

"Oh, George, I've got two long papers due— I don't think I can . . ." She stood there, as always resisting him, so he felt. Always first having to say no, so intact did she wish to seem.

"I never do anything worth doing at two—do you?" he challenged her, teased her, dismayed as he always was by the gap between them, the having to make a bridge. For when he thought of Pen he thought of her as part of himself, yet she had never said she loved him, would not say it, for some complex reason of her own, some stubborn refusal to be bound, to be committed. He slipped an arm through hers and they walked along together, well in step. At least she had not pulled away. They were together.

"But why just today? There's time—there's all year," she said sensibly, brushing back that straight lock of hair which always fell over her forehead, which must always and constantly be pushed back, smiling at him now suddenly as if she were glad to see him after all. When she smiled her face broke open in the most amazing way; it was otherwise very tense and quiet, fine cheekbones, narrow dark eyes, and then a wide surprising mouth which could break into an enormous smile.

"I don't know— I just have a feeling . . ." he said vaguely, for really there was no imperative reason.

"What sort of feeling?" she inquired. Pen had become very logical in the last year due to a course in philosophy she was taking.

"Oh, I don't know." George felt uncomfortable now, pinned down. "I just thought this was a lovely day—and, really—I wanted to see you. We could have tea afterwards." He could not keep the pleading tone out of his voice and felt humiliated. "Never mind," he said crossly. "If you don't want to."

Lately everything had got too tense between them,

that was the trouble. It was ever since he had kissed her, the first night after the holiday. She had been upset. She had said, "I don't want to feel so much, George—please—" such a queer thing to say. But like Pen. She was different from everyone else. That was why he loved her so much.

They were retracing his steps which had been airy and joyful as if he had wings on his feet. But now he was back in the complex tense anxiety of his relationship to her, he stubbed his toe on a loose brick rather painfully. It was annoying the way they had to keep pushing past masses of girls; she had slipped her arm out from his long ago.

"Oh all right, I'll come, George. Don't take everything so hard."

It was a graceless acceptance, but he did not mind. At least now the day would have its meaning, would be moving toward two o'clock, when he would have together in the same room the two people he loved best in the world. It was going to be all right.

"Isn't it a beautiful day?" she said, suddenly scuffing a pile of leaves, like a small child, looking round at him and smiling again, that smile which flooded his whole being like liquor. He was too moved to smile back. He felt his cheek twitching. How much does she know? What does she really feel? he wondered. He felt exposed, aware of the hole in his sock, of the shabbiness of his corduroy coat, wishing suddenly that he did not have such small features, that he were taller, that he were the kind of man women instinctively admired.

Of course she was late. He waited at the head of the stairs in Longfellow Hall while the other members of the seminar stood around, smoking, lazy and casual; he tried to conceal his impatience. She came up the stairs just behind Cavan, slowed down by Cavan's preoccupied progress. He looks—ill—George said to himself anxiously. No, not ill—what was it then?—as if he was carrying a heavy weight.

"Sir"—George waited for the eyes to lift and met a look so naked and intense, that he stepped back. "Professor——"

"Hello, George, what is it?" The look vanished and Cavan turned to him a bit impatiently. Had George dreamed that strange piercing glance that did not see him at all, that was looking only inward, and looking at something terrible?

"I—I wondered if I could bring a guest, Miss Wallace, today?"

Pen stood just behind them, just not on the landing, looking amused.

"I suppose so."

"She's right here—Pen, this is Professor Cavan." It was all now unbelievably awkward.

"Well, since you're here"—Cavan made a gesture of acknowledgment, the barest acknowledgment, and went into the room where they sat round a long oval table, some twelve of them, all graduate students. There was the usual shuffling around, lighting of cigarettes, a request to open the window. George saw everything, as if because of Pen's presence he sat watching a play. Cavan appeared to him as a stranger, hunched forward in a listening attitude, a pad and pencil in front of him, none of the usual professorial paraphernalia and even his reddish hair that wouldn't lie flat, unlike any image one might have of a distinguished scholar; the blue eyes, absolutely humorless at the moment, looked out disturbingly alive, as if they were living eyes in a mask. These eyes glanced over at Pen with some curiosity and then at George. The minute Cavan came into a room, the whole atmosphere became charged. That was the strange thing.

George almost resented Pen's attitude of an uncommitted observer. Would she, in fact, sense the undercurrents of fear, of admiration, of something like reverence but sharper and less comfortable, which this man created in his students? He glanced at her, leaning forward, all intelligence and spring—yes, she would get it. If anyone would, Pen would.

Kovarsky had started reading a paper on Willa Cather. He read explosively and badly, running whole sentences together and then pausing for breath in the middle of one, and was plainly nervous. Cavan was listening intently. He made no notes, but once moved jerkily in his chair and smoked incessantly, lighting one cigarette from another. You could almost see the thoughts crossing his eyes, the questions, the disagreements, the moment of rather greater interest as Kovarsky approached the center of his thesis. George was relieved that this was evidently one of the better papers—Pen would be duly impressed. Kovarsky's theme seemed to be that Cather stood outside the creative stream of the novel in America, that she was a minor master in the classic novel, but had sacrificed too much in the process, that for instance in *Death Comes for the Archbishop* she had entirely evaded the problem of Catholicism in a democratic country, that her individual characters, real and realized as they were, failed to become representative because they were set against an incompletely understood background from a sociological point of view. This, he suggested, was abundantly clear in the late novel laid in Virginia, *Sapphira and the Slave Girl.*

When Kovarsky finished, he leaned back and lit a cigarette, his hand shaking, glancing nervously round to feel the reaction, obviously shy of looking at Cavan, sitting there silent, but dangerous like a bomb which might explode. One reason for the tension in the class was that Edward Cavan never had any ready-made phrases at hand, the kind which smooth over and open the way for relaxed discussion. His teaching was a process of thinking which moved forward right in the classroom by sudden jerks, as if his spoken words were a rough draft which he corrected as he went along, often retracing his path. It was a complex kind of improvising in which, as he talked, he seemed to move outward to include more and more, really a kind of exploration. Sometimes there were astonishing silences when his own concentration, as his forehead flushed, acted on the students like a spell and they waited, breathless, for the sudden brilliant torrent which would break the dam. This happened rarely and only when he was moved. It was happening now.

He lifted his head and looked at Kovarsky a second in a curiously appraising way as if he were trying to fit together the rather stout blond boy sitting there and the work he had just read, as if perhaps he were reminding himself to be gentle, or reminding himself that Kovarsky, the person, must be seen all round, whole, his precocious background in the New York public schools, his passionate reading of the Marxist critics weighed in the balance.

They all wished devoutly that he would say something, anything now.

"I don't know what to say, Kovarsky," he began, looking down at his clasped hands. "You've put the cart before the horse, you see, and so perhaps put the wrong cart before your horse. You have in fact judged before you have had the experience; you have committed the—to my mind —unpardonable sin of applying a preconceived formula to something which you only looked at through this formula, not for itself. You have got to judge a work of art first for what it is; you've got to possess it completely. But how thin your appreciation is, how poverty-stricken because you wore blinders all the time——"

"But, sir"—Kovarsky was red with shyness and perhaps anger—"I did read all the books. I do admire Willa Cather. Surely I said so."

"Perhaps so. But it's a grudging we-must-be-fair-after-all kind of admiration, a thin admiration. Why? Because you had made up your mind before you opened one of the novels that your criterion would be Lewis, Dreiser, maybe —Sherwood Anderson——"

"What's wrong with having a criterion?" someone else asked.

"Nothing, Sawyer, if it's inclusive. This criterion would exclude Jane Austen for instance completely, wouldn't it? Turgenev, probably. I can't overemphasize the danger of this schematic approach. You must learn to read with the whole of yourselves; you must bring love as well as intellect to this kind of analysis—just as in personal relationships. After all, a really fruitful reading of an author of this stature means giving up yourself for a time, means being able to encompass something wholly by imaginative sympathy. These are not mere intellectual matters." His fist was closed, as if he were restraining himself from bringing it down with a bang on the table. "You're going at a fine piece of pottery with a blacksmith's hammer. Naturally it breaks to pieces. How many of you have ever been to the Southwest?" But he did not wait for the answer. "I think this is a serious matter. We're at the beginning of a term. It looks to me—for Kovarsky is not an isolated phenomenon"—and here Cavan suddenly smiled quite kindly. George had noticed before that the release in a passionate moment such as this always made Cavan more able to communicate in a gentle way afterwards, more human in fact—"it looks to me as if you people had better relearn how to read. You've been corrupted by four years of reading for examinations, reading to analyze. You've almost forgotten how to read for experience, and it's high time you did. Learn to love, then you will have earned the right to judge. Anything else is cheap arrogance, believe me." He looked now at Kovarsky in a rather friendly way. "You've borne the brunt of this attack, Kovarsky, I'm sorry." But then as if he felt he had gone too far he added, "But these things have to be said, not only said but felt. I don't care if none of you ever makes a brilliant remark or writes an A paper, if at the end of the course you are capable of homage, intelligent homage, homage which you have worked to get at with the whole of yourselves, intellect, imagination, heart." The words came out now, hard, direct, straight at them. Then Cavan was suddenly silent, took out a cigarette, lit it, and changed his tone completely.

"Well, let's be specific. Any comment?"

George ventured that if the term "classic" was used, it had better be defined, and just what did Kovarsky mean about the classic novel being outside the main stream? Something had been released in the class too and the final hour was a lively one. It ended with a quite passionate discussion on "background," what is involved when the term is used and how in Willa Cather's case the background was intrinsic, a felt and later realized part of all her memories as a child and subconscious memories through her grandparents. The effect of this sort of distillation of family experience on her style, as contrasted with that of Dreiser especially, was discussed and gave Cavan a chance to speak eloquently of style as inseparable from point of view, from the person writing.

"It is the person writing. The limitations of style are personal limitations—look at Oscar Wilde or Pater, look at Thoreau. Willa Cather's style has complete integrity, the power of intense distillation. You don't get this sort of thing out of the air."

As usual when the two hours were up, the entire group followed Cavan down the stairs and out onto the street still talking.

"Is it always like this?" Pen asked George, and he could tell from her look of animation that she had been touched, as he hoped she would.

"No, I told you this was a lucky day."

"Gee whiz," she said, "I guess I'll have to spend the summer reading novels." And suddenly she laughed. "It doesn't feel like Harvard College, George. Where are we anyway?"

George and she stood out on Appian Way, looking at the knot of talkers who had stopped now at the corner before separating. They watched Cavan, with a sudden abrupt gesture of good-bye, break away and go off across the Common alone. He walked fast, his head down.

"Yet," she said turning back to George, her face all

serious again, "there's something painful about that man. It hurts. Why, George?"

Supersensitive where Cavan was concerned, almost resenting Pen's quick accurate intuition, George pulled her away in the other direction, badgering her as they walked to be more explicit. "I don't know what you mean really. What hurts?" And then before she could answer, there was the matter of where to go to be settled. They stood on the sidewalk looking in at the little tables under umbrellas at the Window Shop, tempted by the warmth of the day, though no one was sitting outside.

"But that wonderful chocolate cake, Pen," he reminded her as she seemed to hesitate. He felt ravenous, as if just looking at Pen used up an immense amount of energy. "Those little sandwiches. . . ."

That settled it, and they were able to bring their tea outside, to sit alone among all the empty tables in the late warm sunlight while Pen's question reverberated and echoed, and they came back to it, their heads close together like conspirators.

"Tell me," George urged, though he was afraid, afraid of what Pen's eyes had seen, wanting suddenly to protect Cavan, to throw a cloak of words round him so Pen would never know, never guess the terrible look he had intercepted at the head of the stairs. "Why do you say 'hurt'? It's such a strange word."

"I don't know"—she looked dreamily about her, and he felt she was about to escape him again, withdraw into her inner world.

"You must know," he said urgently. "You can't fling a sentence like that around and not know—it's irresponsible——"

"You sound like my tutor."

"Don't. This is important."

"Oh very well." She leaned her chin on her hand, frowning. "When Professor Cavan talks about things he cares about, it's terrific, but it's"—she hesitated again—"it's almost too much, George. I mean it's as if he were battering down a wall inside himself to get through, and so one feels battered too—it's exciting, but disturbing. You'll hate me for this"—she turned to him now quite seriously—"but should anyone allow himself to be that exposed— a professor?"

"Is that why you said 'where are we'?"

"I suppose so. One expects a professor to be a little less or a little more than human—I think that's it. They all have their attitudes, their little jokes, their ways to protect themselves. But Cavan is just there, with no defenses, nothing between him and the class."

"Except the subject, Pen—or rather," George corrected himself a little stiffly, "an attitude toward the subject. You felt that surely?"

"I was awfully uncomfortable all the time," she confessed.

This George recognized as the truth, and he minded. The class, when they talked about Cavan over beer or in their rooms, had not one of them ever admitted this, but it was the truth. Yet they would not have missed a single meeting for the world. They were attracted and at the same time disturbed, made uncomfortable, as Pen said.

"But it's not what he says"—George turned to her earnestly—"is it? I mean if you wrote down everything he said today, every word made sense—at least to me. It was right at the center of things, wasn't it? Wasn't that what you felt?"

"Absolutely."

George sighed with relief. Such an unequivocal affirmation from Pen was a triumph.

"Well then?"

"I don't know, George," she said quietly. "Do you?"

"He's the greatest teacher I have ever had." But this of course was not an answer, and he knew it. "He comes closer to what teaching should be than anyone—" he added as if a further blank check was needed.

"What should teaching be?"

He laughed. "I was going to say a transfusion, but it sounds absurd—something more anyway than an intellectual exercise— Oh, you know," he ended, reaching across for her hand. It was ice cold, as it always was these days. He looked at it for a moment, lying there quite passively in his as if it didn't belong to her. "Next year I might get an instructorship. We could get married."

He had not meant to say it like this, so casually, but it just popped out as if he had in the last hour reached the end of his tether, and it had to be said.

She withdrew her hand quite violently and sat looking down at her lap, her face closed up like an empty house. "Don't push me, George, please."

"I'm not pushing you," he said irritably. "But after all, we've known each other for a year——"

"I'm sorry, George."

"Is there someone else?" he could just bring himself to ask.

She hesitated, then answered looking at him very

frankly, "Only myself. I don't know really who I am, you see. I don't know what it's all about. It's not my fault."

"Oh, I know," he groaned, "I do all the wrong things."

"It wasn't the wrong thing to take me to the seminar, darling."

So near to misery he had been a second before, so near now he was to happiness because she had said "darling." After all and in spite of everything, it was a lucky day.

VI

Ivan Goldberg sat at the big desk in his ground-floor office
at Warren House sharpening a bunch of pencils very methodically and neatly with a small penknife. Boys banging
in for conferences could cast an eye on him, a somehow formidable presence sitting there rather like a Chinese god to
whom one might make an obeisance, but with whom one
would not carry on a casual conversation. He sat very erect,
the shadow of a smile on his lips, immaculately dressed
(was it true that he changed his shirt three times a day?)
and looking rather more like a banker than a professor, his
keen black eyes always alert, magnified by thick glasses.
This was a face that never relaxed, was never to be caught
off guard. If Cavan seemed to Pen too exposed, Goldberg
had contrived a façade which no one had ever seen through
completely. With students he maintained the upper hand
on principle. He had made it his business to have all the

answers within his field of English and American literature, and he did not range outside it. Absolutely concentrated, with a mind like a fencer's, he was bound to win. He was feared because he had deliberately chosen to be feared; he believed in an absolute hierarchy. His god was the University but he considered himself a high priest to be treated accordingly. He expected a student due for a conference to be there on the dot. As Chapel rang the hour, he adjusted his watch. Perkins was late again.

But it was not after all Perkins who swung open the heavy door into the hall; it was Edward Cavan.

"Have you got a few minutes, Ivan?"

"Of course. Shut the door. Perkins is one minute late and it will do him good to cool his heels." Goldberg came out from behind his desk and sat down in one of two armchairs to the right of it. It was a subtly flattering gesture, as if he would consciously give up the advantage of sitting behind a desk. And it was a gesture symptomatic of his relation to Cavan, the man in the department for whom he had the greatest respect and at the same time the man who was among them all his real antagonist. For Goldberg did not approve of Edward Cavan's emphasis on what he called the periphery of literature—economics, history, all that could be rolled up in the term "cultural historian." He did not follow this modern fashion; he considered himself a purist. Cavan's political activities not only made him uncomfortable, but actually made him suffer. He suffered that a professor of such distinction should make a fool of himself. He felt that it reflected on the University, but even worse, it diminished Cavan's authority, and Cavan's authority was necessary to him. He had chosen his enemy as other men choose their friends and he wanted his enemy to be immaculate, beyond reproach. "What's on your mind, Edward?" he asked, taking a cigarette from a silver case and offering Edward one.

But he regretted the easy question as soon as he had asked it. It was clear and had been for sometime that too much was on Edward's mind for anyone to speak of it casually. Edward was sitting forward in his chair, ill at ease, and more than usually crumpled-looking. He might at least keep his pants pressed, Ivan thought.

"You're not going to like this, Ivan"—Edward looked up a moment, his chin forward a little, his eyes unsmiling.

"Well, what is it?" Goldberg sat back deliberately in his chair, the cigarette hanging from his lips so that the smoke curled about his head and he looked more than ever impassive and judicial, the man who had his guard up in the presence of the man who had no guard.

"You know about the case out in Nebraska, I presume?"

"I seem to have read something about it in the *Crimson*——"

"A Professor Lode in the department of economics there has been fired on the grounds that he campaigned for Wallace. Of course this is not what the official pronouncement is, but one gathers that the trustees have put pressure on the college and they've knuckled under." Edward's tone was, as always in such matters, harsh and belligerent. Goldberg observed this and it hurt him. The man had no business to be so passionate.

"Yes, yes— I do remember the facts," he said warily.

"I want you to head a Harvard committee to protest." Having launched his bomb, Edward now sat back to wait for it to explode. It had evidently been an effort, for Goldberg saw the faint sweat on his forehead.

"I should have thought this was up your alley rather than mine," Goldberg played for time.

"At this point my name would be damaging. I campaigned for Wallace myself, if you remember."

"My dear fellow, you know very well that I will do no such thing."

Edward got up with a gesture of some violence, stood there, as if he was going to walk out, then said very quietly, "What if the professor involved were myself, Ivan?"

"We don't do things that way at Harvard, as you know very well. I presume this is a state university and politics naturally enter in. No, Edward, I have steadfastly refused to be involved in political matters and I don't see why I should suddenly go back on my position now."

"But this is not a matter of politics, Ivan." Edward was obviously forcing himself to be patient. "You can't evade it on those grounds. It's a matter of freedom to think and believe and say what you believe. It's a basic American principle which is being attacked here. It's the opening wedge in a fight against the intellectuals as subversives not only for political reasons but because they're intellectuals. You're just being an ostrich," Edward said, sitting down again abruptly, determined, it appeared, to stay and fight this out once and for all.

"The reason the intellectuals are being lumped together as subversives is that too many of them have played politics as amateurs. If they'd stuck to their last, we wouldn't be in this mess." Goldberg deliberately became gentler and sweeter in tone and more smiling as what he said became fiercer in content.

"Very well," Edward shouted hoarsely, his face quite red now and all pretence of reasonableness gone, "have it your own way. Say we were all crazy and wrong, you still can't condone firing a man without a hearing. You simply can't. For once in your life, Ivan, you are not going to escape into your ivory tower. You just can't do it, cold fish though you may be." Goldberg felt the smile on his own face freeze so that he seemed to be looking out of a mask. Inside it, he suffered. It was a dreadful thing to him to see a man of Edward's intelligence reach such a pitch of passion. What he felt actually was something like love, the kind of love that makes you slap a hysteric.

"You're driving yourself too hard, Edward," he said gently.

"If so, it's the fault of people like you. You speak of intelligence. Have you any beyond the strict little field you have shut yourself up in? After all, Ivan, you're a citizen, aren't you?" But as if Ivan's tone had only really reached through to Edward after his answer, he leaned forward suddenly with his head in his hands. "Do this one thing for me, if not for yourself. It's perfectly safe," he added as if he had let himself show too much feeling.

"We don't speak the same language, Edward. You have no right to call me a coward. Let me explain myself." Goldberg now was the one to stand and walk about the room. "If I give my name to your committee, I'll be badgered day and night by every other committee under the sun for any cause of the same kind. If I give my name, it will end by having no value. Even as a citizen, I feel my work as an educator and a scholar is my real responsibility. I do not have time for extracurricular activities. That is final." He stood with his back to the window, waiting for Edward to storm out of the room. But instead the man just sat there, hunched over, his head in his hands and for a moment Ivan had the fantastic illusion that he was crying.

"You know there is no one I respect more than you as a scholar, Edward," he said quite gravely, the little smile gone at last. He and Edward were so near to being friends, so near to crashing through the thin glass wall between them, that at this moment he felt that if he could only go over and put a hand on Edward's shoulder, the glass would slide away.

They faced each other. But when Edward lifted his head, his eyes were blazing. Not tears but a paroxysm of anger shook him, the more terrible because for once it was controlled.

"Scholarship of the only kind I respect will have a hard time existing from now on, I mean scholarship which has some relation to the world in which it exists," he said, hammering out each word.

"Your book on Wallace Stevens, for instance?" Goldberg fought back.

Edward got up from his chair and stood there like a little bull. "It can hardly be written. But of course this is something you don't know about——"

"I don't carry the world about all the time like an unborn baby inside me, if that's what you mean."

"Maybe it is what I mean. I'd rather do that, ridiculous as it may appear to you, than do what the German professors did—wash my hands of any responsibility, let the Nazis take over, and then wake up in a concentration camp. You can still go your own way, Ivan. You're lucky. . . ."

There was no way now to get back to the moment when it seemed as if they might crash through to each other. For the little smile had come back to Ivan's lips and he was icily polite.

"I realize, Edward, that these emotional appeals—what is supposed to happen to a Jew at the mention of the word concentration camp—are usually effective."

"For God's sake, Ivan, don't be a fool. Of course that's not what I meant!" Now Edward was touched at the quick, and Goldberg had won. They stood with the room between them, and for the first time there was silence. Out of it Goldberg heard his own voice, charged with emotion, so that it surprised him as much as it did Edward.

"Edward, come back," he heard himself saying.

"From where, Ivan?" and it was Edward's turn to smile.

"This morbid sense of responsibility. You're killing yourself, you're using up your marrow, wasting very great powers. It's tragic." But Ivan could not keep the warmth now out of his voice. What was meant to be severe sounded like admiration.

"Aren't you exaggerating now? It is hardly morbid; it is hardly using up one's marrow to make a simple request of a colleague." It was Edward's turn to score.

"You looked exhausted when you came in here."

"So people say. As a matter of fact I came from a rather good seminar, a paper on Willa Cather. I was quite eloquent." Edward rocked on his heels, his hands still in his pockets.

"Oh hell," Goldberg said suddenly, "What's the matter with us anyway? When am I going to see some of the Stevens book?" Goldberg and Cavan had been used to showing each other work in progress, counting on severe unrelenting criticism and enjoying it. This was their real relationship, and Goldberg was making an open gesture toward it in asking the question.

Edward's face clouded. "I'm afraid never," he said quietly.

"You're closing the door between us because I won't sign your manifesto? I can't believe it."

"It's too expensive to keep the door open, Ivan. Can't you see?"

"There's no way to bridge the gap?"

"Apparently not."

"I can't believe it," Ivan said half to himself, but at that second Edward opened and closed the door and was gone. Ivan could hear his voice in the hall apologizing to Perkins for the long wait. The damn fool shouldn't talk like that to a student, Ivan groaned. It's not dignified.

"Come in, Perkins," he said in answer to the knock. "I expect students to be on time. You were more than a minute late."

VII

"Come for a walk, Edward. I feel low," Grace commanded on the telephone at nine o'clock the next morning. "There's no concert, you know. The orchestra is gadding, but it's our afternoon just the same. There might be a few late migrants still worth seeing at the cemetery." She said all this in one breath, because she was so afraid he would refuse, because also she did not know really what mood she had interrupted. "I expect you've done a full day's work, already?"

"I've been sitting in front of a blank page for two hours. Perhaps that's work." His tone was dry, faraway. She could sense the fatigue in it.

"Well, it's a lovely day and a walk will do you good," she answered firmly. "We'd better start at three. It gets dark so early . . ." It was clear that he did not want to talk now, and once that was settled she hung up abruptly. But when she had hung up, she sat for some moments doing nothing, stroking Horace's head absent-mindedly as he lay curled up beside her on the bed, half-hidden under the breakfast tray.

"He's coming, Horace, so we mustn't be anxious, must we?" she said, scratching him now under the chin, as the purrs grew louder. One paw stretched out and she held it a moment in her hand. Little leather palm, she thought. It was such a soft yielding little hand for a moment, but then it withdrew itself quite firmly.

"It's a hell of a world, Ellen," she announced when Ellen came in to take the tray.

"Yes, ma'am. I expect it is, ma'am," Ellen answered discreetly. She was tall, thin and ageless, and nothing Grace Kimlock said shocked her because she didn't believe a word of it.

"Professor Cavan will be coming to tea, Ellen. We had better have some of those scones he likes and some of that ginger marmalade." If love could find some way of expressing itself, she thought glumly. Ginger marmalade indeed. But lately she had been reduced to this sort of thing. Edward is swimming out of my ken, she said to herself. I do not know really where he is, how to touch him. It was this that made the world a hell. "Well it's high time I got up, Horace," she said, "no point in brooding." Her getting up made an earthquake of the calm island of the bed and Horace, offended, got down, gave a tremendous yawn, stretching himself full length, first one back foot then the other, and walked slowly and with great dignity to the door. The day had begun.

It might be a hell of a world, but it was a beautiful day, clear as a bell and cloudless, and so warm that Grace, armed with binoculars and a stick, needed no coat over her suit. By the time she and Edward were through the iron gates of Mt. Auburn cemetery the sun had reached just the point in its afternoon course when the slanting rays flowed through the blood-red dogwood leaves and the brilliant gold maples and set off each berry or sharply cut Japanese maple leaf in peculiar theatrical brilliance like a pre-Raphaelite painting. True aficionados, they did not need to decide where to go, but walked without speaking down their usual path into a round green amphitheater entirely lined with Grecian temples, or variations on the theme of the Greek temple, family crypts set into the hillside. It was like a small classical city, a slightly cluttered Claude or Poussin, as Edward had once remarked.

"Why no one ever comes here, I can't imagine," Grace said, her bright glancing eyes taking it in, the casual air of the planting among the white tombs, that mass of rhododendron, for instance, and in the distance a stand of pines. "It's the most beautiful thing in Cambridge."

"It has everything—even a kind of society." Edward smiled, as Grace took off with her usual insatiable curiosity to peer through the iron-grilled door into one of the tombs, where she could see a little iron chair sitting there in the dark beside a marble table.

"Even a swallow's nest," she said, coming back in triumph. But it was all, she knew, slightly staged by both of them, this walk which was the conscious repetition of so many walks in every season, when they had been carefree, militant, happy—she stopped still. The word "happy" was too dreadful really beside Edward's haunted face. For her sake he was making a great effort to be genial and appreciative, as if she were giving him the cemetery this afternoon as a present and he must make appropriate thanks. But she knew without his telling her that he hadn't slept, even as they walked on into a small dark valley, narrow and enclosed, so that the trees planted on the hilltop soared to amazing heights, seemed to be about to take off into the sky.

"Look at that oak, Edward! What splendor!" The words echoed back as she turned to him, standing passive, rooted, looking at the oak obediently, but not seeing it.

"Yes," he said, "it's very fine."

But we cannot talk to each other, she thought in a kind of panic. We cannot communicate. In the old days, this banter about the tombstones, this "taking in" of every sight and sound had been like an accompaniment to the undercurrent of communion, and that was its charm. They talked about the trees and the birds, but what they were really saying was, "We can talk about these things because all the important things don't need to be talked about."

Now the silence all around them seemed like a threat. They walked on the beautifully kept grass, side by side, and she felt a kind of panic as they left the open spaces and made their way through the pine grove, a narrow dark passage which would lead them out onto the two long ponds where families of wild ducks sometimes came for shelter, and to gobble at the floating green stuff. She had always loved these ponds, but now it seemed as if only damp and darkness and loneliness were there to greet them. Already the light was going, was leaving roots and stones in shadow, brilliant and warm only in the tops of the trees.

But what could she say or do? He walked ahead of her, his hands in his pockets and she followed, helpless as a dog. They had come, at the end of the two ponds, to a stone bench where it was traditional to sit down for a little while, traditional for Edward to take out a cigarette. The fact that he did not do so, but just sat there, was the worst of all. Grace nervously took out her binoculars and swept the trees as if they were tiers of boxes at the opera, but all she discovered was a junco. She had to make a great effort of will not to talk. She sensed that if Edward were to get some peace from this walk she must leave him alone, not pry and not gabble.

"Aren't you going to smoke?" she asked gently, after what seemed an eternity.

"Yes, now that you speak of it, I think I will." He was pulling himself back to her; she could feel the effort it was. "What have you been doing with yourself?" he asked, when he had lit his cigarette.

"What have I been doing?" She had the impression that she had chiefly been worrying about him, but she must think of something quickly. "Fosca came to tea, of course. I had lunch with an old Radcliffe schoolmate of mine. It depressed me. You would think she had never heard of an idea in her life."

"I expect you frightened her"—Edward made a stab at the familiar bantering tone.

"Oh no, I was good as gold. I discussed the servant problem and the high cost of living for hours."

"So perhaps she thinks you never heard of an idea."

"Oh no, she can't think that," Grace said, caught as she always was by his bait. "I gave her a piece of my mind before she left. I simply had to, Edward. She was talking such perfect nonsense, fantastic stories about the corruption among the Socialists in England. She gets it all from her husband, of course."

"People believe what they want to believe"—he got up—"that's what it all comes to in the end."

They stood looking back a moment at the dreamy pond, at the long row of beeches reflected on one side, and the Gothic redstone tombs on the other, their roofs covered with long grass, even bushes. This was the oldest part of the cemetery, perfectly Victorian, before the Greek temple came into fashion. "How many times did we have to listen to the story of Roosevelt's walking on the water? People actually believed it, you know," and he turned away, as if he were suddenly very tired.

Even Grace felt subdued, tamed by his atmosphere of passive negation. They were moving out to one of the uglier and more crowded parts of this city of the dead, and Grace broke away to do something, anything to break the depression which was creeping upon her as if out of the ground. She amused herself by reading the names on the tombstones.

"Good Lord," she ejaculated suddenly, "here's old Mrs. Bowditch. Whatever is she doing here?" Then, as she saw the other names near by, "Oh yes, of course she was a Merritt, wasn't she? She must have wanted to revert." She was astonished to hear, like a reprieve, Edward's sudden amused laugh.

"I expect we do tend to revert," he said, still laughing, and then more soberly, "I wonder what I am reverting to——"

"You're too young to revert to anything, Edward," she

said in her natural tone of voice, acid and commanding. It really seemed as if they were coming out from a long tunnel. Just then, as if to make this sensation tangible, a male pheasant ran out from behind a rhododendron bush, stood for a second quite still, alerted, his head high, as Grace laid a hand on Edward's arm to warn him. It lasted a few seconds, the bird's wild bright glance, his standing there a few feet away in all his brilliance of red and gold and black, and then he was off with a little short run and a loud whirr and disappeared over the hillside.

But they had had the vision. The excitement of it coursed through Grace like electricity. It released for her the words she had been holding back for a half-hour. Now she could say them, her hand still on Edward's arm. "It's all so beautiful, Edward," she said in a rush. "And so short, really," she added, meaning life perhaps. Then, quite gently, "I wish I could help."

"No one can help," he said moving away from her, so her hand fell to her side, and it seemed a rejection. "That's just the trouble." He was not looking at her, nor did he see the tears which had started to her eyes. "It's not your failure, it's mine, Grace."

"Friends should be able to help each other." She drank the shadows all around them like a bitter draught. All the light had gone up into the sky. They were in darkness. "But I'm too old. Don't say anything," she said harshly. "It's the truth." She walked ahead of him now, very straight, up over the hill where they looked down on the large round pond, dominated by the circle of white columns which commemorated Mary Baker Eddy. "All those religions," she said with contempt. "They're no help either."

117

"Darling Grace"—Edward came up to stand beside her—"I haven't done much to cheer you up, have I?"

"That's all right," she flashed back at him. "I'm a tough old bird." She would not yield any further to destructive emotion. And her eyes were eagle-bright now, as she took out the binoculars and hid behind them.

"Anything to see?"

"I thought there was a duck in the reeds," she said shortly. "I find ducks comforting."

"I never felt closer to anyone except my mother," Edward said, "than I do to you."

Had she heard? She turned and went quickly down the hill toward the broad road which would lead them out again. And he followed, his head bent, his hands in his pockets, as perhaps he had walked behind his mother when he was a child, dawdling a little, waiting for her to notice his absence.

"Hurry up, Edward," Grace called impatiently. "It's high time for tea."

Edward sat with Horace on his lap stroking him absent-mindedly and looking at the cold hearth. It was really too warm for a fire, yet the absence of it made the room feel somber.

"I wonder if I ought to get new curtains." Grace looked at the heavy green velvet curtains, faded to the color of olives.

"No, no," he said quickly, "don't think of changing anything." His eyes wandered to the Sargent portrait of Grace with her mother, her mother sitting in the very chair where she sat now, and the little girl with flaming red hair and a narrow intense face standing beside her. "It's a beautiful Sargent, you know, one of the best." She could see his interest flicker for a moment, like a fire which might light and might not. But at least she thought, he is really looking at something and taking pleasure in it.

"I'm leaving it to the Fogg," she announced.

"It's so perfect against the gold walls, so perfect in this room, I can't imagine it anywhere else."

"Oh, I expect the house will be torn down," she said gloomily. "It's a white elephant, God knows."

"You are depressed, aren't you?"

"I need my tea." She felt quite cross. "Where on earth is Ellen?" And she pulled the long tasseled cord energetically. "I really die every afternoon at this time. I just ebb away—" and she laughed a laugh which denied this altogether.

"Oh you'll not ebb away, will she, Horace?" He scratched Horace under the chin affectionately. "She'll go out like a burst of fireworks, a shower of gold—" he chuckled. Had a little ease crept in with the tea? With the warmth, and Horace, and the whole familiar atmosphere of the room and the time? Perhaps Edward felt it too, for he ate two scones and drank down his tea thirstily.

"I forgot to have lunch," he apologized, passing his cup back for the third time, and then as he sat there, suddenly thoughtful, but still relaxed, he said, "I have fought with nearly everybody I care about at all in the college." He seemed bewildered, at a loss to understand why, just what was happening or had happened.

"You're thinking of Damon——" she hazarded.

"No, as a matter of fact, I'm going there to dinner tonight. Julia asked me."

"Oh good," she breathed, fearful of overemphasis. "So that's going to be all right."

"Is it?" But he let that drop. Then he told her about Goldberg and his refusal to sign a petition about the Lode case.

"Oh, Goldberg," and Grace shrugged. What did he expect? Horace, disliking the atmosphere of tension, now got up and flopped down to stretch out full length on the rug, showing the fine seam down his white stomach.

Edward reacted violently to her dismissal of Goldberg. "Goldberg is the nearest thing to a great scholar we have in the department, Grace. You can't shrug him off."

"But he's never been any help to us, surely."

"This is different. It's a University matter." Then he added, "I could trust him about my work. I wanted him to look over the Stevens."

"Well, he can still do that, I expect," she said drily.

"No, I won't see him any more. I told him so yesterday."

"I see. . . ." In small, the University was the world. The same splits broke it into pieces, the same tensions were working inside it, like fine fissures which might suddenly gape.

"No, you don't see," he said irritably. "You can't see. More than anything else that's happened this makes me feel that I don't belong in this community, Grace. I've become a real outsider— Oh, these people mean well. They're my friends, or imagine that they are." He paused and then went on quite quietly and gravely, "But they seem really to be profoundly cut off from reality. It's that."

"I can't see that it's different. We've always been a small minority——"

"Yes, perhaps. But that small minority represented the

rising tide. We were part of something much larger than any small group inside the prison walls, and there were apertures in the walls."

"Well, there still could be. I don't see that withdrawal is the answer." It was her vital energy she pitted now against his apathy. It was not the words she said, but her very attitude, her essence which she brought into play.

"I feel locked in, locked up, stifled," he said.

"It was different in Europe?" She pushed him to re-member, perhaps, the conviction, the warmth which he had brought back from that summer at the Salzburg Seminar, anything now that would wake the fighting man in him again.

"Good God, yes. In Europe the intellectual is still part of life itself. I'm tired of being a kind of governess without real responsibility, without dignity, someone who may be turned out like Lode at any moment at the whim of the employer—and who is only considered responsible as long as he is *not* responsible. They're making eunuchs of us, Grace, that's what it amounts to." But though these were passionate words, the man who said them seemed to be whipping himself on to an emotion he no longer felt.

"That couldn't happen at Harvard, Edward, after all —I mean, about Lode."

"That's it"—he turned on her with violence, with tri-umph—"that's just what Goldberg said. As long as it doesn't happen at Harvard, all's well. As long as it doesn't touch *us*, it isn't real."

"Don't be cross with me. I can't bear it." She had wanted to call out his fire, but she could not bear it when it was directed at her. Everything might crumble around them, but Edward and she would stand fast together. And as long as they did, all was not lost.

"I couldn't be cross with you," he said quickly. "Forgive me."

But when he had left and Ellen came to take the tray and she said, "Well, he ate two scones, Ellen, that is something," there was no comfort in the words.

VIII

It was absurd to be so nervous, Julia thought. She had
changed her dress twice, searching frantically for the right
note, neither dim nor spectacular, and now she was standing in her comfortable old gray chiffon, her one Paris dress,
Vionnet, bought before the war. She stood there at the
long mirror, pinning on a crumpled red velvet rose, but as
she tried to open out the petals, she was not thinking about
this, she was standing in the Hotel Louvois nearly fifteen
years ago, and when the rose fell to the floor, she did not
pick it up. It fell, and she let it fall, as the years had fallen
leaving her now to stand here, marooned (but only for a
moment, for she must look at the roast). Then they had
been, it seemed, at the center of life. Everyone was in
Paris; Edward dragged Damon off to meet Blum, she remembered. They came back lit up, combative, Edward as
usual with a refugee in tow. How many people did he help

123

that year with affidavits, money, above all, time, listening to the painful stories, pouring out warmth?—How long ago it was. Another world. Damon had just got his professorship and Edward was on the brink of beginning the big book, she remembered, stooping now to jab a pin into the floppy rose, but it was really too limp, better put it in the Morgan Memorial bag with the other odds and ends of life it was time to throw away. *Is* the roast burning? She sniffed apprehensively and, forgetting to powder her nose, fled down the stairs.

"Where have you been?" Damon asked crossly. He was looking into the oven reproachfully. He was getting out ice cubes, another reproach, as he liked her to do this for him, it made him so impatient. He was as prickly as a porcupine, and she felt at once that she must do something to change the atmosphere, but what?

"Well, I—I couldn't decide what to wear," she apologized.

"It doesn't matter, does it? Edward won't notice. He doesn't notice anything these days."

"It's for myself," she said quietly. "I need to feel armed."

"You look very nice, you always do," he said, but without seeing her. "Damn these cubes, Julia. Why don't they invent something?"

"Darling, go away," she commanded. "I'm nervous enough as it is. I'll bring in the ice when Edward comes." And then, as he stood there, his hands dripping, she handed him a towel and pushed him out by force.

At least the roast was not burned and the potatoes seemed to be browning nicely for once. Oh please, please let us be calm, she implored the air. Let us be kind. Keep

Damon from getting angry. Make Edward understand—
but the custard looked rather queer. And it was high time
she carameled the sauce, too. We are children, she thought,
lost in the wood. It is time we grew up, she thought, banging about in the kitchen drawer for that wooden spoon
which always disappeared. But as she ladled the sauce in
the immemorial gesture (so she had watched her mother
do it in the big sunny kitchen in Milton), she felt calmed.
Calm welled up in her. We'll manage, she told herself.
We'll find a way. For we really love each other. That is a
fact. She clung to this fact. Can people who really love
each other be divided? The question lost itself in the deli-
cious syrupy brown mixture, just the right consistency,
thick but not sticky—and then she heard the bell. Let
Damon go. Let them meet each other first alone.

"Darling Edward," she said as she came in with the
ice cubes a few minutes later. "Bless you for coming," she
said, carried forward on her kitchen thoughts so that she
found herself kissing him. Then, embarrassed by what
she had done, she explained, "I was thinking of Paris, 1937
—do you remember? It's because of this dress. . . ." She
sank down into a chair.

"Of course I remember," Edward stood with his back
to the fire, his hands in his pockets. "It's a charming dress,
Julia, a work of genius——"

"It must be, if it's lasted all this time," and she sighed,
sighed with pleasure, with relief, for it seemed as if the
enormous tension of the last days had vanished, had been
dissipated like a cloud. There was Damon, stirring the
martinis and smiling, and there was Edward standing at
the fire, just as if nothing had happened.

"Poor darling, you've never had another, have you?

And we thought we would be so rich, at least I did. A professor's salary"—suddenly he laughed—"what children we were!"

"It was a good time," Julia said, as he handed her a martini. "You don't need to feel so superior."

"A very good time," Edward echoed and lifted his glass to her.

"The year before Munich," Damon turned to them from the little table where he had been mixing the drinks. "I wonder—was it really such a good time?"

Edward considered this for a moment. "No," he said earnestly, "perhaps it wasn't. But our star was in the ascendant just the same. We were rising in that falling world —why do I say that?" He stopped. "But there was solidarity, Damon, you must admit. And one felt useful. That summer in Paris I really accomplished rather a lot, in one way and another."

"You were inventing your book," Julia broke in. "And then you went down to the Spanish hospital somewhere in the South, didn't you? And all those German refugees—"

"There was a reservoir of good will to be tapped. That's what I really meant. People listened to one."

"Yes," Damon frowned, "I suppose that's true. But we were such children, Edward. We really were."

"And now we've grown up?" Julia asked lightly.

"Julia thinks I'll never grow up"—Damon ruffled his hair—"and perhaps it's true."

"It's the effect of science," Edward teased (this was an old war between them, a war of many skirmishes, safe skirmishes Julia thought with relief). "You scientists have always been children, you and your dangerous toys."

Julia hardly listened as the familiar tunes were played.

She drank her martini, half listening, more watching the two men's faces, the ever-changing weather in Damon's, his eager flashing look, responsive not so much to Edward as to his own thoughts—and Edward's, opaque, taut round the eyes, concealing (so she sensed) a permanent state of anguish. How could one help such a man, who was not able to talk about himself, whose personal dignity was such that, almost, it precluded intimacy? While she thought these things, Edward had apparently changed the subject. They were talking, she gathered, about the strangeness and rarity in America of children's living on in their father's house, as Damon had chosen to do.

"We did find it strange at first," Julia reminded him. "At first I had every intention of changing things around," she added, with a smile at Damon, "but I wasn't allowed to. Even that stuffed fish in the hall, you know? For years I wasn't allowed to throw it away."

"My grandfather caught that bass," Damon said seriously.

"I've no doubt he did, but that didn't mean we had to live with the corpse for the rest of our lives." But Damon did not really like to be teased about this family feeling he had so strongly, and it was time she thought of serving the dinner, so she got up, only pausing a moment in the door because she felt she must just hear Edward's answer as Damon, wanting to change the subject, asked, "What was your father's house like?"

The question gave Edward pause. He clasped his hands round his knees and rocked back and forth as he launched into an ironic description. "Oh, you know, golden oak, overstuffed furniture, glassed-in bookcases supporting casts of Greek statues with fig leaves applied, reproductions of Botticelli in Florentine frames, little inlaid Persian tables—oh"—he rocked back and forth a moment, evoking it all—"and those glossy glazed brown tiles round the fireplace— Need I say more?"

"Well," Julia made a parting thrust as she left them, "the bass was hardly a thing of beauty!"

But they were safely launched now and Damon would soon be talking about his grandfather. She could leave them.

For the moment at least, anguish, division had been kept at bay. By walking very carefully they might be able to ignore it. Yet—it was there. In the old days they had not had to walk carefully, so Julia thought after supper when they had gone back into the study to have their coffee. And now, in the slight pause as for a moment no voice filled the silence, what was clear was the lack of something. The intangible bond which had made silence another form of communication was no longer there. Silence had become dangerous.

"How's your work going these days, Damon?" The question was a polite one. It had been asked to fill the gap. Julia felt as if tiredness flowed out of Edward like a fog. He drank his coffee down as if to give himself an injection, and turned to Damon, but all the time all around him was this fog. Yet he had enjoyed his dinner—perhaps that was why. He had relaxed, almost, had praised Damon's burgundy, had seemed like a reasonable facsimile of his old self, just as the whole evening because of their united effort, was a reasonable facsimile of all the other evenings. Julia was not prepared for Damon's answer.

"I haven't been able to work for a week, if you must

know," he said quite crossly. Then, as he caught Julia's warning look, he added, "But I've been stuck anyway, as a matter of fact . . ."

Edward got up to hand his coffee cup to Julia for more. For a moment Damon's words lay on the air, as if they had not been spoken. Edward seemed preoccupied. Perhaps, indeed, he hadn't heard. Then, standing at the fireplace again, he faced Damon and said, "We've got to talk about it, Damon."

"Oh, do we?" Julia said quickly. "We don't really, do we? I mean—can't we just be peaceful? It's been such a happy evening," she said, as if she were indeed bidding it now farewell.

"Yes, we do." Damon stood too, laid down his coffee cup and faced Edward. For a second she had the vision of two boxers eying each other in the ring. But no, it must not be like that. She must stand between them somehow, ward off the blows, prevent its happening.

"I don't know what happened at the Civil Liberties," she said, standing and laying a hand on Damon's arm, as if to prevent whatever was to happen if she could, "but surely your friendship is more important—and talking about it won't help, Edward. You know very well it won't." She tried to look into Edward's eyes, but he was looking down. She might have been pleading with a stone. He was locked somewhere deep down inside himself. He was not to be touched. "Sit down, Damon," she said almost roughly, "please sit down both of you." This time it was a command.

"I came here to say good-bye." Edward didn't move.

"No," Julia's voice rang out firmly, "you can't do that,

Edward. It's not fair—and what's more it's childish. One doesn't break off a friendship like ours over a political disagreement." She stood in the center of the room, and she was trembling with anger and revolt.

"I do not honestly think it a strength, nor wisdom, to be as dogmatic as you have become, Edward. It's too much like fanaticism." Damon said this quite quietly—it was a sentence he had evidently been preparing in his mind.

"This is a matter of principle," Edward answered at once. "If the intellectuals can't stand together now on principle, then it's just too bad."

"Oh damn the intellectuals," said Julia, "let's be human beings."

"Exactly," Edward turned to her. "As human beings we cannot afford to start telling tales, snooping and spying on each other, writing letters assuring perfect strangers that none of our friends are Communists——"

"Some of my best friends are Communists," Damon interrupted. He could not resist the joke, but it was a mistake. You don't joke when a man stands up in your house, raw with wounds.

"It's not a laughing matter," Edward said quietly.

"It's too serious, that's why one has to laugh sometimes," Damon said quite gently.

"The great American pastime—laugh it off. Pretend it's not real. But it is real, Damon, God damn it. I know. I say if you begin to compromise you're lost, when it comes to a matter of principle."

"We're not starting a witch hunt by writing a private letter to the ACLU executive—it's just plain childish to say we are."

"I didn't come here to argue with you, Damon," Edward said wearily, flinging himself down into a chair and rubbing his eyes as if they ached.

"Why did you come?" Julia asked. "Oh, Edward, surely for friendship's sake—can't we agree to disagree?"

Edward groaned, then said as if each word were a heavy stone and he were lifting them one by one, "Friendship without solidarity isn't possible, Julia——"

"You sound like a Party member, Edward——"

"I wish I were one," the answer shot back fiercely. "I wouldn't feel so absolutely alone."

"But, Edward, it's a loneliness of your own choosing, surely. You know we love you and honor you and want you always to be our friend. It's not our fault," Julia said, helplessly.

"It's nobody's fault, I expect. We're locked up in separate jails."

But Damon had been thinking and now he made another attempt at reason. "Listen," he said gravely, "we can't fight and win without making some compromises with things as they are. The Communist Party by being a kind of secret society has put itself outside the democratic procedures, Edward. You have to admit that."

Edward lifted his head. "Maybe. But I can't see that putting ourselves outside democratic procedures is any way to fight it."

"Of course. I couldn't agree with you more. We do feel the same way, Edward, that's what you won't admit. It's as if you were deliberately cutting yourself off—why must you?" In some way Damon had come through to a place where he could talk, where, Julia thought with gratitude, perhaps after all, they might reach safety. If only Edward . . .

131

But he sat there, with his head on his hands, belliger-ent, uncompromising, almost as if he could no longer listen to anything anyone might say.

"I'm cut off," he said then, half to himself. "I can't find my way back to you, Damon. It's no use."

If the silence that preceded this exchange had seemed to Julia to have the seeds of danger in it, the silence which now lay between and all around them had become danger itself. If it were not broken, broken soon, she thought—now, she thought— Come back to us, Edward, she said, but the words made no sound.

"It's like a nightmare," Damon said suddenly, getting up and going to the window to stand with his back to the room, rumpling his hair in exasperation.

"I'm sorry." Edward got up, lifted himself up with difficulty. "I'd better go now."

"But where will you go?" Julia faced him at the door as if to bar his passage. "Going away won't help." He would go to those bars in Scollay Square, she supposed, carrying his word *solidarity* like a banner which no one could see, drink with the sailors who called him Professor and treated him like a harmless drunk, walk the streets half the night, and then not sleep. "We can't let you go like this, Edward. It's not possible." She stood in the doorway, thinking, If I could touch him, take his hand, make the simplest human gesture. Why couldn't she? What was it in Edward that made such gestures impossible? These thoughts flashed through her mind as they stood there, waiting for some miracle which would alter the moment, save.

"I'm sorry." Edward looked at her now for the first time, a long look as if he had reached the point where it no longer mattered whether anyone saw what she saw or not. For what she saw was love though its expression could, it seemed, only be pain. Then he pushed past her quite gently, but quite firmly, and they heard the front door close behind him.

"Damon, don't let him go like this. Run after him. Bring him back," she said quickly and then sat down.

"It's no use. You know very well it's no use. He wants to break away from us, God knows why. But he has to do it. That's what I felt tonight."

"It's as if everyone had gone mad," Julia said in a tight dry voice.

"I couldn't say it. I couldn't say any of the things I was thinking. I just couldn't." Damon walked up and down now, as he did when he was deeply disturbed.

"What things, darling? Say them to me." But she was thinking, Edward is alone now. He is walking through the streets alone. He will go to bed alone. There is no one to whom he can say those things.

"I wanted to tell him that people like him are necessary, that there have to be conscientious objectors, guardians of conscience, there have to be the absolute people, and we honor them. But they are not the doers or the builders, in the long run, and I think part of Edward's conflict is that he won't admit this. He wants really to be active, not a speaking conscience, but deep in—that's why the word 'solidarity' means so much to him. Only he can't be, just because he is what he is, noble, uncompromising, absolute. So he's caught." The words came fast now, and Damon was finding his release.

"I wanted to go and hug him and take his hand, but I couldn't," Julia said. "Why couldn't we?" Tears streamed down her cheeks. She paid no attention; they fell down her cheeks like Damon's words, and Damon, walking up and down, did not see them. "Why can't love help?"

"We've done all we can, Julia." Damon flung himself down, his moment of lucidity, of understanding spent, and now only the exasperation, the tiredness, the sense of failure, ready to take over. "Love?" he said bitterly. "Edward doesn't know what the word means."

"No"—she blew her nose—"that's not true. He can't give love or take it, but he knows what it means. He knows all about it," she said, "that's what's so terrible."

part **II**

I

George Hastings did not answer his phone which rang ten times during the morning. He lay on his bed slowly, almost contemptuously drinking down a bottle of whiskey. He had not bothered to dress. The shades were drawn. "Men can't stand too much reality," he repeated from some poem, some play. Who had said it? An imaginary group of professors sat in a circle round him. It seemed to be the oral exam for the doctorate. Who said it? "Auden," he guessed, and met their pitying look. He knew very well that what was driving him to get completely blotto was shame. He had not been able to feel anything, you see, when Jack brought in the paper, white and shaken. I loved him, he was like a father to me, but all I could think of when I got the news was, *Now I'll never get that instructorship. This certainly shoots that to hell.* Pretty fine specimen, I am, the great intellect, but no soul, he thought, taking a long drink. It tasted awful. He disliked it almost as much as he disliked himself. There was emptiness. There was shame. There was nausea. There was whiskey. There was nothing else. No Cavan. No feeling. That's what Harvard added up to—no Cavan, no feeling. Just the intellect and waste. Nothing in between. No feeling. No instructorship. Repeating the same words over and over, they finally became just words, unrelated to anything, discs with words on them floating round in the air. He had set up a cycle that he found he could not break, and suddenly he was terrified, shaking with fear, his pajamas dripping wet. He staggered out into the bathroom and glared at his unshaven face as if it belonged to an enemy. This was not himself, obviously, this sullen object of disgust. The image blurred, and George was sick into the basin.

He was shaking so much then that he had to sit down. Very slowly the room came into focus, the mess of books on the table, the wastebasket overflowing beer cans and carbon paper onto the floor, and the pile of uncorrected themes which he had pushed aside as usual till the eleventh hour. George sat with his head in his hands and looked at it through the eyes of the truculent stranger he had become. Yet last night—far away down a long tunnel in another world—last night, he remembered clearly, as one might remember some forgotten scene of childhood, he had actually begun to write. He had been filled with clarity and power. It had seemed like good work, focused, clear work, the best he had ever done. And while he was doing it, so concentrated, and deeply happy, Edward Cavan had been getting ready to throw himself under an elevated train. As he, George, felt the power shooting up in him like the green drive of spring in a tree, Edward Cavan had cut himself down, and cut so much down with himself that now it seemed to George that half a century had passed and he sat, an old disappointed, self-disgusted man, stewing in his own failure. "The wind at my back," he said aloud. Yes, it was that. The excruciating loneliness, as if the world he had set his faith on had just crumbled to pieces. "The bastards," he said, "the dirty bastards." He was not sure himself to whom this referred.

He had seen Professor Cavan once after their abortive talk at Albiani's, had seen that the door of his office was ajar and stepped inside just for a moment, wondering if maybe this time would be the time when he could ask his question about a dinner engagement. For Cavan was sitting at his desk, his chair half turned so that he faced the window, and he was looking out, apparently waiting for a student, at any rate in an attitude unusually passive for him. When George spoke, he turned quite suddenly, startled out of whatever thought he had been thinking.

"Oh, it's you, George," he said with a kind of relief. Then for an instant, but it was only for an instant, George had the sense that the walls of reserve which always stood between him and his man were shifting, and he caught a glimpse of something—such painful love, such loneliness that he had instinctively lowered his own eyes. It was as if their positions had been exchanged and Cavan was the one who had a question he did not dare ask, and that he, George, had something to give. The deep-set blue eyes had looked out like an animal's eyes, pleading, George did not know for what. Yes, it was like an animal imprisoned. And George had looked away, had said something unimportant about the last paper read at the seminar, as if deliberately to avoid a crisis he felt unable to meet. The whole

139

thing took at most a minute. Then the student Cavan was waiting for turned up.

It was in fact such an intangible experience that George might have buried and forgotten it, if two days later this man had not chosen to do away with himself. Now George knew that he must live through that moment again and again, examine and re-examine it, search it for clues. He felt as if his head were bursting, but he forced himself to get up, forced his shaking hands to run water into a coffee pot, to wash the dirty cup and when, at last, he managed to drink the scalding stuff, he forced himself to shave, put on a clean shirt and trousers. Then, as if all this had banished the truculent terrifying stranger he had become, he made his bed and lay down on it, arms under his head, staring at the ceiling. What could I have done, he asked himself, if I'd known what to do? Nobody wants to look too deeply into an older person's problems, especially into a teacher's private problems. It seems slightly indecent. I suppose, George thought, he wanted something of me that he couldn't ask, that I had to give. But I didn't give it. It was too big; it upset my feelings about things. It broke down walls like breaking down houses. One couldn't cope with such loneliness. I wanted his belief, not his love, his power, not his need. We're all so scared of our feelings —there it was back again. The trap. The trap which had snapped shut on Edward Cavan. For Cavan had feeling, naked feeling, that was his greatness, what set him apart. It was also, George guessed, what tore him to pieces— had he thrown himself under that train out of self-loathing? Out of rage?

No, George turned over on his stomach pressing his head down into his hands to shut out the image. It was too violent an image, it had no reality. It was quite impossible for him to put it beside the Cavan he knew. He could meet this reality at present only with revolt—it had to be shut out, thought away. The message found on Cavan's desk had said something about "the state of the world." But when they sat in Albiani's and Cavan had tried to talk, how could George know how serious the whole matter was? Was this preoccupation with politics Cavan's strength or was it his weakness? Was it strong to take an absolute stand which proved in the end untenable in relation to the facts? Or was it fatal weakness? Oh, if only I could have asked him more, tried to understand, George groaned. How would he ever find his way out through the maze of questions now? Who could help? Everything had become nothing, for the pivot which held it all together was gone. The world had broken in two, not Edward Cavan. Edward Cavan was intact. He had let himself be savaged by an elevated train to remain intact, leaving the world all breaking to pieces, leaving the loneliness inside everyone else, the awful, bitter sense of failure and guilt inside everyone else. We can't get through to him now; we can't share the burden whatever it was. It's too late.

This time George answered the phone. It was a woman's voice he heard. The last thing he wanted was to cope with a woman.

"This is Miss Kimlock," the voice said. Then there was silence.

"Yes," George said cautiously. He hadn't an idea who she might be.

"I've been trying to get you all morning." She sounded quite cross.

"I'm sorry. I wasn't answering the phone." Kimlock?

141

Kimlock? A relative of one of his students? "What can I do for you?"

"I want to talk to you. I'm a friend of Edward's . . ." George felt the silence growing like a paralysis.

"Oh."

The silence was there again. How did one stop a silence?

"I just can't talk." He hung up the receiver. It was brutal but he had to do it. I just can't talk, he said again. They can't make me. They think I have feelings because they do. They don't know about the trap. Pen—the remembrance flashed through him like a wound—saying after he kissed her that she didn't want to feel so much. Cavan throwing himself under a train. The loneliness. No way out. "Edward?" George laughed a harsh laugh. "He wasn't Edward to me, Miss Kimlock. He was Professor Cavan. Get that? *Professor*. I can't help you"—George said all this aloud to the empty room—"you've got to help yourself. He was no friend of mine."

II

Damon finally got off to his eleven o'clock class. Frantically nervous, he could not find his hat, nor his notes for the lecture, but at last after he had stalled the car twice, it hiccupped off and Julia was alone. Her hands dropped to her sides and she sank down into the leather armchair in the study, Damon's chair. She picked up the newspaper, folded it together and laid it beside her, face down, so that the headline was out of sight. The room felt incredibly empty as if—with Damon's electrical presence gone—it had been uninhabited for years, instead of a few seconds. There was a dank smell of tobacco, she noticed, but she had no energy to get up and empty ash trays. It was necessary simply to sit still and attempt to pick up the pieces, pieces of herself, pieces of Damon, pieces of Edward. Until now she had been far too busy trying to soften the blow for Damon, trying to lift the burden of guilt he was carrying, as he repeated over and over, "We failed him. It was our fault, Julia." Her whole will and energy had been bent for the last hours on persuading Damon that they had really done all they could.

"If it's failure, it's failure of something far bigger than just we two, than just his friends," she kept saying.

"It was an act of violent rejection—of all of us. An attack, rather. Yes, an attack," he said, running his hands through his hair so it stood up on end. And then he added, "It's such a waste."

To think that we are part of a world in which such things happen, in which a man like Edward commits suicide. What had gone wrong? Where? She sat looking at the walls, at the photographs of Damon's grandfather and of their two children. And for just a second she felt a kind of relief, as if they had come to the end of something, some long bitterly painful argument which had (as indeed it had) been going on for years. At least now there would be no more arguments. There might be a little peace.

She was astonished at her own cruelty as she thought this. It was as if some aching conscience, which Edward's presence had been, was suddenly stilled. No, she said to herself, a suicide is not a simple death, bringing peace with it. It haunts; it asks a question. She saw that the argument had now gone down to a level where it would have to be fought not with reason, but with life itself. And fighting a dead man was a more complicated, a more painful affair than fighting a living one. It was no end, it was only the continuation on a different level—but at this point, she suddenly felt faint. She sat very still, waiting for the dizziness to pass. When it did pass, she lay back in the chair, her eyes closed.

144

Until this moment she had really felt nothing. She had been frantically racing along trying not to feel, trying to get to some intellectual rational plane where she could turn and face the feeling and not be overwhelmed.

Now it pounced. It pounced because she suddenly saw Edward's face very clearly, and as if for the first time, the long narrow forehead, the disarming reddish hair, the shy lonely eyes behind glasses and the queer tense mouth that could clamp shut so hard. It was solid like a piece of sculpture. Two nights ago this face was a real face; it existed. Now it did not. Death, she thought: people just disappear. They are suddenly not there. He was here in this room, gentle and quiet at first, smiling at Damon's oldest jokes brought out nervously for the occasion; his suit needed pressing; he had praised her French peas; he had all that time been carrying his death around inside him like a secret; and they had not been able to get through to him, to hold him back. "Why isn't love enough?" she asked the walls again, and each time she asked this question the same thing happened. She began to cry. It was like some awful wound inside her; and now she had begun, she knew she would never stop, or so it seemed. But suddenly she sat up. She had remembered John in boot camp. She must write to John at once, quickly, before Damon came back and needed her. So it is that life pulls one forward, she thought; there is no time to weep anything out; there is always a human responsibility to pull one back from the abyss—but here she stopped on her way to her desk and stood quite still. What if there were no immediate responsibility and one came face to face with one's life on its own terms as Edward had? What then? But I must telephone to Bess, she thought, at Bryn Mawr. I shall have to think all this out later. And what would she say to the children? When they asked, "Couldn't you do anything, Mother?" What could she say?

He didn't trust us any longer, you see. He felt we were beyond the pale, out there in that alien world which was closing in on him. The enemy, in fact. No, that was not the thing to say to the children.

They went forth to battle but they always fell;
Nobly they fought and bravely, but not well . . .

What was it? That old poem she had used to recite in school, the romantic appeal of failure. But this will not do, she thought, sitting down at her desk and again blowing her nose. She must summon the whole of herself and write to John. She must tell him. She must explain that such things happened in our time. Masaryk, Winant. It was not a company of weak men, of cowards. She undid her pen. She must say it in such a way that Edward was not diminished in John's eyes; it is rather we who are diminished in our own. Yes . . .

The letter was sealed and waiting on the hall table when Damon walked calmly up the path after his class. At once Julia knew by his walk, by the way he moved, at ease with himself, that his mood had changed.

"Well"—he flung down his brief case—"I might as well not have bothered about that equation. I talked to the boys about Edward, talked for the full hour. It's not a bad thing for physicists, even embryonic ones, to have to deal with a human equation for a change."

"What did you say?" Julia was amazed, almost resented this man's ability to rise like a phoenix from his own ashes over and over. For he had been abject when he left her, the creature of his nerves. Now triumph was written in his very stance. He had become an Olympian again, the great Professor Phillips. So quickly and with just a small exhibition before fifty students or so, he had won. He felt justified. For the students—oh she knew it well—were certainly gathered now in knots over their cups of coffee to praise Damon, to call him a great man.

"I talked about the value of the dissenter in our society. I talked about Edward, not as a hero, but as a human being whose greatness was his humanity and his fallibility, and I talked, I'm afraid"—here he smiled happily—"about the function of a teacher who combined scholarship and passion. Oh, well"—he ended, catching her eye and its cool appraisal—"I did the best I could for poor Edward."

"And you added of course that you were in political disagreement?" she could not keep the irony out of her tone.

"Why so acid?" He looked hurt and astonished.

"Never mind," Julia said quickly, "I'm upset, that's all. I've been writing to John."

"Good. I'll write him myself this afternoon. I'm afraid this will be rather a blow."

This was Damon's tone always about the children. They had never seemed quite real to him, perhaps, except as an afterthought. Or when in some way they reflected himself, won a prize at school, or showed some interest in him. Had he forgotten that John had said his one real grief at leaving college was to miss Edward's course? And Edward had written him a beautiful letter, such a humble letter, so full of love. It was in John's breast pocket when he left. Actually, she remembered, Damon had been a little jealous of that letter.

"Yes, do write to him." Julia pushed the hair back from her forehead as if to push some thought away. "I must just go out and get this to the post office. It may save a few hours." It was imperative now that she get out of the house, away from the urgency and weight of Damon.

Now, for instance, he looked quite stricken suddenly, and begged her to come back very soon, not to linger. It was true that her presence supported him, that he needed her, but she felt herself stiffen. "Very well," she said, "I'll come right back."

"Get Grace for me on the phone will you, dear? I really must talk to her." He said it quite casually. As usual by yielding, she had become a kind of servant.

"Do it yourself, Damon. I don't want to talk to her."

The swing door to the kitchen swung behind her. She was safe in the kitchen, where no one would notice that she was trembling with anger. Expect her to call that arrogant old woman, indeed!

There seemed no barrier between Damon's inner self and his flesh, she thought. He wore himself outside. But her inner conflicts were buried deep. Sometimes looking at herself in a mirror, she felt that she was caught in her body, lost too deep to be found or ever to come out. She envied women who could get angry, throw things. She envied Grace Kimlock, who, she knew, thought her a perfect fool. Someday, she had told herself for years, she would walk out of the house and not come back. But what she did was to take down a mixing bowl and prepare to make a dessert for supper.

She could hear Damon on the phone, the amazing tenderness in his voice, "I know how it is for you, Grace—how it is for all of us, like the end of the world. . . . I haven't seen anyone, except my students. I had to lecture at ten." A note of reserve crept in. "Oh, she's terribly upset, of course. I must see you, Grace. May I come in after dinner?"

Of course. He would only let her go out for a moment, but he would leave her alone all evening. What is happening to me, Julia thought, frightened of her own bitterness? This is not what Edward meant to do. We've got to be more not less than ourselves now. We've got to grow.

But she couldn't help being glad when it turned out that Grace couldn't see Damon till tea the following afternoon. There was a meeting, it appeared, something to do with police brutality, and even the death of her best friend would not keep Grace Kimlock from going into battle, Julia thought with a grim smile.

III

The study in his house on Francis Avenue where Ivan Goldberg sat was so immaculate that it looked like a stage set. Even his desk was empty except for the leather-bound notebook in which he was now writing something. Even the books had no informality about them; they were bound in sets, the English and American classics, the French classics, the great Russian novelists. He could have walked out of this room and left no trace of himself, unless, as gossip had it, it was true that he kept a day-to-day journal in the manner of Gide.

As chairman of the department, he had been on the phone all morning trying to arrange for various people to take over Cavan's seminar and the three graduate students whose adviser he was. Fortunately, Edward had been on half time this term in order to work at his book. Nevertheless, it was a delicate business. His colleagues were all busy at work of their own and did not enjoy the idea of taking on additional tasks in the middle of the first semester, a low ebb in everyone's energy, as Goldberg well knew. On a pad before him were five telephone numbers written in the hieroglyphic hand which so irritated students. He had called them all, but had found no one ready to take on the seminar. So he would have to manage that himself. But this was not as simple a decision as it appeared while he re-arranged his schedule in the notebook. He would, in taking over Cavan's seminar, be walking into hostile territory with his hands more or less tied. Very quietly then, he laid the book in which he had written down his new schedule into the right-hand drawer of his desk, closed it, and took out a cigarette. The geometries and abstractions of organization which were his private game against the demons were all very well, but the moment came when they no longer helped.

He had often noticed that the first effect of shock is anger. A child hurts himself on a chair and is furious with the chair, for instance. So his own first reaction had been to think, The fool, the utter fool to throw away his life, his work— He had said this to Angela who had just looked at him out of her quiet blue eyes and had not answered; so now he was alone, utterly alone with his demons of self-doubt and self-hatred. But why did he feel so terribly alone? After all, he and Edward Cavan had been antagonists always. There's no one left whom I respect—it's that, he told himself, and did not think it strange that he could also call the man he respected so much an utter fool. But he knew suddenly that his main reason, the inner compulsion to write his book had been that Edward would read it, this close analysis of seven great American works of literature, at the opposite pole from Edward's discursive book in which the background and growth of the writer had been emphasized at least as much as the work itself; this was to have been an answer, more than an answer, part of a diptych. In the deepest sense the roots were intertwined. They had been all along working together, for Edward, he knew, respected him, believed in him, only was extremely and perhaps rightly critical of Goldberg's taking so much committee work. Lately Cavan himself had become something of an outsider in college affairs; at the same time Goldberg had become a power. But becoming a power had a price—and the price was that unfinished book which could now never be laid into Edward's hands. He pushed away with a violent gesture the heavy desolation that seemed to be all around him in the air, that settled on the books, that filled his lungs and made him suddenly choke.

It's no good, he thought, none of this is the point. I failed him. It is worse to fail an antagonist worth your mettle than a friend. There had been a moment there in the dingy study at Warren House only three days before— or when was it?—when if he could have made a really human gesture, he and Edward might have come to terms, might have allowed the love buried so deep under their antagonism, to flow out. Admitting this now, knowing it to be the truth, pain and grief took possession of Ivan Goldberg so intensely that he walked up and down hugging himself with the force of it. Why couldn't I? What is wrong with me that I cannot be human as other people can, that I am always so afraid of giving myself away? And what did it mean to be respected and feared if one was not loved, could not be loved because one was not lovable? Edward

had been loved, God knows. Difficult, rude as he often was out of sheer passion, this rudeness was always forgiven because it came from passion, whereas the smooth hard surface he, Ivan, presented to the world was unforgivable like the barren fig tree. "It's too expensive to keep the door open, Ivan, can't you see?" But it was I who shut the door, not he—and all the time there was Edward right beside him in the room, alive. "Oh God," Ivan tore out of the study and up the stairs to find his wife. Angela was reading aloud to Cissy who was in bed with a sore throat. For once Ivan hardly noticed Cissy whose face always lit up in such an enormous smile when she saw her father. He pulled Angela away almost roughly, unable to say a word.

"Daddy's crying, Mummy," the clear piping voice called after them. "Don't cry, Daddy."

Angela, soft, warm, pretty Angela had never seen her husband cry. He was sitting in the hall on a hard bench in the window, hugging himself as if he had a pain, shaken with sobs.

She stood beside him, not daring even to put a hand on his shoulder, as if, bowed over, hugging himself, he had become suddenly majestic and unknown like a god.

"It isn't your fault, darling."

Ivan pulled her to him then, driving his head against her belly as if to bury himself there. Very gently she stroked his springy black hair and waited. The tense racking sobs finally came at less regular intervals, and his hold on her, which had been painfully hard, relaxed. But still he said nothing. They were not people who communicated by words, but by the invisible waves of feeling and breathing and touch and silence.

"I'm s—s—sorry." Ivan blew his nose on an immaculate linen handkerchief. "I'm afraid I frightened Cissy." In a second he was on his feet. "She's very quiet."

They found her sitting up, tense, her enormous dark eyes going from one to the other fearfully. Ivan went over and sat on the bed where he could put an arm around her, could explain that people had to cry sometimes, even grown-up people.

"Why do they?" she asked, turning to look at him with immense curiosity.

"Because they'll burst otherwise."

"Why will they burst?" she persisted like an inquisitor.

"Because"—he hesitated, then bowed his head before his child—"they're so ashamed."

"Don't do it again, Daddy," she said firmly. Don't do it again, he said to himself as he went down the stairs and back to his study to try to work. But how did one change? Work was the drug—he had learned this long ago—the drug that never failed. When Angela brought in his lunch on a tray, he was so absorbed that he did not even lift his head.

The seminar was to meet at two. He had thought at first that he would simply have an announcement posted. But that, he knew, was evasion. It would be better to get it over with, once and for all. So, at precisely ten minutes to the hour, he put on a light overcoat and walked briskly down Kirkland Street toward the Common. It was a cruelly brilliant day; the dazzling light hurt his eyes. And he looked at all this as if he had become a stranger to it, a stranger to the immaculate thrust of the chapel steeple against the bright blue sky, a stranger to the uneven brick pavements of this, his Cambridge, the barberry bushes framing long

green lawns, the Greek revival houses which the college was taking over one by one. He saw it all with a stranger's, an outsider's, eyes.

He had come here fifteen years ago for his doctorate, a year or two after Edward Cavan had moved over from Columbia. Those were the days of their long argumentative walks, when he was the outlander and Cavan the insider, and for Ivan the irregular bricks after the hard cement paths of Urbana seemed like the pavement of Heaven. Gradually in those fifteen years he had absorbed Cambridge and made himself part of it, with the big house on Francis Avenue the final stage of taking possession. He could not imagine life without the Charles River, without the ugly black-faced clock on Memorial Hall, without the queer bare spaces of the Common which he was now crossing, where children rubbed smooth the cannon, and no one perhaps but Ivan Goldberg remembered that it was Lincoln who stood in the middle of the high Civil War monument. But now today these familiar and consoling sights were no longer his. They observed him as if he were a criminal. He felt at bay. This made him walk faster and stand straighter than he usually did. He failed to greet a former student who gave him a tentative smile and saw the smile vanish. Appleton Chapel rang two as he pushed open the door of Longfellow Hall at Radcliffe. He was annoyed to find he was slightly out of breath and took refuge in the bleak instructor's room with its empty fireplace, its memorial plaque and smell of dead cigarette smoke. Here he forced himself to wait nine minutes. Then he climbed the single flight of stairs and faced eight men sitting round a long oval table.

He knew that he was smiling faintly as he always did

when he was nervous. He knew the effect this would have and did have. "My name's Goldberg," he announced briskly as he sat down. They introduced themselves one by one, Kovarsky, Mead, Zausmer, Herrera, Keith, Hastings, Servi, Anangnos. Then there was silence as Ivan Goldberg laid his brief case on the table, took from it a folder marked Seminar, American Lit. and said, "One of you no doubt has a paper to read. Shall we begin?"

It would have been appropriate, it was necessary that he say a few words of introduction, that he break the atmosphere of hostility by some reference to Edward Cavan. But he simply could not do it. It was clear to him that if he even spoke Edward's name, his voice would break, he would disgrace himself and be unable to go on. So in pure self-defense he talked brilliantly about the paper, which was an analysis of the early realistic novels of Howells. He did it the more brilliantly because he did it without mentioning Cavan's name. As he left the classroom he realized that his shirt was soaked through.

"He's a cold fish—" This much he heard as the door closed behind him.

IV

The night had been so strange, so terrible since one A.M. when the phone had summoned him out of a deep sleep to identify Edward's body, that Orlando Fosca felt lifted up and borne deep on the tide, a tide so powerful that it left no room for personal feelings. He had moved through the interminable processes, going to Edward's apartment with the police, finding and reading his last statement, telephoning Isabel Ferrier in California, trying to preserve what he could from the reporters, like an automaton. Then he had gone home and sat for hours in his chair in a state of extreme wakefulness. It was as if an explosion had taken place inside him and he were no longer an old man, but already dead himself and so beyond fatigue, almost beyond grief in any human sense of the word. His landlady had kindly brought him some lunch on a tray. Then perhaps he had dozed off. At any rate it was quite suddenly time for him to go over to Grace's.

He stopped for a moment to look at the chestnut on Brattle Street, his old friend, one of a pair in front of an old house. A branch had fallen in a storm a few days before, and the wound was still there, a naked white gash, though the broken wood and leaves had been carted off. It was strange how intensely he wanted to see the wound closed, tarred over. So anxious about it was he that more than once he had had to restrain an impulse to ring the doorbell and inquire after the tree, make sure that some concern was felt, that surgeons would be sent for. He had known this tree in its splendid baroque flowering, in its summers of openhanded leaves, in its fruitful falls dear to the children, for so many years. Now standing here, in his hallucinated state, he poked a fallen chestnut with his stick till it cracked open to show the bright brown nut inside. And in doing this it was as if his self, which had been floating somewhere beyond reality, came back into him with the force of shock—and with it the full human burden, the full weight of what would be expected of him when he reached the indomitable old woman who waited for him now and whose heartbeat he felt as if in his own pulse.

When he reached the house, he did not stop to ring the bell, but pushed open the door as an impetuous young man might have done, went right to the drawing room where she was standing with her back to the fire, and pressed her to his heart.

Grace, who had been erecting barriers against her grief all day, was taken by surprise. She would have none of the earthquake of emotion which Orlando's unexpected gesture unloosed. She disengaged herself stiffly, turned her back on him, and said rather gruffly, as if the episode had not taken place, "Where's Ellen with our tea?"

He watched the quick angular stride, the decision of her as she pulled the bell cord, watched her with admiration and a slightly disillusioned smile. He had made a huge effort—now it was done he knew how huge—to raise his exhausted self to meet her in the fullness of their friendship, and she had been unable to receive his gift. Strange fascinating little person who, so avidly hungry for life, consistently pushed it away and hid herself from it—even now when, God knows, they were naked enough, stripped down to the quick.

"I tried to get hold of George Hastings, Edward's student, you know—he didn't even know who I was," she said irritably. "He refused to talk, hung up on me. It was most extraordinary."

"Do you think so?" Orlando asked with slightly barbed gentleness. "Do you really think so?" The tide of feeling was ebbing away in him now. He felt so shaky that he sat down.

"Yes." She looked down at him, her eyes blazing, but was it grief? Was it anger? "I do think so—under the circumstances."

"Probably he couldn't talk. People react in different ways, Grace. Poor boy," and he sighed.

"He was rude," she said inexorably.

"Desperate people are often rude, my dear." And now it was his turn to flash her a severe look. "Edward often was."

Ellen, with the tea tray, slipped in like a beneficent shade. Orlando was touched to see that she had obviously been weeping.

"It's hard for us all, Ellen, isn't it?" he said gently.

"Yes, sir." She broke into a sob as she disappeared down the hall.

"Ellen is a fountain of tears," Grace said sharply, as if she were not at all pleased by such exhibitions of feeling. She busied herself with pouring out his tea exactly as he liked it, with passing a plate of very thin bread and butter. She did not look at him, and he wondered how long she would be able to maintain her defenses, how long on this strange afternoon he would find himself regarding her as a psychological curiosity, rather than as his oldest dearest friend.

For the moment it was clear that she wished everything to be as usual, the occasion to be framed as far as possible in the safety of gestures and habits which had been going on for years. Yet it was as if all these familiar gestures had now lost their meaning, lost the content which made them nourishing; they were empty gestures. It seemed to Orlando that this room, where nothing had changed since the days of Grace Kimlock's father, were flying apart, and in a more subtle and frightening way as if he and his old friend were at such complete cross-purposes that they might as well be flying apart.

"Light the fire, there's a dear," Grace said in a gentler tone. "It's chilly here. I feel old and cold, Orlando," she said as if the thought of old age had never before crossed her mind. The fire helped, as a matter of fact. They could sit and say nothing. The fire spoke; they could listen to its language, watch the Cape Cod lighter flame up blue, and the pleated fans of paper blaze and enfold the birch logs in a sheet of brightness. They drank their tea. Then Grace leaned forward, her hands clasped before her, struggling perhaps to break the pattern she had herself set up.

"Why did he do it?" This was the question she had wandered crazily through the day asking and asking and searching for an answer. She had gone for a long walk by the river, had tried to read, had climbed up and down the stairs a hundred times as if to search for a small lost object, her glasses or a thimble. Now she flung the question at Orlando, and he saw the flush creep up in her throat with the force of it.

"I don't know," Orlando said quietly. He passed his cup absent-mindedly for more tea.

"You *must* know. You must tell me," she said fiercely as if he were willfully withholding information. When she had poured his tea and handed it to him, she looked into the fire and murmured, "How could he do this to us, Orlando? that's what I can't understand. I'll never forgive him, never," she said without conviction, as if she were repeating by rote words which had ceased to have a meaning.

"It doesn't matter now." Orlando passed a thin hand over his forehead and held it there over his eyes.

"It matters to *me*, very much."

"No doubt it does. But we won't get the answer now, or perhaps ever, Grace." It did not help at all, but Orlando was now thinned down by fatigue to the point where there was no excess kindness in him, only the bare bones of the truth. "This is not a simple matter. We shall go on living with it for the rest of our lives."

"I can't," Grace said, "I've got to know."

"And if you can't know—for knowing really means being Edward—what then?"

"I'll die," Grace said simply.

This, Orlando thought, is what it is to be young, this

absolute quality, and for the moment he found it peculiarly irritating.

"Don't be childish, Grace. How well did you know Edward?"

"You sound like an inquisitor," she said nervously. She had never seen this stern Orlando before. "You know very well that Edward was like a son to me."

"Do mothers really know their sons?" he asked inexorably. "Don't you understand, Grace, that what you were to Edward was one fixed point, was a sort of security—yes, like the security of a parent, perhaps. You agreed about all the important things."

"Well, didn't that make us close?"

"In one way, yes. But who were Edward's lovers, if he had a lover?"

"I don't know."

"Of course you don't. And neither do I. Don't you see? There are whole areas of Edward's life that we never touched, never could touch."

"People like Edward Cavan don't commit suicide for love—a man of fifty—really, Orlando, what a romantic you are!" She triumphed.

"No, perhaps not. But in a conflict so terrible that it ends in suicide, the whole person is engaged. You'll have to admit that."

"Decent people don't commit suicide." Grace took refuge again in her anger.

"Perhaps not, if you regard suicide as a crime. Do you?" Orlando was relentless.

"I don't know"—and she flung up her hands in a gesture of unwilling abandon. "You're no help to me, Orlando

—and I thought you would be." There was no gentleness in her voice.

"I'm a wounded man," he said stroking his beard rhythmically. When he did this it was always a sign of great agitation, as if he calmed himself as one might calm a cat. "Don't badger me."

She shook her head as if to shake something off. "It's like a nightmare. Nothing will ever be the same again."

"No." Orlando walked over to the long French windows and looked out. "Nothing will ever be the same again."

"Animals are the only comfort," came the relentless anguished voice behind him. As he turned, Orlando saw the room, which had been flying to pieces, slowly focus on the bowed old figure, her hands clasped under her chin, and knew how dear she had become to him in the last few minutes of war.

"How is Horace?" he inquired and it meant, It's all right. Somehow we'll survive this together.

"Horace is all right, indifferent, beautiful as always." But the words did not carry the meaning, as they exchanged a smile, as at last they reached the moment of communion, and Grace leaned her head back against her chair and closed her eyes. "I don't know what I'm going to do," she said in a matter-of-fact voice, not bothering to catch the single tear which slid out and rolled down her cheek. "It's going to be so lonely."

"I think Edward will be with us for a long time to come," he said gently. And then, "The dead help the living."

She opened her eyes and sat up straight. "How?"

"I don't know how. I'm not a mystic, as you know, my

dear. I do not believe in anything like tangible presence"
—he drew in his breath as if he was in physical pain—"and
in this case a tangible presence would be a tormented one."

"It was such a dreadful way to do it, Orlando—so
brutal," she murmured, following his thought. It was not
an interruption.

He passed a hand over his forehead. He had seen
what she had not seen. He found that he was sweating.

"I think perhaps it is that death leaves us the essence
of the person," he said, but it had become a great effort.
At the moment he was nowhere near the essence of Edward. He was fighting off the image, not of horror—it was
not like that. But the sense he had, when he looked down
at the calm empty face above a body cut in two, that Edward was not there, that this was not Edward.

"What was Edward's essence?" she whispered.

"We can't know yet," he answered quickly. "It will
take time. I can only tell you that after Sylvia died it was
more than two years before I could get past the image of
her suffering, before I could even think of her as she really
was. It takes time," he said again, stroking his beard.

At Sylvia's name, a name Orlando so rarely mentioned
and only under the stress of such a moment, Grace turned
to him and perhaps for the first time looked at him, really
saw him, sitting there, his eyes sunk so deep into the bone
from tiredness that he looked like a very old man. "I'm an
egotistic old woman, Orlando. Forgive me," she said drily.
"My dear, you must go home and get some rest. I am going
to get Ellen to pack up a little basket that you can take
home for your supper. You must forgive me," she said again,
as she got up to go to the kitchen.

164

"We're old friends," he murmured, but she had already gone.

When at last Orlando Fosca closed the door behind him and was safely back in his study, he sank down into his armchair, loosened the laces of his boots, leaned back and closed his eyes. For a few moments he gave in to the sense of total dizzy exhaustion, to the relief of being here alone, of not having to go out for supper (kind of dear old Grace to have thought of that soup), of not having to brace himself or to consider others. Damon had agreed to meet Mrs. Ferrier's plane. For a few hours at least his responsibilities were at an end. The image which floated before his mind was that chestnut tree with its great open wound. Something, perhaps, could be done about that tomorrow. He opened his eyes and looked about him, at the familiar wall of books on his left, at Grace's ridiculous penguin in its glass globe, and lastly at the small round photograph of his wife as she had looked when he first met her, the radiant young face framed in fair hair, the large sensitive eyes, eyelids drooping a little, the ghost of a smile. Thinking of her, as it always would, opened the deep reserves of feeling and it swept over him, with a force that made him lean forward and groan, what Edward's loss would mean to the University. This was the great tree standing with a limb torn off, bleeding into the air, that branch rich with leaves and flowers which would never grow back again, never bear its real fruit, that branch which had just fallen with a great crash. And Fosca smiled at himself, recognizing that in spite of all his quarrels with it, he loved the University passionately, in a different way but no less than he had loved his wife. "We can't do without Edward," he said aloud, hatred not love in his tone, for he hated the smug safe scholars who remained, who would never kill themselves because they would never be stretched as Edward had been on the rack of conscience. An Olympian, Edward called him, for he had accused Fosca of being too detached. But whatever virtue there might be in such a stance went out of it if the only struggles one watched from the heights were the petty struggles for advancement, the jealousies over honorary degrees, the endless playing for position which was one side of University life. Edward had transcended all this by sheer passionate intensity. "We can't do without him," Fosca said again.

What would Edward have been if he had not tied himself to the rack?

"He would be alive now." Fosca heard his own groan and sat up. Would he? But Fosca took back the cry he had uttered out of his own grief. One cannot wish the people one loves to be other than they are. An Edward not torn to pieces, an Edward concerned only with literature, would seem a monster.

But standing was not the thing, and he sat down again heavily. The room which had seemed so friendly a moment before, now loomed about him, full of enemies. These objects that do not run down, he thought, glancing again at the self-satisfied penguin in its eternal snow, become our enemies. It was queer the desire he felt to go and smash the penguin.

V

Damon and Julia had been sitting now for half an hour in the waiting room at the airport, unable to relax for a moment as every few seconds a loud voice on the public address system told them that the Paris flight was now ready and would passengers please assemble, or that there would be a short delay for Chicago. Each time this happened they stopped talking and wondered tensely if this time the announcement would be that Edward's sister, who was rushing toward them through the air between New York and Boston, was finally about to land.

"Sit down, Damon," Julia said irritably, as once more they were disappointed. "You'll wear yourself out."

"I'm worn out," he answered. "This is the last straw."

"I don't suppose she's exactly looking forward to this either, poor woman."

"Edward despised her," Damon said impatiently, rubbing his face with his hands as if to rub out the fatigue. "You remember his acid descriptions of the house, the high fidelity atmosphere, and her smug husband, the perfect picture of middle-class indifference and selfishness, both of them."

Julia sighed. There was no point in arguing with Damon when he was in this contrary mood. Better save one's strength. She concentrated instead on watching the minute hand of the clock on the wall inching its way towards half-past ten. With every second of waiting she felt a greater longing to be anywhere but here, in this brightly lit limbo, waiting for Edward's sister, that poor woman who would find no mercy here. "We are pitiless, you know," she said.

"Number Five, Number Five." Damon lept to his feet again. "The St. Louis plane is now landing." Was this it at last? Could it be possible? Damon dashed off to make sure, then signaled her impatiently to join him at the gate. It was all happening more quickly than seemed possible. A man with a brief case pushed in past them; then three excited young girls wearing orchids; what if they failed to recognize her? Julia pressed Damon's arm. There was no other woman alone. She was extremely elegant, Julia noted with surprise, pushing back a strand of hair, wishing now that she had thought to wear a hat.

"Mrs. Ferrier?" Damon asked.

"Yes—are you"—she hesitated, searched for a name, gave up with a shy glance at Julia.

"I'm Damon Phillips. This is my wife, Mrs. Ferrier. Professor Fosca, who telephoned you last night, has no car, and besides he is quite exhausted, as you can understand."

168

"It's awfully good of you to meet me," she was saying, "I'll just see about my bags."

"Give me the checks. You and Julia sit down." Damon ran off impressed, Julia sensed, by the smooth elegance beside her, the air of unobtrusive luxury, the soft silvery gray fur wrap, the slim ankles. Damon, as susceptible as a boy, had evidently already reversed his judgment.

"Your husband is a professor?" Isabel interrupted her train of thought.

"Yes, physics."

"Oh."

"I don't understand anything about it," Julia smiled reassuringly. "It's all a mystery."

"My husband is a surgeon." Julia noted the slight lift of the chin, was faintly amused. Surgeons in Isabel Ferrier's hierarchy were evidently superior to professors.

"So Edward told us."

"Did he—did he speak of us often?" The bright gray eyes looked frightened, and Julia, seeing the fright in them, answered more warmly than truthfully, "Of course." Thank goodness Damon was coming towards them now with the bags and this subject could be dropped.

It was a relief to get out of the garish light into the dark car. Isabel took out a cigarette and offered Julia one. They sat together in the back seat.

"Damon is the worst driver in the world," Julia said, as he stalled the car for the second time. "All we can do is try to relax and count on the innocent's luck. It's flooded, darling, just wait a minute," she said to Damon's back.

"Oh be quiet, Julia," he said crossly. "You make me nervous."

Isabel felt she had been catapulted in the last five minutes into a world as strange as the moon. Anyone could tell that Mr. Phillips was a professor. He seemed in fact like a caricature of one, his thin uncombed hair falling down over his forehead, his face all broken up by lines, his air of agitated incompetence. Henry would have a fit if he imagined she was being driven by a man who stripped the gears every time he changed speed and turned right round in his seat every few minutes to look behind him. But she was not nervous. She was too excited, peering out into the strangeness, a limbo of factories with glimpses of water seen through neon signs, and even once a ship tied up apparently in the middle of a city block.

It was really too queer to be here, driving along through the night with two perfect strangers, uprooted from everything familiar—the plane had become a kind of refuge in the last hours—but here she was nowhere. She wondered if she would ever get back to Henry, he seemed so far away in the sunlight where everything was natural and good.

They had just crossed an immensely high bridge and now swung out onto the water's edge. Damon turned round continually to point out things to her, continually admonished by his wife to pay attention to the road, and for a while Isabel had no time to think. "That's Boston over there?" she asked, amazed that it could look so brilliant, reflected lights in the river, all shining and beautiful like a city in a dream. But then that too was gone and quite suddenly Damon was swerving into a driveway, grating to a stop, and they had arrived.

"We thought we'd bring you here for a nightcap, so it wouldn't feel too strange, but you'll sleep at the hotel just around the corner. We thought you might rather not be a guest, feel quite free," Julia was saying as they walked up the steps of the porch.

Then Isabel was inside the house, so different from any house she had ever seen, slipping her coat off, as she slid down to the edge of a wornout leather armchair with tufts of white cotton batting showing through. On the walls, faded blue, there were sepia photographs of an old man who looked like a minister and two seascapes in big ugly gold frames. Her hosts had gone into the kitchen to get drinks, she supposed, for she could hear a murmur of voices and the sound of ice cubes falling out of a tray. She looked down at the table beside her, where a pipe lay on top of a pile of magazines she had never heard of—*Nature, Science, The London Economist*. In a room where everything else made her uncomfortable, she turned gratefully toward the fire. She felt very dazed. I'm so dreadfully ignorant, she said to herself, to be Edward's sister.

It was a strange thought, one she had never had before—or not since she was a child. In it she recognized that here she came as a representative, for Edward's sake, not for her own. And she was frightened, wished for a second that she had not come, or had pleaded fatigue and asked to be taken straight to the hotel. At least she could look for the bathroom and escape for a few moments. When she came downstairs again, she found them waiting for her, Julia stretched out comfortably with her feet on a hassock, Mr. Phillips standing with his back to the fire.

"You must be dreadfully tired," Julia said, at the same time as her husband was saying, "There's a drink there beside you."

"Sit down, Mrs. Ferrier, and relax," Julia was saying.

171

"I can't," Isabel confessed. She sat on the edge of the chair, in a state approaching panic.

"It's a terrible ordeal for you, all this. We're so sorry"— Damon's cigarette wagged up and down grotesquely in his mouth. She had so dreaded these hawk faces, the faces of the intellectuals, the enemy. Now that she saw they were kind, not like Edward hammering at her all the time, she turned to Damon with childlike relief. "You see, I don't belong here," she said, taking a swallow of her drink. "Edward pushed me out of his life long ago."

The words were so entirely unexpected coming from the woman who spoke them, that Damon peered at her with something like embarrassment and then glanced over at Julia as if to say, You handle this.

"He wasn't easy on any of us, you know. He wasn't an easy person," Julia said.

Would it, after all be possible to talk? Isabel felt as if she were carrying a tremendous burden alone, had been carrying it for years. Was it possible that here in this unlikely room she could lay it down? "I suppose I always hoped that things would change, that he would change— or something—and now I can't get used to the idea that they won't, that . . ." She couldn't finish. The words were all mixed up. And she was grateful for their silence, grateful that they did not rush in to help her out, just waited as if it was the most natural thing in the world to be silent.

"We know so little about him, really," Julia said into the fire.

"But at least you talked the same language," Isabel said quickly. "Edward and I have hardly talked at all for years. He hated everything about my life. Yet I've been

172

waiting, having nightmares, dreading this always—it seems to me—lying awake at night. It sounds crazy," she said. She was almost frightened of the sensation of release. She must not talk too much. She must be careful, said the little voice inside her which made her wear gloves to lunches.

"We've all been anxious about him. We've all felt helpless," Julia said. "That's what's so awful."

Isabel took a long drink, then settled back in the chair, and for just a second closed her eyes. To close her eyes was like drowning, and she opened them again quickly to get away from the sensation of being sucked under, sucked down into places where she would lose all self-control. "But you were part of his life," she said, "he hadn't given you up—" She stopped because she caught the look in Damon's eyes, the look of guilt, of acute distress.

"He walked out of this house four nights ago," Damon said almost angrily. "We had been friends for years."

"Poor Edward, he couldn't help it," she said without quite knowing why.

"What makes you say that?" Damon pounced on her now, and for a second she felt the piercing glance, the glance she had been afraid of, probing her, demanding reasons for what she could only feel, not know.

"I don't know," she said, "but it seems as if Edward was like a coiled spring all the time, coiled so tight, it just didn't break."

"Yes," Julia murmured, "yes, that is how he was." She was remembering these afternoons when he had come as the light was going and sat for an hour with her at teatime, and how the tension in the darkening room grew and grew till he would suddenly get up and go, without a word, leaving her feeling weak as if they had been engaged in some terrible battle.

"You know," Isabel turned to her gratefully. "Sometimes it was as if the spring turned backwards, he was caught in it"—she stopped to clasp her hands together nervously—"I'm no good at saying these things," she said.

"On the contrary," Damon said. She was aware that he was listening intently, that in some extraordinary way she had after all, something to give.

"It was a kind of black anger—like beating your fist on a wall. And he used to do just that when he was a boy. No one could reach him or touch him, not even Mother, at those times. We called it his 'blackness.' When he was a boy he used to get into fights, I mean physical fights, in those moods. Then when he was older and he couldn't do that, it was another kind of destruction. He broke off with me when Mother died." She felt their close attention around her like a shield. She knew that they really cared, cared quite differently from Henry who had simply written Edward off as a hopeless neurotic—as if that solved anything. "You see," she said, looking over at Julia, meeting the compassion in her eyes like a balm, "we didn't tell Edward that Mother was dying. He never knew, because he was at Oxford and Mother wanted him to have that year. But when he got back and she was dead—well, it was the end of us as a family. It was the end of Edward and me," she said, and at last she was laying the burden down. "I still don't understand it, but I remember running up the stairs to his room as if there were a fire, and he was standing at the open window— I ran and held him with all my strength and said, 'No, Edward. You can't. It's the blackness—you know Mother called it the blackness'—and then he pushed me away and fell down on his bed and cried. But he never forgave me." She took a long drink. "I've never told anybody all this. It's so queer I should be telling you. I was so afraid of you——"

"We were rather afraid of you, as a matter of fact," Damon said gently.

"Why?"

"We thought you were a stranger," Julia broke in warmly. "We didn't know."

"I don't believe in any of the things Edward believed in. You probably know that," Isabel said. It was a relief to say it.

"But you believed in him?" Julia asked.

Isabel turned this over in her mind. She was feeling the effects of the drink, or of the plane, or of sheer exhaustion. "No," she said, "I don't think I could. He hurt me too much."

Julia got up. "We've kept you up long enough. Damon, you really must take her to the hotel and let her get some sleep. You've given us a great deal, you know," she said laying a hand on Isabel's shoulder. And then, as if this gesture made her shy, she went on hurriedly, "You'll have a hard day tomorrow. Dr. Willoughby wants to talk to you about the funeral. But try to sleep tonight," she added. "Would you like a pill?"

"Thank you, I have some."

"It seems as if we'd never think this through to the end—not for a long time," Julia added at the door. "But you've been a great help."

"It isn't thinking, is it?" Isabel turned at the door. Damon had rushed on ahead, as usual. "I have to feel my way."

175

VI

Isabel drank two cups of coffee, but found that she couldn't eat. Her bed was strewn with newspapers, and she kept picking them up one after another and rereading these words of grief, anger, recrimination, each one of which was a blow, none of which seemed real, seemed to have anything to do with the boy she had remembered so vividly last night, standing at the window of his room, hating himself. The Edward Cavan whose name blazed across the front pages was someone else, someone more important than she could have guessed, someone around whom a whirlpool of conjecture and recrimination now raged. Boxed on the front page of the *Times* there was a letter, for instance, from a well-known writer to the effect that Cavan was a victim of the cold war, a martyr whose act of despair laid a new burden of responsibility on all men of good will; but in a long column in a Boston newspaper a sports writer devoted a whole column to a kind of jeering and rejoicing, as if an enemy had fallen, and went so far as to accuse Edward of being a coward. Isabel herself felt nothing now but confusion, shame and, worst of all, exposure. How would she ever dare go out, go down the stairs and meet all the eyes? Her quiet talk with the Phillipses had been nothing but a short reprieve, an illusion that kindness would smooth over and make possible these terrible days, and above all that the whole business was a private matter. Now she had to recognize that far more than private feelings clustered round Edward. Already, only forty hours or so after his death, he had ceased to be human, was being made into an effigy, like a stuffed straw man held up before crowds to be cheered or jeered; he, the person, had already been snatched away and transformed to fit people's prejudices and passions, a symbol, she supposed intellectual people might call him. But what was he to be for her now? How would she cope? How find her way? How meet it all? The whole world was her enemy this morning, waiting to pounce and demand of her some answer, some stand. But she had no answer at all, she did not know what she believed about Edward now. Oh, if only Henry were here, she thought—and then cringed. Henry would be meeting the world at home, would be reading the same headlines, or others like them. Even he would be dragged down into the whirlpool, he and the children. No one she loved was safe.

She lay in bed, the shades pulled down, smoking, wishing she could lock the door from the inside and just stay here for the next three days, refuse to see anyone, be ill. Instead she must dress, go out into a strange city and take all kinds of responsibilities—the funeral? Her heart beat furiously. What happened when people committed suicide? And all the time she was really an intruder—Edward would not have wished her here, not have chosen her for this task. What did family mean to him? She dressed angrily, efficiently, determined at least that the façade would be impeccable, that she would not again give herself away as she had done last night because, no doubt, she was too tired to be armed. She would do what had to be done, but she would hold herself back, that self that Edward had so completely rejected. She would go home untouched, unchanged. So she said to herself, writing out determination with the red lipstick, drawing the line of her mouth harshly a little redder than usual.

The man at the desk told her that the church was just a few minutes away. "Just a nice little walk," he said genially. The hotel had been like all hotels, but as soon as she stepped out onto the brick pavement, into the bright October morning, the special quality of the place assailed her, and she became a stranger. She was almost knocked down by a girl on a bicycle, a long red scarf streaming out behind her and a pile of books in the basket. As Isabel walked on, she became part of a procession of students, boys and girls in small groups, a few isolated ones threading their way through, and all moving towards the spires and towers she could see in the distance. They were wholly self-absorbed so that she moved among them like a ghost, watching her step on the irregular pavement, looking up at the old elms and down at their roots humping the bricks under her feet, looking at the churches (there seemed to be a great many). She had now reached a long brick wall enclosing a group of rather formidable Georgian buildings, and here, she was

178

glad to see, a good many of the students turned off. That must be Radcliffe, she thought, relieved to be more or less alone now, with a great expanse of park on her left and in the distance a terribly ugly Gothic tower with a black-faced clock on it, the gold hands just approaching ten. She walked a little faster, for shouldn't the low gray church she was looking for be just along here?

Yes, there it was, with a funny old cemetery beside it, a little plain building, she thought it at first. The tower was square with a small window in the upper part and a beautiful red door at its base. There was something surprising about it, standing here, so sober, with the traffic roaring past, something harmonious and quieting. She walked a little beyond it to look back and see the long windows at the side. She supposed that it was old. For a moment she had forgotten her errand, but now she remembered and turned back, hurrying a little, not knowing quite where to go. She was standing just in front of the red doors, hesitating, when a voice said behind her,

"Were you looking for me? Are you Mrs. Ferrier?"

"Yes, I am."

"Come into my office, won't you?" She had just time to see the bright inquisitive eyes behind glasses, the pale bald head, and then she was following Dr. Willoughby into his office. He reminded her of a plump, cheerful bird, a robin perhaps.

"Sit down. Do you mind if I light my pipe?"

"Not at all." She sat, unrelaxed, holding her handbag stiffly in her lap, while he eyed her, she felt, just as a bird might, shyly, glancingly.

"You must be very tired," he said without especial

emphasis, pulling at his pipe in short puffs to get it going. Then he looked at her again, tilting his head a little to one side.

"I'm not tired, so much as agitated," she said. "The papers were rather a shock. None of it seems quite real," she said stiffly.

"You mustn't pay too much attention to all that, Mrs. Ferrier," he said quite brusquely.

"I can't help it. It's so surprising, as if Edward had been a statesman or—I don't know—more important than I knew. It's all so terribly public, Dr. Willoughby, almost indecent. I thought professors——"

"Edward Cavan was a rather rare and special kind of professor, as I don't need to tell you." Isabel felt that he was playing for position, walking round and round the subject, until he could get a foothold, find out where she herself stood.

"I had no way of knowing. We have hardly seen each other in recent years."

"Let there be no misunderstanding, Mrs. Ferrier," he said gravely. "I had the greatest respect for your brother. I honored him."

"Why?" Isabel asked eagerly, then blushed. "It's a strange question, I know, but surely he had become so fierce, so difficult."

"Yes," Dr. Willoughby withdrew and thought this over. Then as if he had made up his mind, he leaned forward, clasping his hands and speaking very earnestly. Isabel, sensing that some hidden pressure was about to be exerted, pushed her chair back a fraction. "In general people of this faith are apt to be conservative, of course. Among the Protestant group we have been the traditionalists."

"How then did Edward . . . ?" She left the question in mid-air.

"Well," Dr. Willoughby smiled, "he didn't. He was troubled. He came here more than once to talk with me. But there were reasons why he could feel at home in this church. We have a considerable Negro membership, for instance. Then your brother found comfort in the ritual; that was the poet in him. There was also very strong in him the practicing Christian, the Christian who wants to follow Christ as literally as possible. I happen to know, for instance, that it troubled him to be responsible for more money than he needed."

"I believe he gave most of it away."

"Yes," Dr. Willoughby deliberately ignored the slight edge in her voice, she felt, and went on, "but it troubled him to be able to do that. He felt it a barrier, and what your brother wanted most, Mrs. Ferrier, was communion." Dr. Willoughby had raised his voice just a fraction and now looked her straight in the eye; Isabel met the glance, felt as if she were being hammered at and looked down frowning. "Something of what a theologian means by the communion of saints on earth," he went on implacably. "That, in the long run, was I am sure at the root of his socialism. It was not a materialistic view at all, and there perhaps was the fatal irony of his position, also the loneliness of it." Dr. Willoughby picked up his pipe, tapped it out and relit it, perhaps to give her time.

All this, Isabel thought, sounded convincing enough. The man was obviously sincere, yet it seemed as remote from the Edward she knew, shouting at her husband, full of antagonism, even hatred, as a bedtime story.

"He was dreadfully intolerant," she said quite harshly.

181

Dr. Willoughby gave her a quick appraising look and then, rather unexpectedly, got up. "Come over to my house and have a cup of tea, Mrs. Ferrier. Do you have time?"

"Of course." She wanted to say, "I'm helpless. You will all talk to me about Edward; that's what I'm here for." But she followed him out across the flagstoned court, thinking that a cup of tea sounded rather good, amused also by the idea of drinking tea at half-past ten in the morning. Was it a Cambridge custom or only an Episcopalian one? And then would Dr. Willoughby talk about the funeral? For that was what was making her withhold herself, a kind of panic. No mention had been made as yet of suicide, of sin.

She sat down gratefully in the small library where Dr. Willoughby left her, looked at the books in long shelves right to the ceiling, the bright green leather armchairs, the quiet coziness of everything, and she sank down into one of these, at last in a relaxed position, one foot under her.

Here in the moment of silence, for the first time since she had come to Cambridge she sensed Edward instead of only thinking about him. She could see him here among the books, leaning forward, his hands clasped between his knees, leaning back to laugh his unexpectedly buoyant rather light laugh, the laugh of a boy not a man. She remembered those years at Cornell, which he never spoke of without lighting up in the warmth of them, how it seemed he was discovering everything at once, including his own real self, how proud he was of being editor of the literary magazine, how ardently he participated in every side of college life, for at that time he still played tennis, she remembered.

"Where did his happiness go, Dr. Willoughby?" she

asked, on the stream of these memories, while he passed her the cream and sugar. They were still friends then, Edward and Isabel. He had invited her to come to his graduation. "What happened to him? I suppose it's the loss of all that, his enthusiasm, his warmth, the waste that I can't accept." She set her cup down on the table rather hard and repeated, "The awful waste!"

"That's what we all feel."

Isabel observed him, bright-eyed robin of a man, so round and safe, so unshaken, and in one of those flashes of intuition she saw Edward again, standing with his back to the fireplace in her own house, angry, sore, difficult. Yet she knew now how much she loved him, how much she had longed to reach out and touch him. "He had become untouchable," she murmured.

"Yes," Dr. Willoughby said gently, "despair separates. It *is* separation—and that, no doubt, is why it is a sin."

This was the word she had waited for and knew would have to be spoken. It shocked her back into the realization of why she was here and she sat up very straight to ask, "What will you do about the service? I mean, after all, the Burial of the Dead. Can you?" Her hand was shaking so much she did not dare pick up her cup.

Dr. Willoughby got up and walked slowly up and down the small room, his hands behind his back. She was now near to tears and very frightened, so frightened that she hid her face behind her hand, waiting as if for a verdict.

"I shall read the service," Dr. Willoughby said and sat down again. "For as far as I can see he did no evil; he suffered much; who are we to judge?"

"Thank you," Isabel said in a small voice. "That's what I came to ask." Relief flooded her. Unashamedly she wiped her eyes, blew her nose. The church, she thought, is this if it is anything, a place of sanctuary to the self-tortured, even to the criminal, but she took back the word. Dr. Willoughby had erased the word by all that he had told her. And for a moment at least she could lay aside the sense she had had of being attacked, of being pursued by she did not know what exactly. She was relieved to be asked to deal now with certain practical questions, such as the casket. It seemed that she must go to an address Dr. Willoughby gave her and decide what would be suitable. He would call a taxi; it should not take very long. Would she have time before lunch? She was to lunch with a Professor Goldberg.

Dr. Willoughby raised his eyebrows a trifle.

"Who is Professor Goldberg?" she asked. "Tell me a little about these people. I'm so ignorant"—she smiled a social smile. Goldberg, it seemed, was the star of the English department, but by no means an intimate friend of Edward's. Dr. Willoughby was obviously surprised that she was to lunch with him. But she could not press him for his reasons. She was helpless, at the mercy of strangers. Would Dr. Willoughby tell her something about an Italian professor called Fosca? She was to meet him that night at the Phillipses for dinner.

"Sit down just a minute," Dr. Willoughby commanded. "Orlando Fosca," he murmured, tasting the name as if it were an old brandy. "One of the few great men. You've heard no doubt of his history of comparative literature in the Renaissance?" She shook her head. "A classic work in the field. He's a humanist of the old school and I happen to know that your brother was extremely fond of him."

"He sounded so frail," but what she meant was "so

184

old." "It's terrible that he had to be called when—when it happened."

"Tonight perhaps you will see the fire, and then he will not seem frail," and Dr. Willoughby smiled almost mischievously. "He's a socialist of the old school, came here to escape from Mussolini years ago. He belongs to another era, the era of pure idealism before World War One. Because of that he has been able to keep a kind of innocence —is that the word?—which people of your brother's generation and mine have lost. He's an atheist of course. That too is a matter of generation, perhaps."

"You know so much about"—she hesitated—"about all this."

Again Dr. Willoughby smiled his mischievous smile. "You think of a man of my profession as outside politics, I expect, but that only shows that you too are an innocent. We're all engaged in politics in one way or another, Mrs. Ferrier. It's a political age."

"Oh dear," she sighed, "I suppose it is. I hate it all so." It was time, she thought, that she went about the business of the casket and she looked at her watch rather nervously. But Dr. Willoughby was warming to his subject. She half listened, missed the first half of the sentence and heard him say only, "I have a good deal more respect for Orlando Fosca than for some members of my congregation, as a matter of fact."

"Because he's not afraid?" she asked quickly, for she felt again the slight pressure behind the words.

"Because he lives what he believes."

"I see." Isabel knew that sooner or later she would be accused, of what she did not know, but of something. Now she began to realize what it would be. In the last hour she had seen Edward raised up into a communion from which she and her husband, regular churchgoers, had shut themselves out. "The communion of saints on earth," she said with a shade of irony. "Are the Phillipses like that too?"

"Oh, Damon Phillips," Dr. Willoughby said quickly, "is a different kind of man altogether, brilliant in his field, which happens to be physics. Phillips is a restless man." It seemed that he might have said something less charitable but checked himself. "A most likable chap, with a wonderful wife, as perhaps you saw last night. Yes, you really had better be on your way," he said. "I'll just call a cab."

Isabel drew on her gloves. She was beginning to see that she had come into a world where people were concerned with things that she and Henry never thought about at all. She had come unarmed into a place where the pressures were very great and were pressures of a kind that she had never even imagined. How would she ever come through safe, unharmed?

"Don't let them scare you, Mrs. Ferrier," Dr. Willoughby said unexpectedly as he came back.

"I am scared," she confessed, "very. But I expect I shall learn a great deal. How can I thank you?" She gave him her gloved hand.

VII

Isabel, walking with Ivan Goldberg through Harvard Square, thought she had never seen so many queer people gathered in one place in her life. If it was not an old lady with ragged gray hair, hatless and carrying a peculiar green bag stuffed with books, it was a cluster of boys of all shapes, sizes, and colors, or a tiny man with a goatee and flowing mustaches who looked as if he had stepped out of a Tchekov play. But they all wore some mark in common, the mark, she supposed, of intellectual people; they looked as if they needed sleep and fresh air. She was so absorbed in these impressions that she almost forgot the tall stranger at her side, with his air of serene superiority, shepherding her now into a kind of back alley.

"I brought you this way because from here one gets a rather charming vignette. Look, just ahead there, that old brick building and the Christ Church Tower behind it.

Quite eighteenth century, isn't it?" He gave it to her like a present, rather formally.

"That's Edward's church, isn't it? Where I was this morning?"

"Yes."

"I'm taking you to a French restaurant," he announced in his precise way. "We can have a glass of wine, and also it's a bit less exposed than the Faculty Club. I hope you don't mind."

"Of course not." Then they said very little until they were settled in a booth in this rather dark restaurant, filled with excitable people around them, all talking at once. Professor Goldberg studied the menu for what seemed a very long time, and while he did so, Isabel studied him. She was trying to decide why one would know he was a professor anywhere—in spite of his banker's gray suit, his immaculate blue shirt and dark blue tie. Was it the small very bright eyes behind rather thick glasses, or the slightly superior way he had of smiling, or his manner which from the beginning had been, it seemed to her, that of a teacher with a pupil?

"I recommend an omelette, a mushroom omelette, and a salad," he said as if it were a matter of some importance. Then when she had agreed and he had given the order and chosen the wine, there came a pause. They had reached the frontier of small talk and they would have to come to the point. Why in fact had he wished to see her, she wondered? Curiosity? Even malice?

He was observing her now and, troubled by the question in his look, she found herself filling in rather rapidly, setting up a screen of words, as she launched into a description of the casket company where she had just been,

188

the hushed atmosphere, the smoothness with which she had been persuaded into the most expensive possible bronze object, against her better judgment. She told it half humorously but something in his response froze the words on her lips. He was looking out through his face, his mask, she suddenly felt. He was trying to say something.

"I'm sorry," she said, "I don't know quite what to say — I feel so inadequate. Something is expected of me. What"—she attacked out of sheer panic—"for instance do you expect of me?"

Professor Goldberg offered her a cigarette and lit one for himself; the question lay in the air between them for some seconds.

"It's more, I think, what I expect of myself, Mrs. Ferrier."

"I don't quite understand."

"I was bold to ask for your time today. I suppose I am not quite myself. None of us is. We are victims of shock. You meet us under strange circumstances, Mrs. Ferrier." The speech was labored, so much so, that—did she dream it?—it was as if he were making a physical effort and his breath came hard.

"But at least," she said quietly, "you knew Edward. I didn't. When I read the papers this morning, I——"

She saw his left hand clench into a fist and rap the table twice. His face flushed over. "It's disgraceful. A travesty," he said between his teeth. "It will have to stop."

"How can it stop?"

Just then the waitress appeared with a bottle wrapped in a napkin and poured out two glasses of wine. However angry he may have been, Ivan Goldberg tasted it very gravely, pronounced it adequate and then leaned forward, glaring at her as if she were not there, to say, "It's like a terrible machine that has been set in motion—passion, doubt, guilt. We're all caught in the machine," he said, almost as if he accused her.

"No one has told me why he did it," Isabel said, as if to deflect the pressure a fraction.

"He didn't know himself," Ivan's answer came quickly. It was as if he were holding back torrents of words. Would they spill out? Would she have to withstand them? Isabel began to eat bread and butter nervously. She wondered if people could hear what they were saying, wondered whether other people were talking about the same thing. For a second it seemed to her that the room was full of conspirators, heads bent together, avid eager faces, those across the way for instance. "People who commit suicide do not do it for a reason—they may think so, rationalize. Your brother talked about the political tensions———"

"Yes," Isabel said sharply. "I know."

"That wasn't it," Goldberg said almost savagely.

"How do you know?" For suddenly she resented him, resented his swallowing her up in his own conflicts whatever they were, resented his asking her to lunch for some purpose of his own.

"Forgive me, I"—he smoked at his cigarette furiously —"you shared your brother's political beliefs?"

Isabel caught her breath. It was a direct attack and she was not prepared. "No," she murmured. "I hated all that. I didn't understand it. He seemed crazy to me." She went the whole way. Why not? He might as well know the worst.

She was amazed to see that he was relieved. The little smile played around his lips again. He attacked his omelette with relish. What have I done, she thought? I've given him something I didn't mean to give. We are conspirators then, conspirators against Edward, against what Edward meant. He wants me for an ally.

"No he wasn't crazy"—Goldberg looked up with almost a smile—"and he's put us both in the wrong. You know that of course," he said as if he were daring her to deny it, as if he enjoyed it, too. His eyes gleamed behind his glasses.

"Why did you ask me to lunch, Professor Goldberg?" She asked with a trace of reserve. "What do you want of me? I've felt ever since I got here that I was being treated as a child in a grown-up world, treated gently. It's not my world," she said. "I don't belong here. I'm a stranger."

"And afraid, in a world you never made?" It sounded like a quotation, but she did not recognize it.

"Edward was way beyond me even when I was a child," she added. And then, was it the wine? the food? On a wave of self-assertion she went on to tell him the truth, tell this smug professor the truth. "I feel ashamed. I resent what Edward did," she said, "if you must know. And I don't feel guilty," she ended.

"Neither do I," Goldberg said blandly. Would she let it pass? After all, they could part now; they would never see each other again. She did not have to push the thing further into places where she would not be able to cope. She saw his left hand clench.

"It's all so queer. He didn't play safe," she heard herself saying, "and most of us do. I bet you do feel guilty," she ended, looking at him speculatively. "Yes," she added, as Goldberg lowered his eyes, "you do. Why?"

"I shall succeed where he failed. But my success won't mean anything, you see. The one person who really cared, who would have known what my book meant, won't be there to read it. And why?" His voice thickened. Isabel knew there was real feeling here, and she respected it. She did not look at him. "Because he knew and the reason he knew was that he was what he was. Quite a few pilots got killed trying to break the sound barrier, you know—and you might call it suicide, in a way. The first tries were suicidal, actually. Edward was trying to break through a much more difficult barrier, a human barrier, to unite the intellect and life, to make man whole. The poor guy," Goldberg said, and now the torrent of words had come. "He was so innocent that he was terribly impressed because Wallace read his books. This seemed to him a sign, a portent—it was the breaking through toward him from the other side. I see it all so clearly now," and his voice grew hard. "But he couldn't break through of course."

"Why do you care then?" Isabel asked. It was amazing how, when they talked of Edward, all these people lit up.

"I don't know. The strange thing is"—Goldberg looked at her now, really as if she were a human being—"that one can talk to you. And one couldn't talk to Edward——"

"Because I don't make you feel guilty"—she smiled an ironic smile—"I'm nobody's conscience, and Edward, it seems to me, was."

"I hated him for it. I fought him every inch of the way. I never gave in for a moment," Goldberg said half to himself. "Only last week he came and begged me to sign a petition—and I refused."

"And now," she asked quickly, "will you sign it?" The question, she saw as soon as it had slipped out, was crucial, was also perhaps cruel. "I'm sorry. That's not fair, is it?"

"No," Goldberg pushed his plate away. "I shan't sign

it." There was a pause while he ordered coffee and dessert, then he came back to the point. "People don't change, Mrs. Ferrier, even under shock. That's where your brother was beating his head against a wall. He believed that he might change, you see, that he would learn to break through. But he couldn't, any more than I can. The only difference is that I accept certain facts and he couldn't. In the University, for instance—and the University is my passion, Mrs. Ferrier—I am respected and feared, but I am not loved. That is a fact I have had to accept."

It was a confession she chose to lay aside, because she had to get back to something he had said earlier. "But if Edward believed in the possibilities of change, then why did he . . . ?"

"Something snapped, I suppose. No one can stand too much tension."

"Something snapped—as simple as that," she looked suddenly angry. "But it's eating you all up, just the same. And eating me up, too."

"Because, don't you see, it throws a bright hard light —and so is symptomatic—on all our inward divisions. It is an attack."

"I didn't know I was divided," Isabel said quickly. "I'm not."

"Because, I suspect, you have like me deliberately chosen to shut yourself away from the agonies of your time. Don't you say, It's none of my business? My business is my husband, my children—do you have children?" he interrupted himself to ask.

"Yes, two, one in high school, a boy. One girl thirteen years old."

"And I say that literature is my business."

"And we're both wrong?" she asked.

Goldberg pushed the cigarette out hard in the ash tray. "Not wrong, less than we might be, less than Edward was. But we'll live, Mrs. Ferrier, won't we?" He smiled his intolerable smile.

"Yes, no doubt we will." I've got to get away from here, she thought. This man is a devil. He's too brilliant and too unhappy and he wants to hurt me now, and he has hurt me. She looked at her watch, shutting out the thoughts that raced through her mind, with this deliberate gesture.

"Yes," Goldberg said, "you have to go, don't you? I'm sorry I have detained you so long." His face froze. He tapped on a glass with his spoon and looked around for the waitress, then turned to her with a surprisingly human smile, a real one and said, "Do you have half an hour to spare? It seems too bad that you haven't seen anything of the college. After all, this was Edward's life, all this. I'd like to show you a few things . . ."

Isabel hesitated a fraction of a second, saw his face close again, his guard go up, and knew that she must do it, however much she would have liked to go back to her lair, pull the shades down, lie in the dark and smoke and think, perhaps call Henry at the hospital and hear his sane normal voice.

"That's awfully kind of you," she said, allowing the thought of Henry to fade. "No one could be more ignorant than I."

She felt as they walked into the Yard through the high ironwork gates that they were entering a secret world. For one thing there was no traffic here, except human beings on their feet. As they crossed the Square on the way she had been utterly bewildered by the cars, the people moving between the cars, the hectic air it all had. Here inside the Yard, it was as if a quiet hand were laid upon them. Gardeners were busy raking leaves off the grass. Students sat under the trees and on the steps of the library in little knots or alone. Goldberg stopped for a moment at the seated statue of John Harvard, then again to point out the sharp clean thrust of the chapel spire. As he talked about these things, he became a different person; he seemed ten years younger. And the tension of their talk in the dark restaurant had in some way relaxed; for the first time since she had arrived the night before, Isabel felt she could breathe freely. But it was only when he had led her into the Houghton Library and they leaned in that dustless atmosphere, so silent it seemed almost deathly, over glass-topped tables under which Keats's own handwriting lay, that she turned to her companion confidently and felt able to ask the real question.

"But what good is it," she asked as if she had picked up a remark of his where it lay between them, "to be involved in what you call the agony of the times, as Edward was, if you come to the wrong conclusions? How can you be wrong and right at the same time? You say that you cannot agree with his political point of view and you say at the same time that you and I are less than he was——"

"Don't lean too hard on that glass. It might break," he said in a whisper. "Come out," he said, "let's sit on the steps of the library and smoke a cigarette." For Ivan Goldberg this was a most extraordinary concession, but Isabel did not know that. She was only glad and a little dazed and very much in awe of the environment. The steps sounded less formidable than the hushed embalmed room. People would not stare at her as if she were a queer animal strayed into the academic grove.

Climbing the shallow steps, to a place where they could lean against the wall and be in the sun, Isabel wondered why she had thought of Professor Goldberg as a devil. He offered her a cigarette, lit it, and looked up, blinking myopically at the chapel spire just across from them. It soared above the Yard and the trees and all the people like some continual signal, she thought.

"I've never done this before," he announced as if it were a confession. "I've never quite dared."

"It takes a stranger to make you dare?"

"It takes Edward's sister," he said gravely. He took off his glasses, rubbed them, and put them back on.

"You talked about accepting the facts—what then were the facts Edward should have accepted and didn't? That's what I really want to understand." It occurred to her that only because Edward was dead was it possible for her to sit here in the very heart of his world and ask such a question. Had he been alive, his physical presence would have blocked the way—and besides never never would he have sat like this with her, open to question. She shivered.

"Are you cold?" Ivan Goldberg asked. "Here, sit on my coat."

"No, I'm not cold. Only every now and then it's as if —Edward—" she found she couldn't go on.

"I know," Goldberg said gently. "We talk and talk and the words mean nothing."

"Still," and Isabel turned to him with a smile, "if you can answer, please do." Then she looked down at her hands thoughtfully. "You see, in a queer way it's as if Edward had died for me a long time ago. And now every moment he's becoming more alive."

"Yes, that's it," Goldberg said quickly, "he's terribly alive now— I wonder how long he will be." He looked off across the Yard and smoked a moment, then said what he had obviously been turning over in his mind. "There were two things Edward couldn't accept. For one, that his idea of socialism was old-fashioned. Socialism as we are seeing it in action in England, for instance, is growing to be anti-individualistic, bureaucratic, and exalts the state at the expense of all Edward meant. A general leveling down does not seem to mean greater opportunity for all, in fact quite the contrary. It's as rigid as the statism Edward so feared and hated in Nazi Germany, and as formalistic, though of course not wicked. And that is why, I suppose, the Czechoslovakian coup was possible at all. But Edward simply couldn't admit this. What he saw when he was over there was the fervor, the struggle, the hope, and certain exceptional human beings whom he loved and in whom he believed.

"That was one thing; the other was his sentimentality about the working man and about the unions, and his refusal to admit that in American democracy as it is, the intellectual *is* isolated, suspected and never an organic part of political life, at best an amateur, at worst a dupe as Wallace proved to be."

"You make it sound so clear," and Isabel sighed. "Why if it's so clear was Edward important? Why do people mind so much? Why do they feel attacked?"

"Because of the reasons for what he believed. The reasons, you see, were generous, deeply human reasons, even if the conclusions as far as we can see, were unworthy.

197

Who are we, unwilling or unable to commit ourselves, to judge?"

"Must one be 'committed' as you call it? Why can't people go about their business in peace?" she asked passionately. Every time she came close to people's feeling about Edward, Isabel felt as if she were being sucked down into a whirlpool where nothing was clear, where everything was struggle and agony.

"There is a price to be paid for not participating and for refusing to be responsible. I wonder," Goldberg said, and she felt the slight barb in the question, "what price you have paid."

"For staying safely outside?"

"For staying safely outside."

Isabel thought this over for a moment. "That's what you meant then when you said something about what you might expect of yourself, because of Edward—since——"

"Yes," Goldberg said, stamping out his cigarette with his feet. The sun which had warmed them had gone behind a cloud and Isabel felt the chill from the stone steps in her bones. It was time to go. She did not quite understand why Goldberg thanked her so warmly when they parted at the door of the hotel, but perhaps it was that he would not have talked like this to anyone in the college. Perhaps it was that he too was lonely. She smiled as she lay on her bed and remembered that she had imagined these people as safe, as superior, as part of some whole from which she was shut out, whereas she saw now they were terribly divided and exposed, exposed to each other, as naked in some ways as children. Oh, if she could only talk to Edward now. She moved her head back and forth on the pillow as if to keep the tears back by this physical motion.

VIII

"We'll have a fire," Damon said after dinner, as they went back into the drawing room. "I'll just light it for you," he said as Julia brought in coffee. Isabel, noting the three cups on the tray, realized with amusement that here in Cambridge the gentlemen would stay on in the dining room for their brandy while the ladies retired. She had felt all evening like a total stranger in a noisy and passionate world. Especially Grace Kimlock—was that her name?—sitting now as straight as a ramrod on the little sofa by the fire, terrified her. She indeed had the hawk's eyes which Isabel had imagined. In this pause while Julia carried out the cocktail glasses, while Damon lit the Cape Cod lighter and set it under the logs, she felt those eyes upon her. To escape she got up and wandered over to look at a portrait of Damon as a boy hanging over the model of a clipper ship in a glass case which needed dusting. Damon was dressed in a white sailor suit with a whistle round his shoulder on a blue cord, and he was looking straight out, a thin fair-haired boy with very bright eyes. The portrait shone out in the great shabby room as the one thing young and untouched by time, for the dark red curtains at the windows had faded and looked dusty too, and the Persian carpet had taken on a soft pinkish glow. Yet how comfortable the Victorian chairs were, she thought, and how safe one felt here. It had been like this, she felt, for such a long time, had been Damon's father's house before it became his, she had been told. This, in itself, this continuity in one house so unusual in America, filled her with peace. When Grace Kimlock spoke, Isabel had forgotten her.

"I wonder how they ever got Damon to sit still long enough for that portrait," the clear sharp voice broke in. And then, as Isabel turned to answer, she pounced. "You're not a bit like Edward," she said, challenging, "are you?"

Isabel was saved by Julia who came back, providentially, just then. Isabel admired Julia; she moved among them, these passionate, voluble people so calmly and slowly, with such control. And now she turned to Grace and said severely, "Grace, be good. Do you take cream and sugar?"

"Black, please. And why should I be good? We have very little time and 'being good,' which I take it means being discreet and saying nothing real, takes too much time."

"Families are such queer things," Isabel said, half in answer, but she was also still under the spell of the room, its peace.

"What was it like in yours?" Grace Kimlock asked. "Edward used to talk about your mother. She must have been an extraordinary woman, really—she painted, wrote poetry or something, didn't she?—gardened . . ." She looked at Isabel expectantly over the rim of her coffee cup. But Isabel was thinking, That is what a life adds up to, the things one does. Her mother, defined like this, had no reality, loomed up out of focus. How to say it right?

"Somehow she was full of life, it was that. Wonderfully responsive to everything—a child's game, the light on leaves—she was always *there* so completely"—Isabel faltered, turned to Julia—"how little the words mean."

"She shouldn't have died," Grace Kimlock said. "It did something to Edward." She seemed unconscious of the implied rebuke, but Isabel colored.

"She didn't want to die," she said quickly. The fact that Edward had wanted to die rushed into the silence as the three women sat and looked at the fire. After a pause, Isabel went on, "It was Edward's year at Oxford. She wouldn't let me tell him, and she only lived as long as she did because she meant to, willed it, kept her heart beating somehow for his sake. The last thing she said was 'lovely' about a little green orchid someone had sent. That," Isabel added, "was very like her." She was suddenly grateful to these two strangers, to these two friends of Edward's for making it possible for her to talk. "You're quite right, Miss Kimlock," she said quite seriously, "you've startled me into telling things I haven't ever spoken aloud."

Grace flashed a look of triumph at Julia, but Julia, lost in her own thoughts, was looking at the fire. Was it the orchid? Something led her to say, "It's strange but these last years I've almost forgotten that side of Edward, the passionate love of beauty." Stretching her hands to the fire as if from some hunger, she said, "But of course it was always there. Did you ever go to a museum with him, Grace?"

"No," Grace answered shortly. She couldn't really bear what anyone else knew of Edward.

"I did, that summer in France. We ran into him quite by chance at Albi and saw the Toulouse-Lautrecs together. I'll never forget the way Edward lit up then, how he could make one *see*. I expect he got that from your mother." She turned to Isabel, drawing her in again.

"And what did he get from your father?" Grace Kimlock leaned forward to ask for another cup of coffee.

Isabel froze. This was a question she had never asked herself. Her mind raced ahead while she said, "They didn't get on, never did. Maybe they were too much alike."

"Edward never talked about his father."

"He hated Father. He wanted to break away from all that." Isabel felt cornered. Was there no way out? Must she face this tearing in the family again, bring it out to be searched by those hawk's eyes? Her hand was trembling.

"All what?"

"Father was a banker, a Republican of course, and very sure that he was right about everything. He had no patience with failure of any kind. If people were out of work, it was their fault, and so on. He and Edward hit each other head on about everything, as you can see," and she smiled. It was getting less hard as she talked. She almost wanted to tell them now. "But that wasn't it—not really— it was, I think, that father never tried to understand Edward, wouldn't, made up his mind not to. Just like Edward. They walled themselves in against each other. It got so I dreaded every meal because of the arguments. But there was something powerful about Father, very powerful. He had a brilliant hard mind . . ." She faltered and turned now rather shyly to Grace, "I guess that's the real answer to your question."

"He does sound rather difficult," Grace said with a slightly malicious smile.

"I expect he does to you. But surely"—Isabel felt she must fight their sense of isolated superiority, this little self-enclosed world which took so much for granted—"there isn't only one way of looking at things? Surely it's possible honestly to disagree and still to respect people, even Republicans," she added. She turned helplessly to Julia.

"Oh, we're all full of poison," Julia answered gently.

"You're so sure you're right. It seems to me you live here in a kind of—" she hesitated, looking for a word.

"Ivory tower? But didn't your father live in an ivory tower?" Grace laughed a short laugh. "It's rather droll that we should be accused of that. Most people accused Edward of meddling too much in the world, of refusing to stay safely in the ivory tower."

"I don't know," Isabel retreated. She felt again the dry wind of passion assailing her. "I live in such a different world." She thought of Henry, her husband, playing bridge now with the Eriksons across the street, relaxing slowly after his high-pressure day at the hospital, thought of him with nostalgia, the safety, the coziness of their lives where these winds did not blow.

"But you have to take sides," Grace said relentlessly, sitting up a little straighter, "in any world. You have to make up your mind, go the way things are going or fight the way things are going."

"The Republicans have been fighting the way things are going for quite some time," Isabel said quietly.

"Don't think we're sure we're right," Julia broke in. "Damon told you," she went on with a visible effort, "that Edward had shut the door on us, walked out of this house two nights before—" Julia's face looked absolutely drained. This then was the explanation of the undercurrents of violent emotion Isabel had sensed at the dinner table.

"I'm sorry." She felt ashamed now. She should have learned from Dr. Willoughby, from Professor Goldberg that it was all far more complicated and human than it seemed under the surface of this safe Victorian room. Henry would lump all these people together as a bunch of radicals, but it was not as black and white as it looked. Was anything when you came close enough to see? "I wish you'd tell me about it, if you feel you could." The question was addressed to Julia, but Isabel saw her glance over at Grace, hesitate, then decide to take the plunge.

She explained briefly what had happened at the Civil Liberties Union. She was interrupted by Grace who hammered out that to Edward the point in question was not unimportant. But for once Julia was determined and brushed Grace aside firmly. "Isabel doesn't want to hear all the details and ramifications. After all we've lived all this out for years, she hasn't." Grace answered, "Well, it's time she learned. She's an American citizen, isn't she?" Isabel blushed, but Julia pointedly ignored the sally. "Ever since it happened, ever since Edward walked out of the house I've been trying to understand the essence—maybe I can try to say it now. You see, we all felt when Wallace led the Progressive Party that here was a chance to start with a clean slate, to have a truly liberal party without commitments to party bosses, to a reactionary South and so on. It was very hard for many of us to admit that he had been taken in by the extreme Left and that this might be as dangerous as commitments which the Democratic Party has to the extreme Right in the shape of Southern Democrats." Isabel listened like a child at school, but none of it hit home for her. She was painfully aware that what made Grace visibly bristle and Julia obviously suffer meant little or nothing to her.

"Some people are not afraid of the extreme Left," Grace said flatly.

"Right. Edward and Grace stuck by Wallace, and this was the beginning of our fight with Edward. He never forgave Damon, quite, for withdrawing from the Progressive Party before the election. These are the facts, you see, but they are not the essence."

"And what is the essence, Julia?" Grace Kimlock inquired.

"You won't like this, Grace," Julia half-smiled.

"I don't expect to. I don't like any of it."

"I can only say what I think. And perhaps it means trying to define what a liberal is—that word which you so despise, Grace. It seems to me that the true liberal is capable of change, is not rigid, grows in fact. What you see as compromise, I see as recognition. Since the last war, there has been a rather subtle shift toward what I might call enlightened conservatism."

"Compromise—fatal compromise and cowardice," Grace answered quickly.

"That is how Edward saw it, of course. For so many years the extreme Right—in Spain, in Italy, in Germany—has been the enemy. Now we are facing an enemy from the Left. You see, Isabel, all our loyalties and faith have been bound up with the Left. This shift makes deep psychological wounds—we have to admit things that we do not want to admit. We have to draw up new frontiers. This is what is happening now and it is not done without pain."

"I call it ratting," Grace Kimlock sat, straight as a ramrod, her eyes flashing.

"For some of us," Julia went on imperturbably, "the failure of the Czechoslovakian Socialists to hold out against communism was the final illuminating thing."

"Edward felt strongly about that, didn't he?" Isabel at least could fasten onto this fact in the midst of a great deal that was simply bewildering. It was all so queerly religious and intense, that was what bothered her. At home people just voted whatever party they were for and then that was that. You didn't lie awake at night, fighting with your conscience.

"After all, he had been in Prague for a year. Presumably he knew something about it," Grace said.

Mercifully perhaps, they heard Fosca's voice in the hall, as Damon and he came back to join the ladies. "It's not going to be easy, in any case, you may be sure of that." But Damon had already rushed on past him mentally into the next room. "No, no, of course not," he murmured. "Well, you look very cozy in here, I must say. Orlando and I nearly froze to death in there. It's high time we got the furnace going, Julia. Nice fire," he said, standing before it, rubbing his hands. Professor Fosca sat down on the sofa beside Grace, his eyes very bright.

Isabel looked speculatively at these friends of Edward's, two men so different yet in one way also alike. Professor Fosca radiated warmth, but Damon Phillips, for all his charm, was too restless to give one any sense of real communication. He moved so fast that he had hardly let her finish a sentence at dinner, and even when he became as old as Professor Fosca, he would never be like him, she felt. Yet they were alike in that their faces were both lined, faces on which thought had left visible traces. It was that, she decided, comparing them with her husband's clear-cut bronze smoothness. They lived hard (she saw it now), harder than a man who played golf and tennis to keep his waistline down. They would not grow old gracefully. They would not, she thought, smiling to herself, perhaps grow old at all.

She caught Professor Fosca's clear blue eyes watching her. "An indiscreet question, Mrs. Ferrier, but what made you smile such a perspicacious smile just then, you who come to us from the golden untroubled shores?"

"I was thinking an indiscreet thought."

"I guessed as much."

"She thinks we're old fools," Grace Kimlock said with a sniff.

"And you don't think so?" Orlando teased his old friend.

"No," Isabel spoke directly to Grace, "as a matter of fact, Miss Kimlock, I was thinking that none of you would ever grow old."

"I'm prepared to agree with you," Damon said gaily, "but why not?"

But this she could not answer. She could not say—Miss Kimlock might be hurt—that they seemed to her childishly passionate. And Isabel was afraid. They were too close to tragedy. They had been walking round it all evening, and, she guessed, they had deliberately spared her. They had not insisted—except among themselves in that violent argument at the dinner table about socialism in Britain, about the Webbs. "I'm not going to answer that," she said quietly. "We have so little time. Perhaps I'll never see you again," she said, looking at them now one by one, Fosca hunched over on the sofa, his delicate thin hands clasping his knees; Grace Kimlock, upright, at bay; Damon Phillips leaning on the back of his wife's chair and Julia herself plucking a thread from her dress in an absent-minded way. "I must thank you," she said, and it was like a farewell, "for all you were to Edward, all of you."

"We didn't keep him from being desperately lonely," Grace Kimlock said sharply because she was moved. "Desperately," she repeated with a tremor in her voice.

"No," Isabel held her hands tightly together, "I guess no one could do that." Because, she would have liked to say, you shut out understanding by the passion of your convictions. You meet opposition to your ideas with something like hysteria always just under the surface. At the very instant of communication you slam the door shut. "Why? Why does it have to be so painful? Why are we so divided?" The words rose to her lips with compelling force; they were spoken to Fosca. "If Edward could have once talked to me about the things close to his heart without that fearful driving anger, without shutting me out—why am I talking like this?" She looked about her in a panic. She felt as if a high wall had just fallen down, the wall that had protected her, and now she was naked. She had given herself away. "I must go," she said, getting up as if actually to run away. She was beginning to feel the tensions which Edward had felt so terribly, in herself, and she knew that she was very tired, tired and with no peace to rest in, no final resolution of anything, only the everlasting questions which devoured the faces around her, as well as her own.

They were all standing now. They were closing in on her, the enemy, the intellectuals, Edward's friends. "I must go," she said again.

Then she felt the gentle pressure of an arm around her shoulders, a most extraordinary sensation as if some strong fraternal emotion actually penetrated through her dress, through her skin, through her veins and reached her heart, as if the old man standing beside her could transfuse love like blood itself. "No, dear Isabel," he said very gently, "you must stay a few moments. You can't leave now." Very gently he drew her over to the sofa and sat down beside her. Julia sat down on the floor in front of the fire. "He shut us all out, Isabel," she said after a moment. "Oh, he was just a living wound at the end. If you'd seen him as I did——"

"But surely there's something"—Isabel searched for a way to say it—"unnatural in that. I mean, he was a sick man surely."

"We're all sick," Damon broke in almost angrily. "Edward watched his friends making what seemed to him fatal compromises—fear creeping in, confusion at the center, the best energies dispersed from within by doubt and anxiety. It's hard to go back on things you've believed and fought for all your life. Edward couldn't. Are we right? Was he wrong? We live in the dark, Mrs. Ferrier, at best."

"You liberals may. Edward didn't," Grace said acidly.

"We are talking to Isabel now," Orlando Fosca said firmly. "Edward lived close to the heart of the matter, always, Isabel, that was his greatness. But he couldn't communicate the very essence of his belief and that was his tragedy. When he fought you, he was fighting himself."

"But you're not like that," Isabel said gratefully. "You feel these things just as passionately, but——"

"I'm very old." Orlando smiled his seraphic smile. "I do not expect miracles. And then," he said more thoughtfully, "I am not an American, except by adoption, and late in my life. Perhaps I feel the pressures less, I don't know," and he sighed.

"Tell me about Edward," Isabel said out of all that had happened in the last few minutes. "I need to know."

"I do not think we shall understand the entire meaning of his suicide for some years to come. Let us leave it, then. What you must know is that as a scholar your brother was unmatched for fervor, understanding and integrity. We simply cannot do without him. The loss to American letters is immeasurable." The delicate hands were clasped into fists now and the mild blue eyes blazed. The frail old man at her side had become a giant, and Isabel remembered what Dr. Willoughby had said about the fire.

"Yes, I think"—she stammered slightly—"I d-did know that."

"Everyone knows that. What people do not know is what his influence was here, how he challenged the better students, and that he did challenge them as he did because he was involved actively and bitterly in the life outside the college. *That* is the heart of the matter," he ended gravely, "you see."

"I don't see," she said, able to be perfectly honest at last, "but maybe someday I will. I mean that you can be so wrong and so right at the same time, that you can shut out love and yet know so much about it, be so lonely and long so for communion—the communion of saints on earth, Dr.

Willoughby said this morning—strange," she murmured as if to herself.

They had come to the end of the line. The silence, in which they all looked at the fire, grew long but no one noticed it. Grace Kimlock gave a loud unconscious sigh. "We're a long way from that," she said bitterly.

"I wonder," Orlando answered very gently. "It seems to me we have had this evening an intimation of it."

IX

It was a cold gray day, leaves and dust skirling about in a dirty wind, bits of old newspaper flapping against the fence. The few leaves still on the trees looked tired, and Grace Kimlock as she walked down Brattle Street thought all this appropriate, a restless disintegration, Cambridge itself where the green lawns were slowly being eaten up by apartment houses and the old frame houses needed paint, having lost all dignity and charm. Not thinking of Edward to whose funeral she was going, she thought of these things, the constant flow of noisy trucks down Brattle Street which used to be an ample thoroughfare, stately and peaceful. It's all gone or going, she thought, and we are old and tired. She stubbed her toe quite painfully on a brick that the root of a tree had lifted slightly, and stopped for a moment to catch her breath, for she had been walking fast. Just then the bell of Christ Church began to toll, each long low ring reaching out like the ripples in a pond when a pebble falls, reaching out into the cold air, into the wind with imperative and calming solemnity. And Grace Kimlock walked against it, walked fast against it as if to shut it out, for now she was afraid, she was lonely, she felt bitterly that Orlando Fosca was not there to support her, though he had explained that the ushers must be there much earlier, and he must be sure that Warlock, the distinguished poet, was properly met, as well as two Columbia professors. She disliked the idea of the funeral; she would have preferred the college chapel where she felt at home, for one thing. As a Unitarian, the child and grandchild of Unitarians, she would be uncomfortable in the atmosphere of Edward's church. "Mumbo jumbo"—she sniffed—"buffoonery," she muttered to herself, as she turned up past Radcliffe College, now quickening her pace, a wave of sudden excitement shooting through her. This excitement which she could not control, which made her feel slightly trembly all over, was disturbing. She reminded herself that a funeral is not a play. She felt absolutely no emotion, no grief, only this wild excitement as if something were about to happen. For three days they had been waiting for this hour, suspended in the unfamiliar corrupting, disturbing element of Edward's deed—was it that? That there would be some definite end at last, some finality?

As she drew near the church, she saw that several taxis were stopping, as well as two long black limousines; already a steady flow of people, nearly half an hour before the time, hurried in, and then, under the spell of the tolling bell, automatically slowed down as they turned into the path. A very old lady was being helped out of her car by a chauffeur. Grace felt herself an absolute outsider, as if she were about to walk into a drawing room, unintroduced. Just then Mrs. Humphreys came and pressed her hand silently, then moved away. The hush from the church reached out and changed them, laid upon them a mask of false solemnity, she thought. And she hated it all, deciding there and then to add a codicil to her will: No funeral, ashes to be thrown to the wind.

The strength of this decision took her in through the wide-open red doors, to the hushing carpet, to the grave ushers and—thank God—Fosca, who came forward from the group of five or six distinguished men, all known to her (and she was glad to see that Professor Goldberg was one of them). Whatever the newspapers might say, the presence of these great men of Harvard appeased something in her heart, hungry for praise of Edward. Harvard at least would show its pride, was not ashamed to do so, and Grace Kimlock walked down the aisle, her head high. She slipped into a pew near the middle of the church, irritated by the soft music oozing from the organ. They might at least have played some Mozart, she thought.

Mrs. Brimmer knelt down beside her and began to pray. Grace Kimlock on the other hand sat up straight and looked around her with unashamed curiosity. She had to admit that the church looked beautiful. There were great bunches of autumn flowers on the sills of each of the long oval windows and at the altar nothing but white chrysanthemums. She put on her glasses—who was that rather frail young man Fosca was leading down to the front rows, while Goldberg preceded one of the deans? (The church was nearly full now and there were still fifteen minutes.) Warlock, she thought with satisfaction. That, she knew, would have pleased Edward. He had come all the way from New York to pay his respects. As well he might, for she knew how patiently Edward had gone over his last book with him, and how carefully later on he had reviewed it for *The New Republic*—how anxious to be just and helpful.

Just then, she saw the coffin. Somehow she had avoided seeing it before, though it stood far forward before the altar on a high stand, a tall candle at each corner, covered in black. Grace stared at it now, fascinated, tugging at her brooch as she did when she was nervous. But it had no reality—a black box surrounded by candles. It did not mean "Edward." It just meant death, and she did not have any idea what death meant.

At the moment it seemed to mean Mrs. Brimmer constantly turning round and craning her neck, to catch her husband's eye if and when he should come. It meant Professor Goldberg, immaculate and stiff, for once not smiling, wearing his Prince Albert as if he had been born in it, behaving so much like an undertaker that Grace caught herself smiling. It meant the rows and rows of students, girls without hats who had tied scarves over their heads, earnest embarrassed young men, and over all, oozing like honey, the pale sentimental organ music. But as she watched, taking it all in like a person at a play, Grace felt falling away from her, little by little, the self-consciousness and the excitement and finally bowed her head as if to shut out all this, as if to find some still point on which she might rest, from which she might go out towards Edward, in which the occasion might at last take on its reality, and she feel a part of it and not the lonely, egocentric, arrogant observer she had been until now.

It seemed, in the hush as the bell stopped tolling, and

for a moment even the organ was silent, as if they were all suspended in a vacuum, completely separate. Then as more definite music made itself heard, the ushers walked slowly down to their places and Fosca alone escorted Isabel Ferrier to her pew. Faces lifted to see her go past, not knowing perhaps who she was, though "family" seemed implicit in her solemn formally-set-apart arrival, in the black veil which hid her face.

"Who's that?" the incorrigible Mrs. Brimmer whispered in Grace's ear.

"His sister," she whispered back. But Grace thought, as the lonely figure knelt to pray, not of Isabel, but of their mother, so cruelly absent now and always for so many years, she who held Edward's love locked up in her helpless heart, helplessly.

"I am the resurrection and the life, saith the Lord—" The words broke the absolute silence with the force of a trumpet, though they were spoken in a very quiet voice. It seemed to Grace as if in that sudden moment something burst apart inside her. The tears she had not shed until now, had not expected to shed, broke from deep down inside her and flooded her eyes so she could not see, fumbling for a handkerchief, hardly hearing what came next. "We brought nothing into this world, and it is certain we can carry nothing out." One part of her was aware how cleverly Dr. Willoughby was cutting the burial service so that any reference to "the appointed time" was eliminated. But another part of her knew only the pain and the blessing of the opening words, the longing to believe them true, the strange consolation of them, though she could not affirm their truth, and then she knew, with the force of an actual wound, her own intolerable loneliness. She was ashamed

216

of the sobs she held back by sheer force of will, the terror that one would resound in the church like some animal cry, as she felt Mrs. Brimmer stirring uneasily beside her and looked in vain (she could not see at all) for at least Fosca's head somewhere, some *point d'appui.*

For many people in the church that day, there was no way to communicate. There was only the separation. Goldberg, sitting stiffly in the usher's pew, the only Jew among them, held himself forcibly apart.

"So when this corruptible shall have put on incorruption, and this mortal shall have put on immortality, then shall be brought to pass the saying that is written, Death is swallowed up in victory. O death, where is thy sting? O grave, where is thy victory? The sting of death is sin; and the strength of sin is the Law. But thanks be to God, which giveth us the victory through our Lord Jesus Christ—"

Goldberg never entered a Christian church without feeling himself drawn down into a whirlpool of anguish of different kinds. For him the word "Jesus Christ" was a terrible word. He could not hear it without remembering centuries of pogroms, his father's stories of their grandfather's village in Russia and the terrors of Easter when the Christians went forth to kill any Jews not locked up in their houses, the doors double barred and their hearts like animal hearts feeling only the fear of the hunted. Here he was, sitting cold as a stuffed fish among the goyim, for the sake of Edward Cavan. Many times an unbeliever, since he did not even believe (as the old Italian printer did, whom he had taken down to the front rows) that Edward was a fighter in the true cause of socialism. Nothing here today, except the presence of the two Columbia professors and Warlock, the poet, spoke to him of his own loss. He was terribly a stranger, forced into ridiculous clothes to parade his grief among strangers. And his teeth were clenched with the effort not to put on his one defense, that smile of superiority and contempt.

"Death is a dirty trick," George Hastings was thinking. He had hoped for some ultimate saving word that would frame all he had fumbled to say himself. But the long familiar passages from the Bible left him cold. Also he was too self-conscious to feel anything, being, as he was, one of four students chosen to carry the coffin out at the appointed time. Pleased to have been asked, pleased by this sign of his "belonging," he now regretted the honor which lay upon him and kept him from paying attention, for he kept imagining catastrophe—that he would stumble at the crucial moment and the coffin lurch horribly to the floor. Responsibility kept him apart.

It had seemed to Julia, sitting two rows behind Grace Kimlock, that something must happen during the long service to take away the sense of futility—for all his anguish, for all his last desperate gesture to communicate something—what?—Edward Cavan now in the last few moments had in some terrible way ceased to exist. She had been a little disturbed by Angela Goldberg's sitting down beside her. No doubt, Julia thought, she felt lonely in this church and had sought Julia out as someone she knew. Yet it had seemed an intrusion; the consciousness of the silent, slightly resisting presence at her side kept Julia from losing herself, from identifying herself somewhere, somehow, with something, and no longer to be dangling, as she felt, in a vacuum. She had been brought up in this church and did not come back without a pang, without an examination of conscience, since, for some years, she had ceased to practice her religion. The sound of the words was soothing, but they had no meaning. They did not console really or explain the presence here of them all, the presence of Edward Cavan dead by his own will. It seemed to her even that they evaded, that they smoothed over with their golden beauty what had to remain naked and terrible to be realized. She felt that they were all being swaddled up in the hush, among the flowers, in the music of the organ, in the ritualistic solemnity from something which must break through and pierce them alive again. And strangely she began almost in spite of herself, to pray, as if the vertical appeal of prayer might somehow make it possible for the horizontal communion, which she craved, to take place at last. It was a felt prayer, hardly articulated in which the words "understanding," "peace," became key words. "If you could help us to understand and to forgive each other," she said silently, thinking of Damon, far away now among the ushers, Damon who had no idea how much of the time she resented, almost hated him. "Oh keep Edward in our hearts," she prayed, reaching at last the still place in herself which she had come to find. "Make him whole and active within us, able to overcome our guilt."

Dr. Willoughby stepped forward and began a passage which at first seemed unfamiliar, "Who bends not his eare to any bell which upon any occasion rings? But who can remove it from that bell, which is passing a peece of himself out of this world?" But then like a musical phrase, forgotten but bringing back in total recall whole areas long buried, the quiet voice went on, "No man is an Iland, intire of itself; every man is a peece of the Continent, a part of the maine"; if there had been stillness in the church before, the stillness of private thoughts, there now fell a complete intense stillness and the separate individuals became one, lifted like a wave toward the presence of the dead, suddenly alive among them in that communion which he had not been able to find in life—"if a Clod be washed away by the Sea, Europe is the lesse, as well as if a Promontorie were, as well as if a Mannor of thy friends or of thine owne were; any man's death diminishes me, because I am involved in Mankinde; and therefore never send to know for whom the bell tolls, it tolls for thee." Dr. Willoughby paused a moment before leading the congregation in the Lord's Prayer, and in that second of deeply shared emotion, the thing they had all been waiting for came to pass.

Isabel in the front pew alone felt the wave behind her, felt it lift her up beyond herself, like a release from bondage. Tenderness for her brother filled her like a blessing. He's at peace now, she thought. He doesn't have to be torn to pieces any longer. "Forgive us our trespasses, as we forgive those who trespass against us."

Before anyone was prepared for it, before George Hastings knew what he was doing, the coffin was being carried down among them and out of the door. Now for the first time, Edward Cavan, the person, was among them. It was terribly evident that it was he himself who was leaving them in the long box. To George bearing the heavy weight on his shoulder, it had become a gesture of support and love, the gesture he had not been able to make that day so long ago when he could not answer. Only like this, Edward Cavan's will gone, dead, could we be allowed to help, to support, to lift, to love. Pen, sitting at the back, saw his face, strained by the physical effort he was making, but at the same time dreadfully grieving. Why can't I love him? she thought, aching at the barrier between them. What is it that separates us?

They all turned to watch the four young men and their burden out through the open doors. They waited like people who have said a final good-bye and watched a living person go away forever, at loose ends, not knowing how themselves to get up and go, to break the spell.

The snuffing out of the four candles touched Grace Kimlock like a cold wind. She got quickly up and went out as if she were being driven out. How strange to feel the icy October air outside, how strange too and lost she was, afraid to be seen with the tears streaming down her cheeks, running wildly to a taxi alone.

It was so utterly finished for Edward and so utterly unfinished for her, abandoned, wholly abandoned here as if in a strange city, with nowhere to go, she felt—for her own house had become like an asylum to hold madness and inconsolable grief.

"Where to, ma'am?" the driver asked patiently.

"I don't know, anywhere—just drive along the river for a while."

She felt cut off, felt that if perhaps they could have followed the body to the cemetery, seen the earth cast upon it, then she would not have suffered like this, such utter and frightful isolation. But by now the coffin was halfway to the train and would travel miles and miles before it was laid to rest beside Edward's mother in Medfield. They were driving under her beloved plane trees now, little yellowish leaves swept up into the gutters and the river leaden gray, ruffled by the wind, past the bridges, the white and red Harvard Houses. The familiar sights were soothing, the boy in a scull alone was soothing—she sat up and leaned at the window to watch him, blowing her nose—the relief it was, after stifling her tears, the relief of being able to make the comfortable blowing noise!

"Whose funeral was it, ma'am?" the driver, sensitive to her change of mood, asked now.

"Professor Cavan."

"The guy who jumped under a subway train the other day?"

"Yes."

"Gee," said the driver, "tough going . . ."

He was a fat middle-aged man, she noticed, with many wrinkles round his eyes. He looked kind and rather tired and easy-going, and she thought how restful it is to talk to a stranger when one is desperate, restful because one is not responsible and nothing one says matters.

"I go past those buildings every day—Harvard," he said, "and think about all the rich boys up there, studying, learning everything, rowing on the river, taking their time." He laughed a slightly self-conscious laugh. "I never even finished grade school myself. Funny that one of them, a professor, you say, would get desperate. He must have been in a bad way. He was rich too, by what I read in the paper. You'd think he could have taken a vacation——"

The total incongruity of this in relation to Edward rushed in on Grace Kimlock like fresh air in a stifling room. She discovered that she was smiling.

"You can turn back now," she announced, giving him her address. "I'd better go home. Somebody might telephone," she said, suddenly hopeful. "I must be there."

X

Julia and Damon walked home in silence. Now that it was over, the occasion which had supported them, Damon looked haggard and frantic. Julia felt completely passive, an automaton walking step by step across the Common, thrown back into life from the moment of peace, of communion in the church, feeling exhausted as if she could sleep for weeks and not sleep out the exhaustion at the bone. She noticed Damon swinging his arms, playing with his watch chain, like a nervous puppet, adjusting his watch to the Memorial Hall clock as they passed it, scanning the sky, casting, she knew, anxious glances at her, half irritated by her silence.

"Well," he said, obviously relieved as they turned into their own path, "that's over," but it was not clear whether he meant Edward's funeral or their uncomfortably silent walk.

"Is it? I feel it's just beginning," and she did not know which she was answering, for her question fitted them both.

"I must see to the furnace," he said, evading her. "It's beastly cold all of a sudden, Julia."

The heart has gone, Julia thought, in a kind of panic. The heart has just gone. We're left here alone.

When he came upstairs from the cellar she had two old-fashioneds ready.

"I thought—a drink . . ." she said, afraid now that it had been the wrong idea. Perhaps it would be safer not to talk.

"Wonderful." Damon was tearing open the mail, flinging envelopes carelessly torn open into the wastebasket, then he sat down with the *New Yorker*, unfolded it eagerly and began to look at the jokes. It seemed as if he were looking for life, as if they dropped life along the way and now he would pick it up again. Just then he laughed aloud. "Look at this, Julia—it's perfect."

She looked at it, a George Price woman shooting a terrifyingly alive lobster with a pistol. It was very funny, but she couldn't laugh. The laugh stuck in her throat like a bone.

"Don't you think it's funny?" he pursued her in a grieved tone. "Life goes *on*, Julia," he said crossly. "I can't help it."

"I'm sorry. I just can't react. The machine has stopped functioning, Damon. Give me a little time."

He was pulling at his eyebrows sourly, drinking his drink too fast. The heart has gone, she thought again, in panic. We have never loved each other.

"People should be at their own funerals," he said.

"Edward would have lived—what a crazy thing to imagine —if he had known what his funeral would be like." He said it half-humorously.

"It did seem for a moment as if we were sharing, as if we were part of one another. It was that old familiar Donne, wasn't it?" Talk welled up in her like a saving grace. The dreadful arid desert was somehow crossed. They could avoid the emptiness if they talked loudly enough, long enough, drank enough.

"That—and just the people—Tanner and Wadsworth up from Columbia—quite a thing, that—and Warlock," Damon said with satisfaction as if each of these names were a medal to be pinned on Edward's chest. He killed himself, but Warlock came to the funeral, Julia thought bitterly. "Pretty lonely for Isabel, I must say. And now she's got to spend the afternoon trying to get the will straightened out. I hear it's a mess. The lawyers will get everything they can for the family, of course, and that's not what Edward wanted."

"He's an unconscionably long time a-dying." Julia wished that it were really over, that they would not have to talk about it any more, yet she knew they would have to talk about it still for a long, long time, get under these surfaces to their own wounds and somehow lick them clean.

"What a queer thing to say!"

"Was it? I guess I resent this feeling of carrying his death all the time inside me, like a dead foetus—when shall we be free of it, Damon?"

"Oh for Christ's sake, Julia. He's dead now. That's what funerals are for, to make it final—didn't you feel at all relieved? I did." He was quite cross. She had known he would be.

"Yes, I'm sure you did." You move so fast, Damon, do you ever catch up with yourself? she wanted to ask. But what was the use of hurting him now?

"You sound quite bitter."

"Do I? I didn't mean to. I'd better get us some lunch. Pour yourself another drink— I'll only be a minute." But am I right always to smooth things over, never to be honest with him? she asked herself, busy in the kitchen, mixing the salad. Whatever we are, we are together. If he fails, I've failed him. When you marry someone you become a kind of Siamese twin—a woman does, anyway. These were her thoughts as she laid the table, set out the salads, the glasses of milk, the bread and butter. But when she called Damon in, she saw at once that it had been a mistake to leave him alone. He was sitting hunched over, a cigarette burned almost down to the end in his mouth, and when he looked up at her, she instinctively lowered her eyes, made shy by the nakedness of his misery.

"Come along and have some lunch," she said gently.

"I'm not hungry."

"Well, come along anyway and talk to me while I eat. I'm starving." So she lifted him, cajoled him like a sick child.

He groaned, then came and put an arm round her casually. "Precious love," he said, "what would I do without you?" Yes, when he was down to the lowest ebb, he needed her, she thought, and as always she was stirred, she was alive with feeling for him, the instinctive reaction of a nurse to a wound. But would he ever come back to her in love when he felt well, powerful, when he had something to give?

He ate his lunch ravenously, as he talked, as it all

poured out. "It was that Donne thing—I thought of how things were back there in thirty-six—Spain—Edward and I used to go out as a team and talk to church groups all over the state. Do you remember? Drive back late at night and talk. The Al Smith campaign too—the first Roosevelt campaign. Where has it all gone, Julia? God knows, there was plenty of opposition. We were a small enough minority. But it was a clean clear struggle—or seemed to be. I expect we were fooled about Spain and that was the beginning of the mess. . . ." He was not looking at her, but beyond her now, into his own history.

"Really only the Catholics and the Communists can be quite clear in their minds now," she answered. "Everything in between, everything that will not take refuge in a dogma, close the windows and doors, is in jeopardy, in flux— What shall we leave the children?"

"The instinct to resist oppression, whatever form it takes," he came back with a bounce.

It was thus that she loved him, when he suddenly pulled himself up short, shot out with basic conviction, putting a huge pat of butter on his roll and eating it in one mouthful, the spring of vitality in the man! She could see him swinging himself up on his own words as on a ladder —like an acrobat.

"Edward would have agreed with that," she said warmly. "Maybe we've become too complicated, maybe we have to get back to such simple ideas—love, generosity— whatever the risk—"

"Could I have called him back?" Damon asked her straight out.

The question came as a shock. She had no time to prepare an answer. "Darling, I don't know——"

"He called me a coward and a cheat—that's what it amounted to."

"You called him a fuzzy-minded fool—it's poison to remember," she went on quickly, "you were too angry, each of you to say anything worth remembering, Damon. That *is* the truth, and you know it is."

"But if Edward and I could get that angry, could hurt each other that much, then what a world we live in—it's that, Julia, the wild animals we are becoming——"

"I know. . . ."

"What's left?" he said very quietly. The room lurched around them. Everything solid seemed to be dissolving, so Julia felt. Yet she clung to the little scattered pieces of truth, she tried to fit them together. She leaned back and closed her eyes. "You don't really think Edward was right, do you?" All his self-doubt rose up in his question, and she opened her eyes to meet his across the table.

"No. I think he was wrong. How shall I say it? Rationally wrong, somehow right all the same, for himself, in himself. It's like Grace Kimlock. It's much easier to be that uncompromising person than to be you, Damon. It's harder to stand in the middle and try to see clearly, to admit—we have to *admit* it—that we were blind to the danger of communism, that we did not want to see the truth. It's hard to admit that. I know what it cost you to get out of the Progressive Party, even if Edward didn't, couldn't know it." They had not spoken out so honestly to each other for a long time.

The coffee bubbled in the percolator. It was warm here in the big old-fashioned kitchen. And Julia looked around it gratefully, at the pots of African violets on the window sill, at the Currier and Ives calendar of Thanksgiving Day on the wall. She felt released, freed from some prison, the prison of her narrow resentment of Damon. Two days ago she would have been incapable of the real inner gesture of respect and love from which her words had come. If things were right at the center, mightn't one from there reach out into the world in concentric circles? Did it all in the end come back to personal relationships after all? She felt his eyes on her face like a touch, was suddenly shy.

"You're reading my thoughts," she said, blushing, hearing his delighted laugh.

"Oh Julia . . ." He came round the table and kissed the top of her head, then went to get the coffee off the stove. More than the kiss this meant, I love you. For it was rarely that Damon helped her in any way about the kitchen or house. When he did, it was like an endearment.

"Thank you, darling."

They drank their coffee in silence, for there was no longer the driving need to batter down barriers with words.

"That Isabel is a very attractive woman," Damon said, leaning back in his chair, relaxed, smoking a cigarette.

"I suppose she is." Julia hesitated. "I felt so sorry for her. She seemed like a person from the moon—do you suppose she has ever thought about any of this—except to be annoyed with Edward for exposing the family? She seemed so"—Julia discarded the word "innocent" and searched for another—"intact—yes, that's it. She seemed so intact."

"She looked on us as specimens, that was clear," Damon said with a faraway look in his eyes which Julia knew well.

"It's just as well, darling, that she will be leaving soon and can't discover that you're flesh and blood."

"You see too much, Julia," he was half-amused, half-irritated.

"You're pretty transparent, my friend."

"Yes." But his thoughts were running on. "Edward was intact too. Something held them back, stopped them in that family. Oh, Julia, if Edward could have looked at a woman like that——"

"Don't," Julia said. She couldn't bear this. It seemed queer, almost sacrilegious while the coffin hurtled across the country in the train. "Let him rest in peace."

What had he wanted of her all those years, when the children were babies and he had come to sit in the living room at any odd time of day, just to sit there, smoking and talking, and watching her, making her slightly uncomfortable? At one time, she supposed, she had been on the point of falling in love with him, with the warmth of his understanding, with something young and very pure that flowed out from him, so guarded, so shy. It crossed her mind like a pang that she had never taken him in her arms, never hugged him hard, not passionately, but just for love, that all such contact could not take place because of something in him. The loneliness of it welled up inside her and suddenly she put her head down on her hands and began to cry.

"Julia, what is it? Don't, for God's sake." She knew he couldn't bear her tears. It made Damon wild with irritation when she cried.

"It's—the s-sep-separateness, it's the l-loneliness—" not just Edward, all of us, she thought, human beings.

"I've got to work," said her husband, making his escape.

XI

Isabel was ashamed at her own relief. Ever since the funeral she had been buoyed up like an actress who has got through a first night safely after the agonies of nerves and who has come through the fiery furnace of the critics comparatively unscathed. Now she could turn her heart toward home—she would take a plane the next morning. She would no longer have to wear the mask of their grief, nor listen to their interpretations of her brother's life and death, but only to find her own. She was free. In fact she was borne up now by a kind of excitement as she made her way through the narrow cliffs of downtown Boston, busy, grimy, but giving her a sense of security, of a world she could understand. Here Cambridge, the University, were as she wished them to be, unreal, noble no doubt, oh yes, touching, even important in their way, but here she felt, looking up at the serried windows of lawyers' offices and firms of all kinds, here, the business of the world got done. This was real in a way she could better understand, which did not frighten her.

Almost she looked forward to the meeting ahead, in which it seemed, she would have to go over the will with Edward's lawyer. This would be a factual affair, a matter of signing documents. Pain, confusion, guilt—these would be formally held at bay. There would be no terrifying old lady with piercing eyes to read her thoughts, no foreign delicate old man whose clear blue eyes accused her of things she could not even imagine. Last night she had gone to bed in a state of exhaustion, wondering how these people managed to live in an atmosphere of such strain, such self-accusation, constantly worrying about responsibilities which seemed to her nebulous in the extreme. What did it matter really whether some physics professor voted for Truman or for Wallace? And why would doing either one be called treachery? She was willing to grant that Edward had been probably a wonderful professor, but wasn't that enough? And why did they have to rub it in, insist, beat her over the head with it? It seemed to her that night that these people elevated talk into a semblance of action and mistook words for deeds. But this, as her husband often said, was the trouble with intellectuals anyway. "They build their own mazes and get lost in them," he had said more than once, with a comfortable chuckle. How childish it all seemed to her, just as they had appeared to her like children that night at the Phillipses', precocious children who did not know anything about life. It was another thing to perform a delicate operation on a lung, to heal the sick as Henry did. That, she felt, was real. And if these people

232

ever went into politics and got their hands dirty, that might seem real too.

She was walking quite fast and realized that these thoughts had taken her past the huge stone door of the office building where she was bound. Now, turning, going back, retracing her steps, she retraced her thoughts until she stood still, looking up at the huge wall above her and, for some reason, was forced to remember something else— that wave of exaltation which had lifted her for a moment in the church. Well, one must be allowed such moments— that was what a funeral was for. Now, standing on the street watching a newsboy call his papers in a halfhearted way and the traffic bumper to bumper in the narrow street, here in the noise and activity of real life, she felt that Dr. Willoughby's choice of the great passage from Donne had been an indulgence, a loving but inaccurate gesture toward Edward's beliefs. "No man is an Iland—" But no one ever was more an island, she thought, than poor dear Edward. In his isolation from ordinary human realities he had come to fatally wrong conclusions, as far as she could see. Could this be called "greatness"? No, it was time to face the facts.

Over there in Cambridge in the noble world of abstractions it had been moving for a moment; she had even wept. Here she saw it for what it was. "People don't crack up because they feel part of the world—that's just nonsense," she said, going through the revolving door in a swirl of self-assertion.

She was going to the sixteenth floor, an appropriate height from which to look down on the tragic facts, on which to examine Edward's final wishes. She had no idea how much of the money he had inherited was still available; she suspected that Edward had given most of it away long ago. But of course it would be very pleasant if there were a legacy. . . .

"Come in, Mrs. Ferrier." Mr. Wainwright was a small nervous man, very brisk and neat, wearing, Isabel noted a pink shirt and black tie with a gray flannel suit, which didn't go at all with his rather wizened kindly face and made him look rather like a monkey. There was someone else there, an elderly tight-lipped man who introduced himself as Mr. Rand and who came, she did not understand why, apparently from Iowa.

Mr. Wainwright offered her a cigarette from the silver box on his immaculate desk and apologized for bringing her here on the day of the funeral, "but I understand that you are anxious to catch a plane tomorrow."

"Yes, what do I have to do, Mr. Wainwright? Sign something?"

He leaned forward, to pull out a folder containing some papers which he opened on the desk. Then he took out a pair of old-fashioned steel-rimmed spectacles, put them on his nose and looked up over them at her with a faintly troubled air. All this was done methodically, slowly, and as if he was preparing a speech and did not know quite where to begin.

"The estate is some fifty thousand dollars, mostly in property, Mrs. Ferrier"—he peered at her kindly and interrupted himself. "Your brother was a very generous man," he said with a smile.

"I know that," she said quietly. She was calculating rapidly that he must have given away roughly a hundred thousand.

"Unfortunately, the will is not altogether clear. I believe we shall have to ask the Courts to appoint an administrator. You see, I'm afraid your brother was in a rather troubled mind and did not realize that there might be legal difficulties. As a matter of fact, there are two wills, one very much written over and the second one, which we take to be the real one, witnessed two years after it was made. This presents certain problems."

"I don't understand anything about all this. I leave it all to you, Mr. Wainwright. But may I ask just what is involved?"

"The main bequest is to Cornell College." Mr. Wainwright made something like a bow in Mr. Rand's direction. "Roughly thirty-five thousand dollars."

Mr. Rand leaned forward and coughed. "Cornell is deeply indebted to your brother, Mrs. Ferrier."

"Yes," Isabel said crisply, "I expect Harvard will be a bit miffed."

They exchanged a discreet smile. It was pleasant to be a part of the miffing of Harvard apparently.

"Edward owed everything to Cornell. He always said so," she added graciously.

"He left his library to Harvard, however," Mr. Wainwright added. "There are several bequests—including one to you Mrs. Ferrier—of one thousand dollars each." Isabel caught her breath. She knew now that she had hoped for much more. It was indecent to be disappointed, but she was disappointed. "There will be no problem about these. They are quite clear in both wills."

"What is the trouble then?"

"It's a matter of, roughly, five thousand dollars given to various organizations in which your brother took an interest. But unfortunately it's just here that there is some confusion—this is a codicil; it is crossed out and revised in three places. Money to be given to the Joint Anti-Fascist Refugee Committee seems now to be willed to"—Mr. Wainwright picked up a typewritten page much written over in ink, and looked at it, searching for the name—"*The Socialist Monthly*." He looked up with a question in his eyes.

"I know nothing about such things," Isabel said quickly.

Mr. Wainwright leaned back in his chair, placing the tips of his fingers together to make an arch.

"We would on the whole prefer that these questionable bequests—the writing is not clear and there seem evidences of hesitation—as well of course as the matter of witnesses—be settled by the Court. In such cases, it is usual for the family to be the beneficiary. The law, as you no doubt know, is apt to tend towards recognizing the rights of the family—when there is doubt, of course—and there *is* doubt, Mrs. Ferrier. Very considerable doubt, I might add."

"It's all rather unpleasant," Isabel said. "Who are these people? Won't they try to get the money?" It sounded rather crass.

"Yes," Mr. Wainwright pursed his lips, "that would not be without precedent," and he smiled a small smile. "This sort of organization, more especially, is apt to be rather touchy. They will consider it a matter of principle, no doubt."

Mr. Rand coughed, crossed his knees and assumed an air of judicial consideration. "If, as I understand it, the will reads that all amounts not directly specified are to go to Cornell—please forgive me, Mrs. Ferrier"—he smiled at her indulgently—"but you understand that I am speaking for the college, and must defend its interest—then, I would think that Cornell might have a prior claim?"

Money, Isabel thought, does queer things to people. She felt hot all over. She felt unaccountably angry—surely not about five thousand dollars? Why did she feel so angry then?

"Well, that will be up to the Courts, surely," she said. "It's none of our business."

"Precisely. With your permission," Mr. Wainwright included them both, "I shall go ahead and ask that an administrator be appointed."

"Well then," Isabel said, shutting her bag, and pulling on a glove, "there is nothing more for us to do, is there?"

"Not at the moment, Mrs. Ferrier."

"Surely I can go back tomorrow?" she asked in a panic. I have to go back, she thought. I can't stay here. They're all enemies. Even Cornell in the last few moments had become her enemy. I'm all alone here. It's disgusting to be made to fight about five thousand dollars.

"I see no reason why you can't," Mr. Wainwright said soothingly, "but"—he took off his glasses and rubbed them with a handkerchief, rather ruefully—"you will probably have to come back—if the will is contested—and I fear —I fear we must expect that."

"Oh. . . ." Isabel felt stunned. Was there no way out? "And what if the family gives up all claims?"

"I wouldn't advise that," said Mr. Wainwright, sitting up quite straight in his chair, "No, I wouldn't advise that," he said. The implication was that justice was not to be trifled with by any human impulses of irritation or generosity. "And after all, five thousand dollars, Mrs. Ferrier. Perhaps I shouldn't say this—I say it as a friend of your brother's and *ex officio*, so to speak—your brother was perhaps not always quite sound. I mean, these organizations, two of them at least are on the Attorney General's list. We would not really wish your brother's money to go into such hands, would we, Mrs. Ferrier?"

"Certainly not," said Mr. Rand emphatically.

"It's his will after all, not ours," she heard herself saying to her own astonishment. "Maybe that was what he wanted."

"Ah yes, of course, no doubt," Mr. Wainwright said hastily, "but the question may be whether—how shall I say it?—whether it was really his will, I mean—forgive me, but his mind was evidently somewhat unbalanced, Mrs. Ferrier——"

"If that can be proved, I presume it would invalidate the entire will," she said with a smile, not looking at Mr. Rand though the smile, a smile of triumph was meant for him to swallow if he could. She had taken a dislike to Mr. Rand.

Mr. Wainwright looked rather smugly at his hands.

"You have a point, Mrs. Ferrier. You have an undoubted point."

Doubt? Confusion? Guilt? Had she imagined that they would not come up with her in the elevator to the sixteenth floor? That they would be left behind on the street with the newsboys? Was nothing of Edward to remain pure? Was it all to be dragged through the press—even his last will and testament? Even this, then, was a mess like all the rest. She felt it like ashes to eat, inside her, all around her, and she suddenly bowed her head, hid her face behind one hand as if to hide from the exposure, from life itself.

"Couldn't he have left a clear will?" she groaned. But no, it was all mixed together, his body, his beliefs, his money, his blood all thrown down for the dogs to tear. There was no escape from what Edward had done. It was everywhere.

Mr. Rand and Mr. Wainwright exchanged a glance.

"You must get some rest, Mrs. Ferrier," Mr. Rand said quite gently. "All this is very upsetting for you."

"Yes," she said drily, getting up, "yes, it is."

She had the key to Edward's apartment in her pocket. Professor Fosca had given it to her and suggested that she might like to go there, perhaps to take back with her some small object. The settling of the estate would no doubt involve the sale of his belongings, but meanwhile there was no reason why as a member of the family she should not take what she wanted. Actually, last night, she had thought with pleasure of finding something to give to each of the friends she had met; she had looked forward to this one small positive gesture she might make while she was here. Now, although she hailed a taxi and gave the address on Mt. Vernon Street quite casually, she wished she could avoid this confrontation of things, this voluntary immersion into Edward's atmosphere. She wanted above all to get away, to flee before some final defense she held hard against her like a shield, was battered down. And, as the taxi turned up Park Street and she found herself among grass and trees with the fine brick façade of the State House and its golden dome before her, she felt quite definitely that she was moving out of one world and into another. In the world of office buildings, she had been in some way, protected—or thought she was. She had not been prepared

for the violence of emotion which gathered quite irration-
ally in her around Edward's money, but still this was a
matter of resenting the sordid quarrel ahead, a business
matter. Business might be sordid, but it could be dealt with
rationally. It was, in essence, impersonal. And as far as the
will went, the responsibility, thank goodness would be
with the law. It did not lie inside her own consciousness.
If there was guilt, it was Edward's for allowing his conscientious scruples to affect in such a disturbing way the
matter-of-fact business of a will.

Now the taxi took her like fate into a world of private
houses. She could not but feel their privacy, their distinction, the ineffable reserved air of them, brass knockers
brightly polished, white doors gleaming to set off the warm,
old, delightfully various red of the brick. Why had Edward
chosen to live here rather than in Cambridge? Was it a
deliberate gesture of setting himself apart from the academic world? Was this apartment, where in a moment she
would be, the habitation of some part of him held in reserve, not shared with students and faculty—in fact, his
private life?

Isabel stood in the street and looked up at the long
French windows on the second floor. There was no way
of knowing from here that the apartment was frightfully
empty, that it lay there, lying in wait, ready to pounce,
ready to say "Intruder" to anyone who now forced the door.
She felt the key in her hand. After all, she did not have to
do this. She could walk down the hill intact. No one would
ever know. She could escape whatever lay in wait for her
up one flight of stairs, the flight of stairs down which Edward had walked with his life in his hands four days before.
The temptation was very great. Almost she did not resist

it. But now she was looking so hard at the windows, it seemed as if they held her like eyes and she could not, quite, turn away. It was not, after all, possible to do that.

She read the name on the mailbox, saw that it was stuffed with mail, but she had no key and could not open it. Dead letters, she thought—what questions did they ask which would never be answered? What cries for help or consolation or advice lay there? She was conscious suddenly that death breaks an enormous delicate web, that thousands of tiny threads which held Edward to earth had all been snapped, and it was not only his life, but all the lives that touched it, willfully snapped and left dangling. What anguish great enough to make one able to do this? She leaned against the door, pushing her way in and very slowly, as if she carried a heavy weight, difficult to balance, mounted the stairs, touching the wall on her right as she went. And as she climbed step by step, it seemed with each step as if something fell away, so that year by year had gone when she reached the landing and stood at the door itself, not Isabel Ferrier, but Isabel Cavan—a young girl whose mother had just died, whose brother had just died— absolutely naked and alone and terrified. It was all she could do not to cry out, "Edward, where are you?" as she opened the door and stood with her back against it, closed behind her, blinded by tears, by the aching need of his voice, so warm always in greeting, aching with the need of someone to lead her to a chair, make her a cup of tea, someone to be there, not this utter emptiness and silence.

The tears were an affront now that she was all eyes, needed above all to see. She forced them back, rubbed her face harshly with a handkerchief. Then she sat down in an armchair by the empty hearth. Sun poured in through the long windows on the velvet curtains faded to amber, not a diffused light but a long wide beam in which motes of dust danced, and which fell on the bookcases and lit up a long row of Henry James's novels in dark-blue bindings. Just in front of her over the mantel was a painting of Southern France—or perhaps New Mexico she thought as she looked at it—a small orchard through which one saw the outlines of a bare brown hill rising, but all this set low on the canvas so that what gave the painting its quality was the wide expanse of sky, the spaces it managed to suggest. On a low table beside her a copy of the *New Republic* carried an ugly black headline "The Un-American Dream." She turned it over. It seemed, at the moment, irrelevant. For what caught her now after the first rush of emotion, was the extraordinary quiet aliveness of the room. She picked up the ash tray beside her, inlaid enamel, bright blue and white, and turned it over. This Edward must have brought back from the Balkans two summers before. Perhaps someone had given it to him—he loved little presents, presents that meant places and people. She recognized over the bookcase a Picasso pen-and-ink drawing which he had bought while still in college—and the awful row there was when their father found what it had cost. But that Chinese horse —that she had not seen before. She was feeling her way slowly into the room, into its life. It was not what she had expected—what had she expected? Some sign of violent disturbance, of breakdown? It was almost suspiciously calming here. A man did not walk out of a room like this to commit suicide. Whatever tore Edward to pieces was somewhere else, and so it seemed almost that he was not here, that what she had feared, the confrontation, would not take place. And it was too still, a stillness through which

242

the roar of a car going up the hill in second broke with ugly harsh insistence, bringing her to her feet.

Edward, she felt herself crying out inwardly again, where are you? In the bedroom, the narrow Spanish bed with its carved head, lay there like a corpse, a heavy dark green spread over it, the corners tucked in under the pillow. Beside the bed, a pile of books, books which in the final analysis had not been able to help him. She noticed among them a leather-bound *Imitation of Christ* which his mother had given him at Christmas the year before she died. It had been obviously much read. There was a Bible, a volume of critical essays by a man she had never heard of, a biography of Beatrice Webb, four small volumes of poetry by modern poets. One, a first book obviously, was dedicated to E.C., she noticed. The others were Wallace Stevens, Marianne Moore and a worn and much-marked copy of Yeats's *Collected Poems*. In the old days when she was Isabel Cavan, Edward had liked to read things aloud to her, and she opened the Yeats half fearfully as if she expected some ghost to rise from the pages, some answer to her question to be spoken aloud. But Edward was not going to give himself away, even now. The book was full of notes but they read like notes for a review. And this was not the moment for poetry, she thought, pushing aside the pang for the girl she had been, Isabel Cavan, who read poetry late into the night and who had a brother alight with enthusiasm for it. All that was long ago, too long to be resurrected here in the dead apartment, the emptiness.

Instead she moved over to the desk, set against the wall. Here she sat down facing his wall, her chin in her hands. There was nothing at all on the desk, not even a notebook or pencil. She reached out a hand to open a drawer, half opened it, then shut it again. She had not come here to pry. For what then? She sat facing the wall, absolutely still, not even thinking, as if here she had come to a dead end in herself. Imagination had stopped working like a run-down clock.

Yet actually she felt tremendously agitated, so nervous that she dared not look round. The apartment was full of presence, of intimation, of some silent communication. And suddenly she knew that what it communicated was absence. There was no one here. There had been no one here when Edward was alive. He had lain alone on the narrow bed unable to sleep (he had always suffered from insomnia even as a child). It was a dead house with a suffering, violently alive man locked in it, unable to get out, sitting in front of a wall. And all the lovely things, and their associations, the friendships they memorialized, the places, the times were there as if to plead against loneliness, to keep loneliness, separation, isolation at bay, as he himself held it rigidly away from him like a poison, flung himself into his work, made the careful notes in the volumes of poems early in the morning, or rushed off to a meeting of one of those suspect organizations where, she knew suddenly, he perhaps felt some communion, some temporary fugitive sense of common identity.

Why? That was the question she asked the wall. But walls have no answer and without knowing it, without being aware of what she was doing she looked around for a mirror. There was none. There was only the shadow of herself, Isabel Cavan, standing behind Isabel Ferrier. She had not come here so fearfully then to be confronted by Edward, or Edward's life but by her own. The answer to the question was inextricably mixed up with other questions, and these other questions were what she had feared. "No man is an Iland." Edward was not. Somewhere he was "attached to the Maine," and in a flash of realization she saw the coffin, lurching in some freight car, but moving slowly towards its rest in the grave beside their mother. He might have been confused at the end about where and to whom to leave his money, but about this there had been no confusion. He had asked to be buried beside his mother. How could so much light hold so much darkness in it? For their mother, it seemed, had been a creature of the light. Isabel never thought of her without thinking of gardens, of sunlight on flowers, of the patient hands, rough from much gardening, transplanting seedlings or putting stakes in to hold up the falling chrysanthemums. She could not think of her without thinking of the way her eyes brimmed with light—there was no other word, very large blue eyes that sometimes looked gray and sometimes deep blue, it depended on the time of day, on what she was wearing. And she could not think of her without the acute memory of the high tension, the strain of wild poetry in her which even marriage to their father had not subdued.

Must one hate one's father if one loves one's mother? Edward's answer, given without hesitation, had proved to be "yes." In the marrow of his bones even when he was a small child he had been aware that she was stifled, that something that should have been free and glowing was bound back, held still by a marriage where passion had not been able to transcend almost complete incompatibility. What it had done to Isabel Cavan was to make her long above all for a life without strain, for peace, for a relationship without ecstasies but also without tensions. She had always been the peacemaker, moving between her father and mother like a little thread, sewing them together again, unwilling to allow them the separation both perhaps deeply desired. What had it done to Edward, this marriage he had entered into and suffered as if it were his own— even as quite a small boy. It had made his loyalty intransigent and narrow, deepened him, tightened him, matured him—and, in the end, murdered him. It was the wall before which he sat, in his fifties. Whatever his friends across the river might say about the state of the world, the tensions—we find our way out into the world from childhood. The pattern is set there. And his pattern had been to witness, to suffer wholly with and for his mother, but to be unable to act to save her. To be a witness, what could suggest a more terrible responsibility? To have no human responsibilities such as marriage and children had been to her, but to be left, naked, the witness always, the one who is aware and can do nothing?

For a brief time in college it had seemed that he would be able to free himself, but his mother's death, the illness kept from him at her wish, so that he might accomplish all that he dreamed that year in Oxford—that had locked the prison door fast. You can't save people from their lives, Isabel said to herself. Mother was wrong there—binding him hand and foot where freedom had been her intention. . . . Well, he was out of the prison now.

Isabel walked out of the bedroom and went to the French windows and pushed them open. She lit a cigarette and stood smoking it. Someone passing by, she thought, would imagine I lived here. She smiled. It was almost a shock to lay for a moment the image of her own house against this one—that sprawling modern house with its swimming pool, its deep freeze to which packs of children went constantly to open pints of ice cream, air and sun and wind flowing in and out, and cocktails for Henry when he came home, tired, wanting only to relax over a game of bridge after dinner, untroubled, in the midst of life, voting the straight Republican ticket, secure behind the walls of their life. Walls? Yes, said Isabel Cavan, taking a long look at California from Boston, at Isabel Ferrier's life from Isabel Cavan's. We have paid something for peace of mind. What? Her eyes, roving round the room again as if in search for something fell on the *New Republic* she had turned over. She went and picked it up, disliking the rough cheap paper and the thick black headlines. It seemed to shout and yell, so one could not trust what it said, yet she found herself reading—people were losing their jobs, professors in state universities, because they believed in the things Edward had believed in, as he, driven by the same guilt no doubt, guilt at their own safety and immunity, by their desire for "solidarity"—she remembered suddenly Edward using that word, apropos of Walt Whitman, was it? Long, long ago.

Here, in this room, so empty of any human ties, swung as it were a little above the human world, where her brother, the witness, had sat in his silent agonies of isolation, she felt suddenly dizzy with what she saw, what opened out, the whole world like a cry, like a need—

But this is an emotional response, she told herself quickly. Unless Edward had committed suicide, I would not feel it. . . .

XII

Because he hadn't seen Pen since the awful thing happened
—and that was three days ago now, George counted—he
felt as if he were coming back to her from some strange
land, from a long journey. He was always nervous as he
turned the corner onto Shepard Street and looked up at the
lights in the dormitories. There was something about this
female world, about stepping into Eliot and being looked
over by the girl at the switchboard and the one or two
other fellows sitting in self-consciously relaxed attitudes in
the living room waiting for their dates, which made him
feel out of place, old and cynical on the one hand, on the
other just ill at ease and gauche. It had happened more than
once that one of his English students was there, for in-
tance, and this for some reason was especially embarrass-
ing. He adjusted his tie, scuffed at some leaves like a school-
boy and turned up the cement walk, through the big white
pillars at the door, berating himself for his embarrassment.

He asked in a firm voice for Miss Pen Wallace and sat down on the bench in the hall to wait. For once there was no one around.

"Hi, how've you been?" she was saying, as she stood up. They exchanged the meaningless greetings meant for the lighted hall: "I like your dress," "Oh, good, you've seen it enough times, God knows." These words, under which their real selves floated in suspense, carried them through the door. But as soon as they had turned off the cement path onto the brick of the street, George took her hand hard in his, and they walked like that as far as Avon Street in an oppressed silence. George wondered sometimes if she had any idea how charged such moments were for him, how locked up and stifled he felt as the great rush of his feeling when he first saw her, even after a few hours, was being dammed up to reasonable proportions.

"Oh Pen . . ." he said.

"Where are we going, darling?" Her light bright voice denied the appeal, but that was the way she always was. She had to get used to him too, to get back to being human after those long hours of concentrating on a translation of Horace or some medieval Latin text. George reminded himself of this and tried not to feel rejected.

"I'm broke. Beer at the Midget?"

"That seems to be our direction." She was looking around her with that eager look, as if she could not have enough of life, as if when she emerged from the dorm everything hit her freshly. He followed her glance to the white frame house they were passing, the old pear tree, the rather wild garden where uncut stalks of autumn flowers stood about, and a cat with its paws tucked in sat on the step.

"Oh, I do love Cambridge," she said. "I do love these houses, and all the trees. Who do you suppose lives there?"

"Some old maid, I expect." She felt the unresponsiveness to this game they usually played together with enthusiasm.

"I know, George," she answered something he had not said, "only, let's wait till we're settled. Then we can really talk. Forget it for a few moments, darling"—she turned her face, looking at him gravely—"it's not that I don't know," and she slipped her hand through his again, so it was all right. But after that, they both felt a little stiff and walked fast as if they were hurrying to a shelter.

Once Pen stopped to smell leaves burning somewhere in a distant garden and sighed. "Sometimes I feel as if I were saying good-bye to everything every moment. It's awful to be a senior. I didn't know how awful it would be."

This brought back to George his recent doubts—would he be here next year himself? But he would not start off on this with Pen. It was too shameful. What did it matter whether he got his instructorship or not? And he swore suddenly under his breath.

"What?"

"Nothing."

The bright lights of the Midget were ahead of them now. But this was home, unlike the dormitory, and they walked in boldly, looking around to see who was there, hailing a couple in another booth and then sitting down opposite each other for that long look of arrival, what Pen meant by being "settled."

"You look awful, George darling. What have you been doing?"

"Nothing"—he frowned—"drinking—thinking—hating those lousy little Groton boys who don't bother to show up for English A." But he didn't smile, just ordered two dark ales in a businesslike way and lit Pen's cigarette and his own.

"Well, you certainly have a champion in Alice Evans." Pen, he knew, was trying to get him to smile, but he wouldn't fall for it. "She bores us to tears with tales of how wonderful you are, and when Towser came to lunch," she went on rather nervously, "the poor guy had to listen to how wonderful *you* were till he actually got quite cross."

There was no rise in George, susceptible though he was about his teaching, catching at the crumbs of praise, like any other of the teaching fellows who lived in a strange state of isolation, sinking or swimming on their own, and as touchy as prima donnas.

"You don't need to, Pen," he said in a tired voice. "Not tonight."

"Sorry, I guess I got off on the wrong foot. I guess I'm scared," she said, puffing at her cigarette as if she had never smoked one before, then suddenly stamping it out as if it tasted bad. "I guess this has been a pretty tough time for you, George. I'm sorry, dear."

The waitress brought their beer and George felt the tight knot inside him relax a fraction. When Pen said "dear," she meant it. "Darling" meant nothing at all.

"I'd just got to the point when I thought I knew what I was doing— I almost called you that night, I was so excited"—he found it unexpectedly difficult to talk. It was as if there were some obstruction in his throat and his voice came out deep and queer which bothered him— "Now it's like a whirlpool. I just go round and round."

"It's thrown the whole college, George. It's not just

you. Girls in the dorm cried and carried on like nobody's business." There was, he noticed, a slight edge in her voice.

"Well, you understood something about it at that seminar, didn't you? Do you remember what you said, that it was altogether different from any course you'd had, didn't seem like Harvard?" He asked sternly. He had not liked her tone.

"I'm glad you took me. Awfully glad." But she was following some track of her own. "What I don't get is the political angle, George."

It struck George like a blow, the coldness of her tone, the perfect detachment. There was something relentless about this girl, something relentless even in her eagerness, her brilliance, something which didn't want to give, didn't want to feel. It was their old battle, but now on another level than sex. Recognizing it, he felt exhausted.

"I guess I'm too confused to talk," he said miserably.

"But to commit suicide for political reasons seems to me crazy," she pleaded. "Don't you think so?"

"Masaryk did."

"Who was he?" she asked absent-mindedly.

"Good God, Pen, you live in this world, don't you?" He was suddenly furious. "Maybe you don't."

"Well, don't blow up. I remember now, of course. But he was right in the middle of things. There was no way out for him. This seems like such a waste." The warm light flowed back into her face, and she said quite humbly, "Talk to me, George. Try to tell me. I've felt so queer and lonely, not being really part of all this. Except"—she reached across to him with a look—"I've known what it means to you in your work."

252

"It's not that," he said quickly, brushing his work aside.

"Tell me, George, try to tell me," she said, becoming again the girl he loved and not the antagonist he had seen a moment ago, the unyielding girl, the girl locked up against feeling.

"Well"—he did not know how to begin, where to begin—"you see, one of the things that bothers me is that I'm not a political person either. None of us are, really, are we?" He looked to her now for support, for justification. "I mean, my generation didn't have that kind of faith. Are we wrong, Pen, are we terribly wrong?" he asked desperately, and went on without waiting for her answer, "I have a feeling now that Cavan must have felt that nobody really cared, you know. Lately it must have been lonely to be himself, terribly lonely. The things he believed in aren't working out, you see."

"Did he talk about it?" Pen asked.

"No"—and then the taut look came back into George's face—"I expect he knew I wasn't really interested. Besides, you know how it is, I saw him in conferences—we had work to do." Sometimes he could see thought in Pen's face like something flowing across it, a tangible reality. "What are you thinking?"

"I don't know," she said, brushing her hair off her face with one hand, leaning forward so her face almost touched the beer glass, in that odd concentrated position he knew well, and found slightly irritating for he always had an impulse to say, "Sit up," she was so curled over, stoop-shouldered, turned inward. "They seem very young some-times——"

253

"They have something we haven't got. I think maybe partly they believed in the wars they fought——"

"My father, for instance," Pen said, going on where she had left off. This was their relationship, this meant they were in the groove, a kind of dual monologue in which they thought of things they would not have thought of alone, yet which seemed at times to have little connection with each other. "My father gets so het up, runs for office, works himself hoarse and exhausted and never gets anywhere."

"You never told me that. I thought your father raised some queer kind of flower——"

"Oh yes, wood peonies. But he goes on periodic political binges as well. He's a single-tax Republican—in a small Connecticut town. You can imagine!" Suddenly they were laughing. They drank their beer down soberly, but then each time they looked up and caught each other's eye they were overcome with laughter, why they didn't quite know, the folly of their parents' generation, perhaps, perhaps just pleasure in having come through to this easier moment, of being safe from all the problems for a moment, safe and altogether by themselves as if they were on an island of laughter alone.

"Oh, I do love you, Pen."

"I know, darling. . . ." She still had the laughter and he had lost it.

"No, you don't know. You don't really want to know, do you?" George asked gently.

"Talk about how young they are," she commanded, evading him.

"I know what you mean. It's like innocence. But Cavan was different—too intelligent perhaps. Why do I talk about him like this?" George broke into what he was saying, "It's disgusting."

"I don't see why."

"Everybody prying into him, trying to get underneath, trying to break it down and analyze it, something so awful he died because of it, and all we do is peer and pry—and don't know what it was, and never will know what it was—"

He had got Pen's real attention now and he felt it, like a rising wave of power inside him.

"Why did you love him so, George? What was it?"

"Did I love him?" George balked at the word. He was startled by it.

"Well, if you didn't, why are you so upset?" She could be so darned logical at times, it was peculiar.

"Well for one thing," he said in a hard voice, "he would have got me an instructorship next year, if you must know——"

"I've thought of that," she said gently. "But that's another thing. I mean your feeling about him."

"I'm sorry. Maybe his passion for excellence, the standard he set, the breadth and depth of the standard," he answered her now, on the rising wave. "For instance, this. Years ago when I was in a seminar. We read papers and he used to get up and stand at the window while we read them, or wander around sometimes. I read one of Thoreau's poems and right in the middle of one poem I stopped and said, 'God, that's good!' I just had to because the line struck me just at that moment. Cavan was sitting and he rapped hard on the table with his knuckles and said, 'Yes! Yes! Yes!' That was all, but I've never forgotten it, the concentrated passion of it. That was the quality he had as a teacher, and I begin to think he had it partly because he had it about everything. I mean, would he have cared in the same way about literature if he hadn't been involved in human affairs themselves? That's the real question, Pen."

"You mean we don't care enough? We're not, as he seems to have been, passionate people?—you mean, we're afraid?"

"Want to play it safe, don't stick our necks out, sit tight—all the rot about a sheltered life. Cavan as a professor at Harvard was never sheltered, never allowed himself to be."

"And cracked up," Pen interrupted the fine flow flatly.

"God damn it, yes, and maybe that's better than becoming a fossil!" George had raised his voice.

"What's eating you, George? Such profanity!" came a man's voice from the next booth. Hoffman's head appeared over it, assistant professor giving one of the Humanities courses. George flushed and subsided.

"I was talking about Edward Cavan," he said stiffly as Hoffman, conjured up like a puppet, stayed there, owlishly.

"Yes, the poor guy," Hoffman shook his head, "couldn't take it, I'm afraid. A bad business. You were working with him on your thesis, weren't you? Bad luck, old chap. I'm sorry," and with that, mercifully, Hoffman got up and took his check.

"You see what I mean?" George muttered after he had gone. "He's got about as much feeling as a stuffed cod. I suppose he thinks he may get promoted now." And then as if the full impact of this hit him after he'd said it, George sank back. "Imagine it, Pen! That idiot in Cavan's chair. Oh my God——"

"It is rather grim," Pen said earnestly, "but he won't get it of course. There must be a good many sharks after the dead body. He wouldn't really have a chance, would he?"

"I don't know." George waved to the waitress for another ale. "You're a cynical little piece aren't you?" he went on, glad now of a chance to change the subject.

"I don't think so. I save my strength. I should think you'd be dead at the end of the day, old chap, old boy," she mimicked Hoffman. "Take it easy, that's what I always say——"

"Oh by the way, Pen, an old bird called me up—what was her name Kitman? Armlock? Something like that. Some friend of Cavan's. I was awfully rude to her, I'm afraid— I was drunk, as a matter of fact. Ever hear of her?"

"Not Grace Kimlock?" Pen sat up straight for once.

"Yes—yes—that must have been it. Why, do you know her?"

"I've met her—she's a distant cousin on my mother's side. As a matter of fact, she's a good egg, George. You'd like her, and it's quite true—I remember now, Edward Cavan was always there. They must have been great friends. She's a loon about anything political. My father calls her raving mad and thinks she's a Communist. I wouldn't be surprised, as a matter of fact. I'll take you there if you like—if you care"—she seemed to hesitate now. "You might apologize in person."

"I'd like to," George said quickly. "I'd like to very much."

"She devours young men. You'd better look out. She'll have you running errands for the Party before you know it——"

"You're not serious, Pen? She's not really a Communist?"

"Of course not, silly. She's just one of these old Boston pinkos who trots up and down Beacon Hill to make speeches at State House committees and prides herself on knowing the Irish politicians by their first names and imagines that without her, no good would come of Massachusetts law. You know the type—as a matter of fact, she's quite a darling," Pen said unexpectedly. "I always meant to see more of her." She smiled across at him, happy because this was like a present she could give him. "You look bemused, darling."

"Gee, Pen, that's wonderful," he said again.

"I'll call her up tomorrow." Pen got up.

"But tomorrow isn't this minute. Sit down again. You haven't finished your beer."

"I've got to get back and study, George. I really must," she drank it down standing. "Come on. . . ."

It was the beginning of the end. Always when George saw Pen it seemed as if their meeting rose on a curve and then at a certain moment, the high point of the curve was passed. When was that moment? He had never been able to seize it, but only to realize that it was gone, that they were slipping down. In all this year they had come to no place of real understanding. Always he must wonder if she would let him kiss her at the door, just before the public dormitory world took her back again, never could he take anything for granted, even after all these months. He could feel her stiffening withdrawal as they turned in to Shepard Street and she lit a cigarette. "It's all a game," his roommate would say, "they do it on purpose, have it all figured out," but Pen was not like that. There was some wild natural force in her that made her leap away at a touch like a deer. She would not say that she loved him. She would never never say it. Now as they walked side by side in the damp autumn dark, walked past the lighted houses where safely married people sat and read, had a place of their own, George felt she was a stranger, a total stranger. Talking about Cavan hadn't helped. The only thing that might have helped would have been if he could have laid his head on her breast a moment and rested there.

"What are you laughing at?" she asked.

"Oh, the craziness of it all, the way people try to meet and communicate and never quite do," he said bitterly.

"Yes," she spoke quickly, "I know."

This was the moment to take her hand and pull her towards him in one splendid masterful gesture, but he was paralyzed, paralyzed by the dormitory lights, by the imminence of parting so his throat felt dry, and he walked very fast, almost running.

"I'm afraid I haven't been much help, darling." He could feel her quick breathing beside him and locked her hand into his, all the sexual impulse dying away, in the force of his feeling about Cavan.

"Some things, I guess, people go through alone. Talking doesn't really help. But it's all right, Pen." For one second he looked down into her clear, aloof gaze in which there was, after all, no tenderness because she was afraid to let it through.

And then, without even saying good night, he turned and ran down the path, wanting more than anything now to be alone, to be free of her, to smell the autumn night and walk himself into exhaustion.

"Good night," she called after him. When he turned back to look she was still there, and she waved.

On Garden Street, out of sight, he slowed down and took a deep breath. He was thinking now not of her at all, as if on the stream of his feeling for her, he had been carried out to a new understanding of Cavan. What if this kind of frustration and paralysis were not bound to one person and one's relation to them, but to everything around one? "These doors that close in one's face, this trying to get through as if one were a prisoner in a cell knocking patiently on the wall, but nobody answers. . . ."

Standing on the street where so many people lived, seeing how the light from the street lamp shone gold on the golden maple leaves, hearing the steady pulse of the crickets in the grassy gardens, this peace, this intimacy which was Cambridge enveloped him in its gentleness. The long tension he had held unbroken in himself for forty-eight hours was released. For a moment at least he stood outside his frustrating love for Pen and the confusing painful grief for Edward Cavan and felt consoled by simply being himself. He thought of his students and what he would say to them tomorrow. He felt that his one responsibility now, and it was Cavan who laid it upon him and whose death demanded it, was to get through, was not to be stopped, was to arrive at communion with other people somehow and at communion with a whole self in himself.

EPILOGUE:
NOVEMBER 1954

The old chestnut tree on Brattle Street had flowered and shed its leaves five times since Orlando Fosca had been so troubled when a branch was blown down, had had an impulse to go in and ask whether surgeons had been sent for, had stopped to see in the wounded tree a symbol of the University itself, just so wounded by the death of Edward Cavan. The tarred break was hardly noticeable now; on her short walks Grace Kimlock sometimes wondered exactly where the branch had been, how the tree had looked; one no longer felt absence in the air, or looked for leaves where there were none. The absence of Orlando himself was another matter. A dozen times a day she felt the impulse to phone him, then sat down with the instrument in her hands, abstracted until Ellen roused her. Orlando had died quite suddenly a year before, late at night, of a brain hemorrhage while he worked at his desk. He was found only the next morning. Since then Grace Kimlock had felt surrounded by ghosts, for the first time in her long life really afraid of the present, a present which bewildered her. There seemed nothing to hang onto at all in this time when the renegade and the informer were the heroes of the day and the things one had always taken for granted like honor, trust, the very foundations of the human compact, were being subtly undermined. Lately she had almost entirely withdrawn from public life, and saw only very old friends like Damon. She was quite suddenly an old lady.

Yet on this morning she woke with some of her former battling self back in play; as if to underline the importance of the day she took out the cameo brooch Edward had given her with Pallas Athene on it and clasped it firmly to her new bright blue blouse, and as she peered at herself in the mirror to be sure it was not on crooked, she lifted her chin and gave a little wry smile, as if to say, "We're not dead yet, old thing."

In the kitchen Ellen and the cook noted that she had eaten almost no breakfast. "She's that excited. It's about Mr. Phillips, you may be sure, the poor man. He's to be questioned, you know. They're after him," Ellen said gloomily. She was not very sure who "they" were, but she had heard Grace telephoning all day yesterday, summoning the thinning ranks to the open session of a Washington Committee sent down to look into communism at Harvard University.

"She's afraid he'll lose his temper, the poor man, that's what she's got so nervy about," cook answered.

"As well he might," Ellen answered. "Prying into people's affairs——"

"Well it's a dangerous time and you never know," cook said shaking her head. "They have to do their job like the rest of us."

"Miss Kimlock says it's a dirty job. That's what she told me. She told me they hadn't caught any Communists anyway. It's just for publicity, that's what she told me," Ellen said quite belligerently.

Cook, unperturbed, chuckled. "She's agin the government. Always has been. You'd think she came from the old country the way she carries on against them all——"

"And a good thing too," Ellen said, quite hot. "There's nothing wrong with the old country."

"Now, now, I didn't say there was, did I?" and cook chuckled again, her arms deep in soapsuds. "Well, we'd best get on with it now, Ellen, if we're to get through and see it all on the television. She's set on our doing that, you know, told me five times if she told me once that she intends for us to watch it."

Ellen sighed as she took a bunch of silver up into her towel.

"What's the matter now?"

"I was thinking of Horace. I never thought I'd miss that old cat the way I do, throwing up good haddock the way he did, turning up his nose at anything you'd cook for him. It's a strange thing the way he used to sit outside the door just waiting like a saint, never a mew out of him."

"Times have changed," cook said gruffly, "we've seen a lot come and go these last years. It's a sad business altogether."

Yet in the general gloom which the kitchen reflected there were points of light. In the last years Grace had got very fond of Pen and George, safely married at last when

George got his assistant professorship. The way George dropped in when he was tired after a day of conferences with students was almost like Edward. But he was gentler than Edward, a great asker of questions; Grace found herself digging out old scrapbooks about the Anarchists, telling George about Sacco and Vanzetti, reliving it all for him, and especially lately when he was bothered, so he said, by the extreme conservatism of his students. "I want some ammunition, Grace," he'd say, with a twinkle in his eye. "What was that Holmes dissent you mentioned the other day?" And Grace would smile. "That's the kind of thing I used to dig up to give to my professors. It seems queer you should want it for your students. Do you suppose they'll all grow up to be fierce old radicals in their eighties?"

With George and with George alone she could sometimes laugh. And now she was waiting for him and Pen to pick her up and drive her to the courthouse. She had already had a talk with Julia on the telephone. Damon was closeted with his lawyer, but Julia said he was in good form and that they had all warned him about not losing his temper. "We'll just hope for the best," she said. "Damon has nothing to hide."

No, Grace thought, he has nothing to hide, but he has publicly denounced the methods of this committee all over the country. Damon and Julia had been pouring money and time out in defense of their friends and the many unknowns caught up in the general hysteria. Damon was safe in his professorship—at least so far—and Harvard had made a strong stand. But the committee was sure to bait him, and they must have something in mind, something to spring or they wouldn't be televising.

Grace's spirits rose as she got into George's battered

old Ford, where she was squeezed in between him and Pen. She felt absurdly young, excited suddenly, a little breathless.

"The place will be packed, of course," George said, stepping on the accelerator. "Goldberg is coming, by the way, told me so yesterday." George grinned. "He had the air of a martyr going to the stake."

"Well, he's been very good," Pen answered. "Not only dedicating his book to Edward Cavan—that took some courage, I expect—but the way he's stood up lately and spoken out. I must say I'm amazed."

"I'm not," George said, "he's not as cold as he seems—and then he told me once that he had refused to be on some committee Edward asked him to be on only two or three days before he died. It seems to have bothered him a good deal."

They had got through the traffic in the Square and were out on the river now, speeding along with the Harvard Houses coming into view and swiftly left behind them; the bridge where George had stood so long ago with his book alive in his hands sped away. "At least he's got his book out, which is more than can be said for me," George said, perhaps half consciously remembering the sense of clear power he had felt, that power so diffused and scattered now by full-time teaching. Could it have been five years ago? Where had it all gone?

Pen, seeing his face set, reached over to touch his shoulder. "Next year you'll have time, George. You really will."

"*If* I get the fellowship——"

"Well, Goldberg's backing you, isn't he? What more do you want?"

She lit a cigarette and handed it to him. The thing was that the coming event had made them all tense, nervous, too aware of all that had happened, lifted out of the day-to-day scramble by this high tension hour.

"What time is it?" Grace asked. She had not been listening. She had been thinking about Edward who had been spared this at least. It was a long time since she had thought about him so vividly. It was a long time since she had cried out, "Edward, Edward," in her sleep, waking over and over again in the dark, frightened by her own voice. It was as if Edward as a presence had been swallowed up. Only sometimes late in the evening at a dinner party, perhaps, when the guard was down, his name might be mentioned. He was spoken of then as a wounded man, with just that shade of smugness which the healthy feel for the ill. Only Orlando Fosca had never used this tone, perhaps because he alone felt no guilt. But the others pushed the thought of Edward away, just as she, sitting in the car, pushed it away from her now. "Of course you'll get the fellowship," she said, patting George's knee rather roughly.

It was just as well that they had come early. Already, a half hour before the doors were to open, there was quite a crowd gathered outside the courthouse. Grace, lifting her head a little, so she could see, drank in the smoke of battle and felt excited. It was a curious group. She recognized members of a militant Catholic organization; there were shabby old women; there were students; there was Goldberg to whom she nodded. She tried to read the faces, to separate those who had come to see "the Reds" baited from those who had come on the side of the accused, to show where they stood, to be heard if possible. But there was no way of reading the faces—and it seemed strange, the secretiveness, the fact that people could show so little to each other what went on inside them, the fact that this group, patiently waiting, concealed violent passions, fear, fanatical religious zeal, hatred, love. But nothing of this showed. For the moment they were a community of people waiting, united in suspense which, for the moment, was merely physical, waiting for a door to open.

Everything changed as soon as a guard pushed back the doors. The passive crowd separated into furious entities pushing each other aside. Grace was almost knocked down and only saved by George's arm from being shoved hard against the jamb. In what seemed seconds the courtroom was filled, filled with rumor and the buzz of excitement. Here people would be judged, flanked by the flag of the United States and the state flag, looked down upon from the high place where the judge in a trial case would be sitting; they would be judged by a group of Senators who made their own rules yet not with any of the usual protections, nor by the usual procedures and they would be judged in front of television cameras. The crew was busily at work now, bringing in standing lights; every now and then a flashbulb went off, practice or a view of the crowd?

Grace felt suddenly afraid for Damon, afraid for them all. She was actually trembling. She looked sideways at George and saw the pulse in his forehead beating. Then she forgot everything and became nothing but a witness, a witness of whatever was about to happen. It had become a play, in which half the actors had been well rehearsed and the other half were at their mercy. It was all so smooth, the filing in of the chairman of the committee followed by two assistant counsels and someone else whom Grace did not recognize. She was struck by the youth of these faces, the untouched look they had; even the chairman, dressed conservatively, with what she felt was a falsely grave look —for in a moment he turned to the young man beside him and made a *sotto voce* remark which brought smiles to both their faces—even he, the Senator himself looked at first glance easy-going, young, quite open as he said scarcely audibly, "The committee will come to order." He reminded the photographers that they would not be permitted to take pictures while the witnesses were testifying. Where were the witnesses? Grace realized suddenly that she had not noticed Damon come in, but there he was, sitting at a table his back to her talking to his lawyer, a gray-haired pink-faced man, who seemed quite at ease. The Senator was making a speech now, very dignified and sure of himself. He thanked various state officials for their co-operation, advised the Massachusetts State Commission sitting in the jury box on his right that he would be glad to ask the witness any questions they might wish asked and made it clear that he was at their service. He then turned to the marshal and suggested that he allow as many people as possible into the room, since "this is supposed to be a public hearing."

There was a few moments' wait while a few more people were squeezed in. Then the doors were closed. Grace did not take her eyes off Damon's back; he was very stooped and looked, she thought, tired and old, as he leaned forward talking to his counsel. There was something vulnerable about his back, about his thinning hair. He looked so human and frail below the monolithic faces on the judge's bench that she trembled for him.

"Mr. Damon Phillips."

He raised his right hand. "Do you solemnly swear to tell the truth, the whole truth, and nothing but the truth, so help you God?"

The whole truth, Grace thought. Who can know the whole truth? Who can promise to tell that?

"I do," Damon said in a loud firm voice. Of course, Grace thought, as the interminable formalities began, this will take hours. She felt wildly impatient and began to doodle frantically on an envelope, while the counsel's name and address were recorded, while the Senator reminded the photographers again that they would not be allowed to take pictures during the hearing. Then he leaned forward, after shuffling through a sheaf of papers handed to him by the young man on his right, and began his questioning. Damon had to spell his own name, explain his position at Harvard, that he had been a professor some fifteen years, that before that he had been an associate professor for five years, that his field was physics, that his salary was twelve thousand dollars, that during the war he had for a time worked on a project remotely connected with the atom bomb.

"Mr. Phillips, in nineteen forty-three and nineteen forty-four, when you were working for the government of the United States is it a fact that you were active in the Harvard Teachers' Union?"

"That is true," Damon said patiently.

"Your salary was at that time ten thousand dollars. I take it that you did not join this union with the idea of striking for more pay?"

There was a ripple of laughter in the audience.

269

"I did not join it, Mr. Chairman. I was one of its original founders, and the union was founded in nineteen thirty-five."

"What exactly was its purpose, Mr. Phillips?" The chairman leaned benignly toward the witness and seemed all attention. Actually Grace felt that he was not interested at all and that all this was building up toward a point which was the real point. The answers did not matter. The questions themselves would lead inevitably to a trap.

But Damon was seizing the opportunity with both hands. He launched into a detailed description of the motives underlying the union: some Harvard professors had felt that they were too detached from the community. The union was an affiliate of the AFL and through this affiliation they not only came to know the problems of high-school teachers in the community, but also could take action on issues in local government and even in state government. Damon gave as an example the stand the Teachers' Union took at a time when the President of Harvard was openly coming out against child-labor laws, which they had supported.

"If I am right you also actively supported the Communist government in Spain during the Spanish Civil War?" the chairman asked, rather impatiently.

"We supported the duly elected Republican government of Spain against a fascist minority who were out to capture it by force, yes." His answer shot back. There was a faint booing at the back of the hall and scattered applause, in which Grace joined fervently.

Damon was doing a little too well, Grace realized. He had taken the bit between his teeth and was galloping off. The chairman looked a little less bland now.

"You are aware that the Joint Anti-Fascist Refugee Committee is on the Attorney General's list, I presume? That it has been publicly named subversive, that it was subversive in nineteen forty-one, in October of nineteen forty-one?"

"I am aware of that."

The chairman leaned over to his counsel and was handed a canceled check.

"I have in my hand a check for twenty-five dollars made payable to the Joint Anti-Fascist Refugee Committee, and signed in your name. I will hand you this check and ask you if you have seen this check before."

"Obviously, since it is signed by my name."

"It is dated October eighth, nineteen forty-one. At that time it was publicly known that this was a subversive organization. You were aware of that fact?"

"Yes."

"Do you know what the word 'subversive' means, Mr. Phillips?"

"I think so."

"You *think* so? You a professor at Harvard, engaged during the war on top secret work for the government *think* you know what 'subversive' means? Perhaps I had better inform you, so that you may not only think but know, Mr. Phillips. The Joint Anti-Fascist Refugee Committee was according to the Attorney General's Report, a Communist Front organization. Did you 'think' so in nineteen forty-one when you made out a check for twenty-five dollars?"

"Yes."

"Are you a member of the Communist Party, Mr. Phillips?"

"No."

"Have you ever been a member of the Communist Party?"

"No."

"Yet in nineteen forty-one you were giving them active support, giving them money." The chairman looked quite grieved. "Are you professors just dumb or what?"

Damon pulled his eyebrow and his face flushed. "This was a matter of conscience," he said with a troubled look which Grace felt would do him no good.

"Your conscience told you you should support the Communist Party?"

"As far as I knew the money collected by the Joint Anti-Fascist Refugee Committee was going to a specific hospital in France where Spanish Republicans wounded in the war were being taken care of. Some of the money may have been going to other things of which I do not know. I did know about the hospital and wanted to support it."

"You thought that your judgment was superior to that of the Attorney General of the United States?"

Damon bowed his head. He swallowed twice.

"Shall I repeat the question?"

"I suppose the answer is yes in this case." Damon cast a worried look at his counsel.

"As a member of the Harvard University faculty you no doubt consider yourself a man of superior intelligence, superior it would seem even to the government of the United States. This is very interesting. Let us take a hypothetical case. Suppose this government had been at war with a government of which you approved, a Communist-run government, and suppose your conscience told you that your own government was in the wrong, would you feel free to give secret information to the enemy?"

Damon hesitated and rubbed his forehead with one hand, then said very quietly, "In time of war I would consider it my duty to support the government of the United States."

"But not in time of peace?" The Senator leaned forward blandly. Someone laughed. There was a hostile stir from one section of the courtroom.

For a second Grace had the vision of the hundreds and thousands of American faces sitting in parlors and kitchens watching Damon's haunted look as he glanced backward at the crowd, as he again ran his fingers through his hair. Then she was distracted because she had suddenly noticed Julia for the first time, down near the front, sitting very erect, her eyes never leaving Damon. When Grace came to, she heard the chairman ask.

"Did you know a Harvard professor called Edward Cavan?"

George Hastings put a hand gently on Grace's arm, for at Edward's name she had jerked to attention, half rising out of her seat. They could feel the tension in Damon, could see him catch his breath before he answered slowly and with emphasis.

"Edward Cavan was my very good friend."

There was absolute stillness in the courtroom.

"A very interesting statement, Professor. Let me remind you of some of the pertinent facts about this very good friend of yours." The Senator lifted a paper from those in front of him and read, "He was a member of the Socialist Party as early as nineteen twenty-nine; he was active on a committee for the defense of the Communist, Harry Bridges; he campaigned for the Communists in Spain; he spent the winter of nineteen forty-seven in Prague and came back to write several articles analyzing the situation there and praising the Socialist government for its tolerance of Communists; he supported Wallace and campaigned for him in nineteen forty-eight; he did not leave the Progressive Party after it had been exposed as a Communist Front." These facts were read slowly and matter-of-factly. Now the Senator lifted his eyes and raised his voice a fraction. "Edward Cavan committed suicide in October of nineteen forty-nine." There was a slight pause for effect. "Do you agree that these statements are true?"

"Yes."

Oh, Damon, Grace thought and it was like a prayer, poor Damon. Would he be forced now to deny Edward? She felt a dreadful impulse to get up and run away. It was too painful.

"Just what was the bond between you, a professor of physics and Edward Cavan, a professor of American literature and an avowed supporter of communism, Mr. Phillips?"

The chairman was smiling slightly, a superior smile, a patient smile, as if to say, you can have all the time you want, you know, to walk into my trap. So Grace interpreted his look. Just then George leaned over and whispered to her, "Don't worry."

Damon coughed, took out a handkerchief to wipe his mouth. He hesitated for what seemed a long time, then said as if he were weighing each word, "Our bond was that we both believed that being a professor, whatever one's subject, does not excuse one from the responsibilities of citizenship."

The chairman leaned back comfortably, "And you interpreted the responsibilities of citizenship—I presume you mean as citizens of the United States—"

This sally was greeted by a guffaw from back in the audience, and general giggles. It was all Grace could do to keep from shouting, "Foul play." The chairman proceeded "that you interpreted these responsibilities as meaning support of the Communist Party," here he raised his eyes and looked out at the audience, hammering the point with one hand, "a secret subversive party dedicated to the overthrow of the government to which you say you felt responsible. I must say that for such brilliant minds, your reasoning must appear peculiar to say the least to the average loyal American." Then he turned quite paternally, it seemed, to the witness. "Your close friend, Edward Cavan, seems to have admitted that he had been hopelessly wrong."

Grace clasped the arms of her chair with her hands. She was suddenly furiously angry. But she lost the chance to speak out because George laid a restraining hand on her. "It won't do any good," he whispered. "You mustn't."

"You have had five years to reconsider your own position." The chairman leaned forward and spoke quite confidentially, "Have you come to any conclusions which might be of help to this committee, Mr. Phillips?"

Without a second's pause Damon shot back, his shoulders squared. "I have come to some conclusions. They would not be of help to this committee." He's getting angry, Grace thought. Oh dear, that may be the worst thing. Yet in her heart she was glad.

The chairman showed no consciousness of the change of tone. "When we have damning evidence against an individual in a position to influence and indoctrinate the young, we must be given proof of good faith. In your association with Edward Cavan over the years, as a founder of the Teachers' Union especially, you admit to having worked closely with Communists and with Communist groups. I do not know what your conclusions are, Professor"—here the chairman smiled discreetly—"but I have here a series of names. The committee will be grateful if you show your good faith by telling us what you know about Paul Humber."

The trap, Grace thought, is sprung. After the long preliminaries, she felt almost relieved. All eyes were focused now on Damon.

"May I confer with my counsel?"

"You may."

Damon and his counsel conferred for a few seconds.

"May I be permitted to make a statement, sir?"

"A witness may make a statement provided it has been handed in to this committee twenty-four hours before the hearing." The chairman leaned over to his counsel and whispered something.

"May I confer with my counsel?" Damon asked.

"You may."

There was complete silence in the courtroom, silence and attention. The chairman tapped with his pencil a moment, then yawned, and leaned back in his chair.

"May I say, sir, that I had no idea that Edward Cavan's name would come up today. My statement has to do with the conclusions you asked for some moments ago."

The chairman leaned forward on the bench and said categorically, "You may make your statement when you have answered my question. Was Paul Humber a member of the Communist Party at any period during the time that you knew him?"

"I am sorry, Senator, I shall have to refuse to answer that question on the grounds of conscience."

There was a slight edge in the chairman's voice now and he spoke quite slowly. "Your conscience had led you before, by your own admission, into rather curious paths. It permitted you some time back to give money to a Communist organization against the express advice of the Attorney General. I'm afraid I shall have to order you to answer the question."

Damon leaned forward for a second to catch his counsel's eye, then stood up again. "I am sorry, sir. I have already said I cannot inform on my friends, or former friends."

Grace gave a loud sigh. She was sitting up very straight now, her head high and she whispered, "Bravo, Damon," so loudly that several people turned round to stare at her.

The chairman was not smiling now. He looked very grave. "You are saying in effect that you put friendship above the security of the United States?"

"I am not willing to give the names of former associates who were not to my knowledge engaged in any criminal activity."

"Have the record show that the witness is ordered to answer the question and persists in his refusal. There is, as you perhaps remember, such a thing as contempt of Congress, Mr. Phillips."

"Disgusting," Grace said loudly. Something in the way she said it or in her appearance released the tension and the courtroom rocked with laughter. The chairman frowned.

"If there is any more disturbance of this sort," he said

coldly, "we shall have to ask for order," and he made a sign to the marshal which clearly suggested removing Grace if necessary.

"Sir," it was Damon again, quite unruffled. He actually had one hand in his pocket, and Grace guessed that he felt relieved that at last they had come to open war. "Sir, may I make a statement, the one I asked to make some time ago?"

"I ask the questions here, Professor. You answer them," the chairman said shortly. Then he leaned over to counsel and after a whispered conference, looked up. "Very well, you have a statement? Make it."

Damon took a deep breath. He spoke now very slowly as if he were weighing each word, but he spoke very distinctly as if he were anxious that the entire courtroom could hear. "You asked me whether I had come to any conclusions in the years since the suicide of my friend, Edward Cavan." There was a ripple of interest in the crowd, then absolute silence as all strained to hear. Although Damon's back was turned to them, it was as if the people assembled in the courtroom sensed that this was a crucial moment for him. Many leaned forward. Grace sat up as straight as she could, though she could not stop her chin from trembling. For some reason what flashed through her mind was Orlando's saying "We shall not know for a long time about Edward." Damon coughed that slightly nervous cough she recognized as meaning he was feeling something deeply. For a second he half-turned and caught Julia's eye or looked for it obviously. "I have come to the conclusion," he said, for a second facing the courtroom and then turning back to the chairman of the committee, "that although Edward Cavan may have been wrong in his belief that Communists and

Socialists could and should work together, in the essence of his belief he was right and many of us were wrong." Again he paused, before speaking more quickly and with a certain thrust. "That belief was that the intellectual must stand on the frontier of freedom of thought, especially in such times as these when that frontier is being narrowed down every day. He feared—and we know how rightly," said Damon, his voice suddenly trembling, "the increasing apathy and retreat of the American people before such encroachments of fundamental civil rights as are represented by this committee." He said the last words loudly and slowly, looking the chairman full in the face.

They were greeted by an uproar in the audience. It was as if the long tense attention had to burst out now, as if a match had been set to a bonfire and the whole room blazed with emotion. From one section of the room there were boos and groans, and when Grace heard this she stood up and began shouting she did not know what, rage and enthusiasm mixed in incoherent passionate words. Some people applauded her; others turned to stare at her; a few shouted back, but now she was on her feet, caught up in a wave of excitement, nothing could stop her. "Don't you understand what's happening here?" she shouted. "We have to defend the Republic as that brave man did. . . ." She had pushed George roughly aside, but now a guard reached the aisle and she felt a hand over her mouth. Before she knew what was really happening, she had been hauled out of her chair and was being forcibly though gently pushed through the crowd, some of whom watched passively, fascinated, no doubt, by the sight of this man lifting an old lady out by main force. She did not struggle, she was too surprised. The chairman was pounding with

279

his gavel as she called back, "You can't do this," just before the doors closed behind her. Then she, George and Pen found themselves outside, closely followed by the cameramen who had got some action at last.

She was panting so much with exertion and emotion that for a moment she couldn't speak, pinning back her pin which had come undone, pulling her hat back into shape.

"Dirty disgusting business," George said through his teeth. Grace saw that he was dead white.

Pen looked as if she might be going to cry. "I didn't know Damon had it in him."

"Well"—Grace surveyed them in the flush of her triumph—"there's one courageous man left anyway. Edward would have been proud. We can hold up our heads again —at last."

"We'd better get out of here." George was suddenly aware of the circle of grinning faces around them, cameras pointed. "Your name, please?" one of them asked Grace, notebook ready.

"It's none of your damned business." George made a dive for the camera and missed it.

"I'm glad to give my name. Grace Kimlock is my name," Grace said clearly and with perfect dignity. "You can say if you will that the liberals aren't dead yet." Did anyone but herself get the nuance in this? It was the accolade to Damon, the first time she had ever used the word "liberal" in a congratulatory sense. Then she added, with a kind of bravado, her chin lifted, her eyes twinkling, "I haven't been put out of a courtroom since the Sacco-Vanzetti case."

"Your age, Miss Kimlock?"

"Seventy-five."

"Quite a girl," one of the men said, and they all laughed.

"Shut up, you dirty bastard." George would have knocked him down, except for Pen's intervention.

"Come along, you two. We're making an exhibition of ourselves," she said firmly.

"He'll be cited for contempt, of course," George said when they were safely in the car, lighting cigarettes. Grace, feeling the reaction, was shaking all over and wondered if the children noticed. For them, she knew, it could not be such a moment as it had been for her.

"What does that matter?" she said, "we can hold our heads up."

After they had quieted down a bit and were driving along the river, Pen said thoughtfully, "It's only the beginning, of course."

"Yes, but it has looked like the end for so long," Grace answered quickly. "You see."

"What I liked"—and George smiled as he said it, a sudden young happy smile—"was that it was Edward Cavan's name that really got Damon going. And it might have been disastrous; I was scared there for a while——"

"Damon Phillips has guts," Pen broke in.

Grace looked at the river and her eyes were shining with tears. "I think more, he's generous. It's a liberal trait," she added, but only she knew what a handsome apology it was.